The Lawyer in Shizukuishi Sleeps with a Wolf

Akira Sugano

Illustration by Yamimaru Enjin

New York

Akira Sugano

Translation by Yui Kajita

Cover art by Yamimaru Enjin

Yen On
150 West 30th Street, 19th Floor
New York, NY 10001

Visit us at yenpress.com
facebook.com/yenpress
twitter.com/yenpress
yenpress.tumblr.com
instagram.com/yenpress

First Yen On Edition: October 2023
Edited by Yen On Editorial: Anna Powers
Designed by Yen Press Design: Andy Swist

Yen On is an imprint of Yen Press, LLC.
The Yen On name and logo are trademarks of Yen Press, LLC.
The publisher is not responsible for websites (or their content) that are not owned by the publisher.

Library of Congress Cataloging-in-Publication Data
Names: Sugano, Akira, 1970– author. | Enjin, Yamimaru, illustrator. | Kajita, Yui, translator.
Title: The lawyer in Shizukuishi sleeps with a wolf / Akira Sugano ; illustration by Yamimaru Enjin ; translation by Yui Kajita.
Other titles: Shizukuishicho no horitsuka wa okami to neumuru. English
Description: New York, NY : Yen On, 2023.
Identifiers: LCCN 2023028698 | ISBN 9781975366308 (trade paperback)
Subjects: LCGFT: Light novels.
Classification: LCC PL875.5.U33 S4513 2023 | DDC 895.63/6—dc23/eng/20230626
LC record available at https://lccn.loc.gov/2023028698

ISBNs: 978-1-9753-6630-8 (paperback)
978-1-9753-6631-5 (ebook)

10 9 8 7 6 5 4 3 2 1

LSC-C

Printed in the United States of America

Contents

Characters

Fuuka

Sora's younger brother. He normally takes the form of a white wolf, but when he is alone with Sora, he can turn back into human shape. Good at cooking. His name is spelled with the characters for *wind* and *fire*.

Sora Oushuu

Former public prosecutor. As a certified fraud examiner, he investigates financial malpractice in corporations and has his own law firm.

Tamuramaro

Former sei-i taishogun, commander in chief, of the expeditionary force against the Emishi in the Heian period; born in the eighth century. In the present day, he makes a handsome living as a highly competent attorney lawyer. He has been watching over Sora and Fuuka for a long time.

I

The Lawyer Has a Complicated Relationship with His Lodger

He had only one answer, and he believed in only one thing.

But even so, lately, he could hear the sound of his bones creaking inside his body from time to time.

In fact, he thought he'd just heard the rasp of them again. But Sora Oushuu fixed his eyes on the broad-shouldered man in the dark-gray suit sitting diagonally across from him.

"It's not for me to pass judgment on how excessive the embezzlement was," Sora said.

He was in the conference room on the fourth floor of Daitokyo Bank's Mejiro branch, located in front of Mejiro Station. From where he sat, he could see the edge of some lush greenery outside the window, the neighboring campus of an old university. It was the second Friday of September; green leaves rustled against the clear blue sky in the late summer heat.

"Going forward, your bank should give a clear indication of how you intend to assess the act itself in terms of its malice, its intentionality, and its recurrence," Sora continued. He turned to a man named Nakategawa, who was sitting on his right, dressed in a dark-navy suit; Nakategawa served as both the general manager and the deputy general manager of the branch.

Sora was a certified fraud examiner: a specialized profession in which he was commissioned by business corporations to investigate any fraudulent activity and, if anything was detected, to ascertain the responsible party and compile the relevant evidence.

The conference tables formed two rows in the room, and a man named Etou—the head of the corporate sales division, who was being accused of embezzlement—sat on the other side, his face twisted into a grimace. The man in the dark-gray suit sitting next to Etou was his attorney. It was just the four of them facing one another in the large conference room: Sora, Nakategawa, Etou, and Etou's attorney.

"'Should,' you say?" the attorney said in a low but airy tone.

"I don't see any sign of remorse in Mr. Etou," Sora went on. "Besides, this isn't the sort of crime you can sweep under the rug by simply repaying the entire sum and taking disciplinary action."

"Are you suggesting," Nakategawa blurted out anxiously, "we should report it to the Financial Services Agency as well as the prosecutors? I have no authority to make such a decision on my own."

"With these figures, it's only reasonable to suspect some foul play when the person in question can repay the sum in full. We're talking about over a hundred million yen here. It hasn't been made clear why Mr. Etou would be able to make the entire payment in the first place."

Sora turned his icy gaze on Etou in front of him.

Etou glared back. "The money was pooled. That's why I can return it as is. I've already told you a number of times," he snapped. He had passed his boiling point long ago.

For a thirty-one-year-old, Sora still looked quite young. His features were well-proportioned, and most people would guess that he was intelligent from his appearance alone. His voice was steady, neither high-pitched nor low, and his expressions didn't change much, either.

As a certified fraud examiner, he was an outsider hired by corporations to prevent fraud, if possible, or to handle the issue internally before it became a public scandal—although, strictly speaking, these tasks were normally the purview of the company's internal audit office. Since he would be called in when that internal system proved ineffective, Sora was used to being accosted as a persona non grata. In fact, he never concerned himself with other people's feelings while carrying out his duties.

"Mr. Etou, I apologize for putting this question to you once again. Are you certain you are the sole perpetrator? Do you assert that there was absolutely no involvement of any criminal organizations?" Quiet and calm, he intoned the same question he had already posed to Etou many times.

"Certainly—"

Etou was about to add *not*, but the others could sense some hesitation.

"Mr. Nakategawa. If, in fact, the head of the corporate sales division was methodically passing on to a criminal organization funds that amounted to over a hundred million yen—money that your customers have entrusted to your bank, essentially..."

Sora paused and glanced at Etou, who showed no hint of either repenting or confessing.

"If that is indeed the case, and if the bank proceeds to cover up the crime, imagine what would happen when the scandal comes into the open. The people's confidence in your bank would be irrevocably destroyed."

"Well, that is true, but...," mumbled Nakategawa.

"If it came to that, Mr. Etou would certainly face imprisonment for corporate embezzlement," the attorney remarked to Sora in his low voice. He looked at Etou, his client, with a strangely indifferent expression.

"Imprisonment would be appropriate. Hundreds of millions have been flowing from your bank to criminal organizations, effectively funding their unlawful activities—systematic fraud on the elderly, drug dealing, violence. The mere act of backing them calls for severe punishment. I would like you to acknowledge the full magnitude of your actions."

"That was never my intention!" Etou stood up, knocking over his chair. His face was red with fury, and he was trembling with anger.

Sora returned a steady gaze at the panicking man. Over the last two weeks, Sora had investigated Etou, collecting information on the transactions in his account and on the records of suspicious activities in his private finances and entertainment expenses. He had everything he needed to prove Etou's embezzlement. Only a single issue remained: to ascertain whether Etou had a connection with a criminal organization for his personal gain.

On his laptop, Sora typed up the words Etou had just spoken. "I've made a record of his words, Mr. Nakategawa."

It was Nakategawa, not Etou, who gave a heavy sigh of resignation.

"I can also confirm… I heard him clearly."

Just when the battle seemed to be settled, the attorney interjected once again in his nonchalant way. "As I understand, today's hearing was on the condition that it wouldn't be recorded. You are only writing down what you heard, yes?"

"What more do you intend to do?" Sora demanded sharply, turning to the attorney. "Mr. Etou has committed a serious crime. Now that he has practically admitted to his link with a criminal organization, you must realize the bank will want to report it to the prosecutors as quickly as possible."

"Everyone's doing it!" Etou shouted desperately, still standing.

"Everyone? Who exactly do you have in mind?" Sora looked at Etou but kept his voice low. "Please, do tell."

Etou bit back whatever he was going to say.

"Systematic embezzlement of over a hundred million yen and feeding funds to criminal organizations—no, not everyone does that," Sora went on. Etou's fists were clenched tight. "Did you ever stop to imagine how your own greed might lead to someone's death?"

His quiet yet ruthless words sliced through the air like a thin blade.

"Allow us to reconsider our position," said the attorney. He picked up his black briefcase, full of documents, clearly preparing to leave. "Come with me, Mr. Etou. For now, they have no power to force us."

When the attorney gave a pat on his back, Etou finally breathed out a sigh.

"We can't force you," said Sora, "but you have no right to settle the matter yourself, either."

"I'm a lawyer like you, so I have no intention of helping him escape. Please send me a written report on Monday. After confirming the facts, we will discuss at length how he can atone for his conduct." The attorney waved off Sora's concern with a laugh. "At this point, nothing more will happen, I can assure you."

Without explaining precisely what he meant by that last remark, the attorney nudged Etou toward the door. Etou glanced back one last time and glowered at Sora, but his dirty look had no effect on Sora's feelings or any outward expression thereof.

"You're so sure you're always right, aren't you? You and no one else," Etou spat out, irked by Sora's unfaltering air. "You think you know everything…!"

"What I do know at the present moment is how malicious this case is," Sora replied bluntly and honestly. But there was something in Etou's words that disturbed him.

"Shall we, Mr. Etou?" As calm as ever, the attorney ushered Etou out of the room. He was smiling, as if to shrug and say, "What else can we do?"

Sora bristled as he watched them leave.

Nakategawa threw up his hands as soon as the door had closed behind them. "Honestly, I didn't think the case was this serious when I called you on board, Mr. Oushuu."

When it was discovered that the accounts of the Mejiro branch didn't balance out and the internal audit office could only provide vague answers, Sora was brought into the investigation. One by one, Sora interviewed the main people at the branch whose positions allowed them to move large amounts of money. He found out that the companies the bank had financed under Etou's guidance had undergone unnatural bankruptcies, and some of those companies didn't even exist. His next move was to hold a hearing for Etou himself and file a report, but then the attorney came on the scene, and now the investigation was dragging out needlessly.

"Just the fact that Etou has the means to hire that attorney suggests he has some private funds hidden away somewhere." The services of a formidable opponent like that would cost a considerable sum.

"If you ask me, Mr. Oushuu, I think you could charge more for your work. Not just for the accuracy and speed of your investigation, but, my goodness, your ears don't miss a thing! I was sweating bullets—I felt like a criminal myself. You really are outstanding." Nakategawa gave a weak smile, putting a hand to his heart, as if to act out what he just said.

"As a rule, I only charge the prescribed rate."

Although there wasn't much demand for a certified fraud examiner, the regulated rate was not particularly low to begin with.

"It's just like you to say that, Mr. Oushuu."

Sora couldn't bring himself to feel grateful for Nakategawa's compliment. What was the point of telling him he wasn't charging enough? "Don't you think it's expensive to hire a third party to audit the internal accounts?" he asked.

"It's a low price to pay if we consider the bank's reputation and trust," Nakategawa replied. "If we can deal with the matter internally, that's the optimal outcome."

If they really valued their trust, Sora couldn't understand why they chose not to make a criminal accusation as soon as they identified the likely suspect. He simply couldn't fathom why anyone would want to carry out fraudulent activities. Embezzlement, corruption, appropriation, illicit donations, and bid rigging could all be exposed upon investigation.

"It's a pointless, worthless crime," he murmured under his breath.

Nakategawa listened to him in silence.

Sora simply couldn't imagine what went on in the minds of people who chose to take part in such atrocious and obvious embezzlement.

"You're so sure you're always right, aren't you? You and no one else."

Etou's jarring words still bothered Sora. And most of all, he kept on seeing the gaze of the attorney in his mind, as if he was still standing in front of him. It was Sora's nature to firmly stand by his belief—it was impossible for him to imagine what drove those criminals to do what they did. And yet he frowned slightly as he felt another wave of unease.

The clear tones of the higurashi cicadas rang through the air, signaling the end of summer.

"He sure does look like a Japanese wolf."

A familiar old man called out from a bench by Sanpouji Lake. Sora was taking a walk in Shakujii Park, which stretched from east to west over a wide, oblong area in Nerima Ward of Tokyo.

"You always say that," replied Sora.

Since the extensive case at Daitokyo Bank had finally reached a point where he could prepare a written report, Sora had slipped off his leather shoes and suit jacket as soon as he got home. Still in his white business shirt and navy trousers, he had changed into sneakers and stepped out into the park.

His straight black hair had grown a little too long. Even so, people often told him that he looked "cool and clean." He got "cold" a lot, too.

The old man was sitting with his wife on a bench. Mr. and Mrs. Kashiwagi were both in their seventies and lived in the neighborhood of Shizukuishi, same as Sora. They ran a calligraphy class there.

"We saw a painting of a Japanese wolf only yesterday, and they look so similar. It was on TV, a documentary about extinct animals. That wolf wasn't pure white like our dear Fuuka, though." Tatsuko leaned down from her seat, gazing affectionately at something near Sora's waist height. "Right, Fuuka, sweetie?"

"Woof."

There he was, an enormous white dog resting calmly on the ground, the very picture of a Japanese wolf.

Lately, Sora had been too busy with the Daitokyo Bank hearings to take Fuuka on walks, so they'd rushed out of the house as soon as he got home.

"Can I pet him?"

"Fuuka seems to love it when you pet him, Ms. Tatsuko." Sora, as always, spoke slowly and respectfully in his mild, midrange tone. Everybody in town called the couple "Ms. Tatsuko" and "Mr. Rokurou." "Don't you, Fuuka?"

Neither the couple nor Fuuka would have been able to imagine how his gentle voice became so frosty at work, chilling the heart of the branch manager who had been next to him.

"Coo, coo." Fuuka hummed happily, his large body snuggling up to Tatsuko.

Sora held the end of a long red leash, as was required by law, but he was always careful to stay close by so that it never got too tight.

"So what breed is he?"

Rokurou, who taught a free and easy style of calligraphy to the children of the town while being a professional calligrapher himself, asked this to Sora not for the first time.

"He's a mix. He was still a little puppy when he was given to me. I had no idea he'd grow so big; it feels like it happened overnight. I basically just work to make sure I have enough for him," said Sora, joking about the food expenses.

Fuuka lowered his head, as though he could follow their conversation.

Sora bent down and whispered, "Sorry," in Fuuka's ear.

"Why don't you get him checked sometime? He really does look exactly like a Japanese wolf."

"The last record of a Japanese wolf is in the Meiji era, so it's been more than a hundred years now. Siebold's[1] papers are almost all gone as well. Fuuka's just a slightly large hybrid."

"You talk as if you've seen it with your own eyes," Rokurou teased. He seemed impressed by Sora's knowledge of the Meiji era and of Siebold from some years before that.

---

1. Philipp Franz von Siebold was a nineteenth-century German physician and botanist who studied Japan's flora and fauna, including the Japanese wolf. He is very well-known in Japan.

"...I like history, so it slipped out."

"You really are studious—our learned lawyer. I'd expect you to make brisk and efficient work of our divorce, too. You'd make sure you divide everything equally between us. Of course, we'd pay you the appropriate fee in full," said Tatsuko with a warm smile. She often brought this up, no matter what Sora said.

"I know I always say this, but I'm not that kind of lawyer. I used to be a public prosecutor."

"But there's a sign in front of your house that says OUSHUU LAW FIRM."

Two years ago, Sora had bought a house with an office space in Shizukuishi. For a young legal practitioner, it was a rather expensive purchase. Although he had just enough in his longtime savings to use as seed money for the property, it was a spacious house in an expensive neighborhood where maintenance costs were nothing to sneeze at.

"I'm not cut out to be an attorney. My firm is for doing stiff and stuffy legal work. I'm what they call a certified fraud examiner—not the kind of work where I can be of service to people like you. I sneak into companies to investigate."

Sora, usually quiet and serious, did his best to work his facial muscles into a playful grin. He didn't want the people in his neighborhood to see the man he became when he worked on cases like the one in Mejiro. Once he was back in Shizukuishi, he could forget everything about work.

For Sora, time slowed down in this tranquil place.

"But we've already decided that you should be the one to sort out our divorce. Brisk and efficient, if you please," said Rokurou, echoing Tatsuko's request.

"Well, I suppose you two can never get divorced, then. I can't possibly take on such a difficult task."

The couple's request might have sounded like a joke, but it was well-known among the townsfolk that the two childless calligraphy artists had thought about splitting many times, and for good reason.

"I can't name anyone I could entrust with such a heavy responsibility, so I'm afraid I can't make any introductions, either."

Even if it wasn't the Kashiwagis asking him, he would never be so reckless as to accept such an important piece of work offhand. With Rokurou and Tatsuko, he was doubly cautious.

"You're an earnest man, Mr. Lawyer."

"I'm stubborn, I know. I'm sorry."

He knew full well that this obstinate inflexibility, which revealed itself not only in his work but also in other areas of his life, was simply his nature. He bowed to Rokurou apologetically.

"Why're you apologizing? It's a good trait to have. You're earnest, and you have a strong sense of responsibility."

"That's right," Tatsuko chimed in. "You know what responsibility is."

To Sora, his disposition felt like a liability, but the couple turned it into something positive in their frank, breezy manner.

"...I do hope that's the case." Sora himself couldn't see the bright side, and he looked down.

That day, as with all other days, he had no doubt he'd carried out his work properly, and yet there was a darkness that lingered over his heart. He was touched by the couple's words. Whenever he talked to them, he felt like he was drinking a glass of cool, refreshing water in the desert.

"By the way—could you take this, dear? It's close to the expiration date, so it was on sale at the shop. It was such a good deal, I just got greedy and bought too much," said Tatsuko brightly, picking up three bags of Shimabara somen noodles off the bench.

"Oh, I couldn't. You're always giving me something." Sora waved his hands and tried to refuse, but the noodles were already right in front of his face.

"Go on. Take them. You know old folks like us can't help worrying over young people living by themselves."

"Come on—let us be busybodies."

Sora gratefully took the somen packs and stowed them away in the reusable bag he always kept in his pocket.

"Thank you so much."

Though she said she "just got greedy," Sora knew their intention was to bring the food to him from the start. He didn't know when it began, but the Kashiwagis had formed a habit of asking after him and checking whether he was eating properly as a single man. He didn't exactly look thirty-one years old, as he'd said he was, so that was most likely where their worry came from. His house, too, was unsettlingly roomy.

"All the same, I won't be assisting your divorce settlement."

Sora could only smile back to thank them, but the ever-present coolness in his expression could be seen as icy by some.

"Your big brother doesn't budge, does he, dear?" Tatsuko joked, stroking Fuuka.

"Coo, coo."

"They say wolves and dogs used to be the same kind of animals," said Tatsuko as Fuuka nestled up to her. "One lives together with humans; the other can tear them apart. Maybe that's the only difference, and we humans give them different names for our own selfish reasons."

"Fair point. However..." Sora agreed with Tatsuko about humans and their selfish reasons, but he paused to crouch down and look closely at Fuuka.

Fuuka's jet-black eyes set a stark contrast to his white fur, and sometimes the lighting made his pupils shine a bright red—as if a passionate flame blazed within.

"What is it?" Rokurou asked instead of Tatsuko.

"The *ritsuryo*[2] of the world, the codes of law, are created by humans, so whether an animal would live together with a man or butcher him makes quite a big difference."

"*Ritsuryo*, eh? Another quaint word. You sure do love your history, don't you, Mr. Lawyer?"

"Yes."

---

2. The *ritsuryo* were a system of criminal and civil codes adopted by Japan in the latter half of the first millennium, primarily the seventh and eighth centuries, following the structure of China's system. This was one of many elements of Chinese culture adopted by Japan around this time.

Sora had quit the Public Prosecutors' Office after serving there for two years. And now, it was two years since Sora had moved to the Shizukuishi area. The people in the neighborhood started calling him "Mr. Lawyer" because of the OUSHUU LAW FIRM sign in front of his house. Over time, he'd somehow become accustomed to this honorific title.

"But, y'know, don't wear yourself out thinking over all that," said Rokurou with concern. He knew Sora well by now.

Tatsuko petted Fuuka again and added, "It's true."

But Sora couldn't help it. The distinction between good and evil, as well as what it led to—the exact sort of things the old couple had just advised him not to think about—were constantly on his mind both at work and in everyday life.

"Even if he is a Japanese wolf, Fuuka is adorable," he said.

Still crouching, Sora looked into Fuuka's eyes, no longer red, and rubbed his cheek against his companion's fur. Fuuka was exceptionally cute, but there was much more to him than that. Sora pressed his ear against the fur and listened to his heartbeat.

"We better get going, Fuuka. It's time for dinner."

Sora wasn't very good at sidling out of conversations with vague answers. He kept on stroking Fuuka, keeping his eyes on the same level.

"Coooo." Fuuka gave a whine that was surprisingly soft and loving for such an enormous animal, and nodded. Even though he could hear and understand the conversations of the people around him, Fuuka never minded.

"See you later, sweet boy."

The Kashiwagis waved at Fuuka, and Sora said good-bye with a slight bow. Sora and Fuuka set off in the opposite direction from the train station to get to the end of the park. They left behind Sanpouji Lake and emerged out of the park on its west side. A little way off from the main street where the buses ran, in its own corner, was the district of Shizukuishi.

"Our selfish reasons, huh. If people accepted that and said they didn't mind getting torn open or killed, that'd be the end of any problems for Japanese wolves," he muttered absentmindedly.

But people, including Sora, didn't think so—*couldn't* think so. Killing a human was a crime.

"Coo?"

Fuuka glanced back at Sora with a soft call. It seemed he didn't have a care in the world and believed Sora shouldn't, either.

"Never mind—it's nothing. How about some somen for dinner? What should we make?"

Smiling at Fuuka, Sora quickened his pace to let Fuuka trot on as fast as he liked. He'd wanted to take him out on a walk first thing when he got back from work, but in the comfortable evening air, they ended up staying out much longer than he'd planned. Fuuka stared at the bag hanging from Sora's hand as though he was mulling over how he wanted to eat the noodles. Sora had been aware for quite some time that Fuuka resembled a Japanese wolf.

"I suppose they didn't know too much about dogs… Oh." Just as Sora was murmuring to himself, a big drop of rain fell right in front of him.

"Rain's coming!"

"Woof!"

They broke into a run in the sudden shower, which the forecast had surprisingly missed.

Sora kept Fuuka on a red leash as per the rules, but he could never get used to it.

The neighborhood around Shakujii Park was connected by bus lines. Right near the Shizukuishi bus stop, there was a house with an office that anyone would've thought was far too large for a young lawyer living by himself.

"We're soaked already."

The house was an old, traditional Japanese-style home, two stories high. Facing the road was a handsome row of light-green bamboo leaves, protecting the office from view. Sora and Fuuka passed through the small gateway next to it and ran up the little path across the lush garden to their front door.

"Totally drenched! Is the somen okay, Big Brother?!" The loud voice of a young man, bright and cheerful, rang in the entrance hall of the house.

"It survived. Safe in the bag."

"Even though it's the Shimabara kind?"

The young man laughed. He was bigger than Sora, with shining, silver-white hair down to his shoulders. He threw himself on Sora and hugged him around his waist like a little child.

"Hey, you've grown so big now. You used to be smaller than me back in the day. Not by much, but still."

If he had been walking about around Asakusa, the young man might've been mistaken as a foreigner who'd fallen in love with Japan. His large figure was clad in a robe made of white silk, brought to Japan through a trading route with the continent. Different in design from a normal kimono, it was meant to be worn under formal attire with the sash tied around the stomach instead of just above the pelvis.

"Really? I've always been pretty much as tall as you."

"As far as I remember, there was a time when you were smaller. You're my little brother, after all, so why not? Come on—you go take a bath." Sora spoke to him gently, stroking his silver hair.

"Wanna come with me?" asked Fuuka.

"Remember, anyone who sees us would think we're adult brothers. The bath isn't big enough for two; it's silly to squeeze in together."

"No one can see us inside anyway." Fuuka sulked, but he still beamed at Sora.

"Go on. You go first, and I'll take my bath after."

There was a small garden around the front door and the living room beyond it, and the bamboo thicket, the trees, and the flowers were gleaming wet.

"Why don't you go first, then, Sora?"

"When it's pouring rain, the little one should warm up in a bath first." Sora gently brushed Fuuka's hair out of his face.

Fuuka looked like he could be in his midtwenties. "You're always so sweet, Brother. I guess I should hurry up, or you'll catch a cold."

Like an obedient child, Fuuka leaped up on his long, sturdy legs.

"Ow!"

The red leash was still around his neck, so when he tried to dash off, he flipped back down to Sora's lap.

"I'm sorry, Fuuka! I keep forgetting… Wish I didn't have to put this thing on you," said Sora, taking off the leash in a hurry.

"I'm the one who keeps forgetting. What else can we do? I'm a Japanese wolf once I step outside." Fuuka looked up at Sora and gave a lighthearted laugh.

"Not even a Japanese wolf. A white dog."

Sora buried his face in the chest of the man on his lap, then pressed his right ear against him. He was listening intently, holding his breath as if to make sure he heard every heartbeat.

"You like to do that once in a while. How come?" asked Fuuka.

"It makes me feel safe."

Sora gazed into Fuuka's eyes, which took on a reddish cast. He couldn't laugh as freely as his precious little brother.

"I'll take out a towel and fresh clothes for you. And make sure you dry your hair, all right?"

"All righty," Fuuka chirped like a little boy, despite having the body of a grown man. He walked off toward the bathroom on the office side of the house.

Rain always leaked through the slightly old wooden hallway, so Sora reminded himself to wipe it up later as he watched Fuuka go.

"If he was a white dog all the time, I'd have to bathe him myself. It really helps that he turns back into a human at times like this."

Sora listened to the bathroom doors opening and closing, and his face softened into a brotherly smile.

In front of the small office hung a modest sign—more like a doorplate—that read OUSHUU LAW FIRM. Because of that sign, the people of Shizukuishi were still convinced that Sora was an attorney, even after he'd lived there for two years. The house was too spacious for just one person; the kitchen at the back of the first floor alone spanned about a hundred square feet.

"Sora, wanna have the somen that Mr. and Mrs. Kashiwagi gave us?" Fuuka asked as Sora came into the living room after a bath, drying his hair with a towel.

"Yeah, let's do that. It's a nice gift."

Both the living room next to the kitchen and the bedroom next to the bathroom were Japanese-style rooms of around 140 square feet. There were also two more rooms upstairs—not that Sora and Fuuka had any particular need for them.

Sora had bought this house when he realized that his little brother was no longer a child and had somehow grown into a rather big adult—and a rather big dog. They just couldn't make do with an apartment or a rental property anymore.

"Shimabara, huh," Sora murmured, sitting crossed-legged in a T-shirt and sweatpants in the living room.

"Are you remembering something sad? Should we have Morioka reimen noodles from Iwate instead? There's boiled eggs."

Fuuka, who heard Sora's voice darken, came over from the kitchen. Instead of the white silk attire he'd been wearing just after his return to human form, Fuuka had put on the black T-shirt and jeans that Sora had left for him in the bathroom. Fuuka flung his arms around Sora from behind.

"Wonder how those noodles came into the country," said Sora. "It's completely different from the reimen in Korean restaurants."

The name Oushuu—which Sora had taken for his law firm as well as his current last name—originally stood for the entire land in the north, not just the city of Oushuu in present-day Iwate Prefecture.

"If *you* looked into it, I bet you'd find out why in a second," said Fuuka.

Sora had chosen to settle in Shizukuishi because it was close to Shakujii Park, where he could take walks with Fuuka in dog form, and it was only a short train ride away from central Tokyo. But he'd been taken by the name of the town, too, which had ties to the north. That was why he'd bought this house despite the high price.

"I haven't looked into what it's like in the north nowadays," Sora replied. "We can never go back, in any case."

"You don't want reimen? Then somen it is."

"Wait. Um, Fuuka."

Even though the house was far away from the train station, and rather old at that, it had still proved to be too expensive. Sora finally blurted out the secret he'd been keeping from his brother.

"Someone's coming."

"Now? Who? If we have a visitor, I'll turn into a dog again. But can't we have some somen first?" Fuuka's face fell; he was sorry to miss the Shimabara noodles that he'd been looking forward to.

"The somen...? Well, that's true—you can't eat them if you're a dog. But no, there's someone coming to stay. A lodger."

"Huh? What do you mean?" Fuuka peered into Sora's face with wide eyes.

"We're going to rent out the rooms upstairs, since we're not using them."

"Nooo!"

Sora had known Fuuka wouldn't like it, of course, so he hadn't been able to bring himself to break the news until now.

"It's okay. I made sure the credit company looked for someone who met all our requirements, and there's nothing personal in the transaction. The lodger will just live upstairs and go to work every day during office hours. I asked for someone who wouldn't spend weekends inside, too."

The credit company was to act as the point of contact between the lodger and Sora, including collecting the rent. Sora had presented an astonishing number of conditions for the tenant, including a penchant for outdoor hobbies.

"But why? Do we have to?!"

"Living here turned out to be more expensive than I expected. We've somehow pulled through for two years, but the maintenance costs are high, and I admit the new job hasn't been taking off."

Sora had left the Public Prosecutors' Office after only two years and opened his own firm as a certified fraud examiner. He got a certification for it because he thought he'd be more suited for a job that didn't involve criminal prosecution.

"My current project is nearly done, but I don't have anything else lined up. I'm in a pickle."

"But didn't you like your old job?"

Fuuka still had no clue why Sora had quit in the first place.

"Well…"

Sora didn't know quite how to reply.

As a public prosecutor, he'd had to deal with all kinds of criminal cases. When he was prosecuting cases that involved discrimination, violence, and murder, Sora's own desires hadn't sat well with the scope of the law, and he'd noticed his desire to act outside its limits.

"If it was a matter of liking or disliking it, then yes, maybe I liked it. The only problem was it wasn't for me."

Sora chose his current profession because he wouldn't be anywhere near the death penalty. He was still conducting hearings, just as he had done in his previous work, but no one would die at the end of a corporate embezzlement case. For Sora, in his current state, that made a very substantial difference.

"I prefer the work I'm doing now, but there's not much demand."

He'd noticed too late that business corporations in Japan weren't so eager to hire a certified fraud examiner, which was a profession that originated in the US. Japanese companies were completely averse to bringing a third party into their affairs.

"Then let's move somewhere else. It's pricey here, right? We've moved houses a hundred times before—why should we live with a stranger just to stay in this one?"

Fuuka bit his lip and shook his head like a little child, despite his mature features.

"I see your point, but…"

Fuuka was right. Before they'd settled here two years ago, the brothers had moved from one place to another countless times. Once, they even packed up and left after just a week in a new town, when small children in the neighborhood started gossiping excitedly about the big white dog transforming into a human being at night. Though Fuuka shouldn't have been able to change into a human in front of other people, children seemed to be an exception. They could see time in a way that grown-ups couldn't.

"Would you rather move out than live with a lodger, Fuuka?"

On the low dining table in the living room, the packs of Shimabara somen from the Kashiwagis sat in a row. It wasn't the first time the old couple had given them something to eat. It was clear they cared a good deal about the young man living by himself with his big white dog.

"…I dunno."

Fuuka noticed Sora gazing at the somen, and he flumped back on the floor with his arms and legs spread out.

"So you don't wanna move, Sora? That's something new, isn't it?"

They had moved so many times in the past that their spacious house was almost empty, with only the bare minimum of clothes and food, alongside Sora's books and tools of the trade in his office.

"Well, we did buy this house."

Even the real estate company had thought Sora was a dubious customer. He looked younger than thirty, and the house seemed to be a purchase beyond his means. But he had paid for it all up front. Though he'd never settled in one place, he had gradually accumulated his savings in his frugal lifestyle. He'd invested all of it and made enough profit on the market to prepare the sum. His years of experience working part-time in Kabuto-cho—the Wall Street of Japan, where the Tokyo Stock Exchange and many security companies were located—paid off.

"I mean, I do like this house, too. It's cozy and peaceful," said Fuuka.

The house was a traditional Japanese-style home, built fifty years ago. Spacious but old, it was practically worth just the price of the land. That was another reason Sora could afford it. But they'd had to renovate the kitchen, bathroom, and more, so he ended up having to spend more than expected. It wasn't easy for him to keep up their life.

"Do you remember Mother and Father, Fuuka?" Sora asked suddenly, bracing himself.

"Nope, not at all." Fuuka's light tone surprised him.

"Me neither." Sora smiled wistfully. For some reason, relief washed over him, tinged with a slight loneliness.

Mr. and Mrs. Kashiwagi lived in the same neighborhood, two blocks away to the east, and they often asked Sora if he was eating enough. Perhaps Sora's words when he moved in had left an impression on them—he'd meant to be modest when he mentioned that the house went over his budget—and ever since, they'd been concerned about whether he had enough to eat.

Sora wondered whether this was what having parents was like.

"I like them, too, the Kashiwagis," Fuuka said, smiling. They rarely thought about their parents, so he guessed the couple was on his brother's mind. "But I just can't live with a total stranger."

Fuuka had a point. Although Sora had asked the credit company to find "a trustworthy working adult who only comes back home to sleep," there was a limit to how much a contract could restrict the lodger's lifestyle. There were bound to be some occasions when the tenant and Fuuka would have to be home by themselves. For Fuuka, that would be a new experience.

"I'm always the only one in your life, Fuuka." Deep down, Sora wanted Fuuka to have something different.

"I don't need anything else," Fuuka said casually.

Sora thought that was fine, but he also felt something had to change. Without thinking, he buried his face in Fuuka's chest again and listened to his heartbeat. It was less something he did automatically and more like a compulsion.

"Is it comforting? Anything wrong?"

Fuuka's childlike quiet made Sora aware of his own anxiety. He tried to trace that anxiety back to its source and found an unpleasant memory there.

"Someone told me at work today, 'You're so sure you're always right.'"

"You *are* always right, though, aren't you?"

At Fuuka's simple answer, Sora let out a long sigh.

"Well, I don't think I am, Fuuka," he said, as if he was explaining to a child, and stroked Fuuka's bangs.

If Fuuka stays with me like this, that's all I need. As soon as the thought crossed Sora's mind, overwhelming dread gripped his chest.

"The tenant will be here soon."

It's for the best, to have someone else here. It has to be.

If a stranger lived with them, Fuuka might grow up more, and he might even turn into a human. If he did, then he would be sure to stay with Sora, and Sora would have nothing to worry about anymore.

"Why don't we try living with them for a few days? And if it feels impossible…let's sell the house," said Sora. He felt bad for not talking this over with Fuuka beforehand, so he would be sure to do so before making another big decision.

The mediating company had already signed a contract with the new lodger. Sora picked up the unopened envelope with the paperwork. Under ordinary circumstances, he would never have left any documents he received unexamined, but the case at Daitokyo Bank had been unusually rough going thanks to that attorney hired by the opposition.

Struggling to reach the stage of preparing a report, Sora had been neglecting his daily chores.

"I'm sorry I didn't tell you sooner, Fuuka. The suspect who embezzled a huge sum of money brought in this attorney, and he's been an absolute headache."

"I don't know what you're talking about. At all." Fuuka pouted and rolled around on the tatami floor.

Fuuka couldn't go outside by himself. The only person he could be human around was Sora. So when Sora was at work, he couldn't go for walks, and all he could do was stay home by himself. For Fuuka's sake, Sora wanted a spacious house, at least.

"I should've picked some countryside town, but what little work I get is mostly from companies in central Tokyo."

"Why'd you even go into law, Sora? I'm here for you whatever you do, but just wondering."

Fuuka turned to Sora with a quizzical look. He didn't understand what Sora did, but he was suddenly curious why his brother had studied law, taken the national bar exam, and chosen it as his profession.

"Who knows?" Sora laughed without answering and opened the envelope. Just as he was pulling out the papers, the doorbell rang. "I see they're punctual. That's a good sign."

The credit company had called to tell him the lodger's last name and that they would be arriving at six o'clock.

"Let's say hello and make sure they know they'll be living here as a lodger, not sharing our living space. Come, Fuuka."

Sora stood up and prompted Fuuka to join him.

"Say hello? I'm gonna turn into a dog anyway."

"Doesn't matter. I'll still introduce you as my family." Sora took Fuuka's hand, and Fuuka beamed.

Sora pushed the button on the door phone, certain that it was the new tenant. "Hi, this is Oushuu. I'll get the door in a moment, so please come in through the gate next to the office."

Fuuka got up and hugged his brother like a little boy, and they went to the front door holding hands. Though they were two grown-up brothers now, Fuuka would transform into a big white dog the moment someone else was in their presence.

Sora stepped down to where the outdoor shoes were kept, and after slipping on a pair of wooden geta sandals, he slid open the front door.

"Welcome. I suppose it's a little too early to say good evening."

There was a man standing in the doorway—but Sora and Fuuka were still holding hands. Fuuka hadn't transformed into a dog.

"Hello, I'm Tamura, your thoroughly vetted new tenant."

The man introduced himself airily, in a deep, calm, but somehow cavalier voice. He wore a well-tailored dark-gray suit, his jacket draped on one arm, and he had a sturdy build, with facial features that matched his physique.

"Tamura..."

Dumbstruck, Sora stared at the man standing there with a black suitcase.

"Aaargh! Tamuramarooo!!"

As human Fuuka screamed, the man gave an amused smile.

"You made somen with ponzu sauce and spicy sesame oil, fried summer veggies, and shabu-shabu pork? And with grated daikon radish, no less. Seriously...why so fancy?"

It was just past seven, and Sora, Fuuka, and Tamuramaro were sitting at the low dining table in the living room, having slippery-smooth somen garnished with everything Tamuramaro had just described.

"I can't stop eating!"

Apparently, Tamuramaro was relishing every bite of the somen, special summer shabu-shabu style, which Fuuka had rustled up all by himself.

Tamuramaro sat on the front-door side of the living room, drinking a can of beer he'd brought in a cooler bag and enjoying the somen. Fuuka sat on the kitchen side, glaring at the man with a look of discontent, distrust, and disquiet.

"Such a pretty shade of purple, these eggplants. And they're so juicy with the ponzu, Fuuka. Thanks for cooking, as always," said Sora, sitting on the office side of the living room.

"I see, the little slits you made helped them soak up the flavor... You're really something, Fuuka. Can't get enough of the grated daikon and the chili sesame oil, or that tang of garlic. Since when did you turn into such an impressive cook?"

Though he was the same age as Sora, as his tenancy documents confirmed, Tamuramaro sang Fuuka's praises like some older uncle. Sora did look younger than thirty-one; meanwhile, Tamuramaro gave the impression of a mature man at ease.

"Well, I don't have anything else to do. I picked it up 'cause I wanted to make good food for Sora."

"Fuuka even makes spicy sesame oil from scratch."

"Wow, you're all grown-up now... This goes great with beer. It would've been perfect after a good bath."

"Go home when you're done! Why're you even eating with us anyway?!" Fuuka barked before Sora could say anything.

As manly as ever—to the point that it irritated Sora—Tamuramaro tugged his shirt open.

"You look like a grown-up, but you've got a rude mouth, Fuuka. Funny, isn't it? You two were born from the same parents, but everything about you is completely opposite. Even your hair, black and white." He swigged his beer, studying the brothers, and shrugged. "You're like the black and white stones in a game of Go."

"Sora's mature enough for the both of us, so I don't have to be!"

"Fuuka, what kind of reasoning is that?"

"But it's true—you are!" Fuuka, still in his apron, tied his silver hair into a ponytail, leaned over the table, and glowered at the intruder. "I'm never gonna live with you, ever!! You've got no right to show up at our house! I never wanna see you again!! I thought we'd seen the last of you ages ago!"

"Fuuka, I don't mind you watching TV during the day, but..." Sora sighed, guessing Fuuka must've picked up even more phrases from some violent TV series.

"But I like the drama."

"If you can, watch some educational programs, too."

"You think educational programs can teach him manners?" Tamuramaro cut in, looking incredulous. "You're more like a mother than an older brother now. You studied at school, didn't you, Sora? Don't let the TV teach your brother."

Sora wanted to make a biting retort, but no words came. Instead, he mustered up the courage to share with Fuuka something he should have shared long ago. Something he had failed to mention, even though he'd been meaning to for many years before Tamuramaro arrived at the doorstep that day.

"I have something to tell you, Fuuka." Sora quietly laid down his chopsticks.

It was a little bewildering to see just how much Fuuka had grown—he wasn't much different in build from Tamuramaro now.

It wasn't just the size. Until just now, their first reunion with Tamuramaro in a long time, Sora hadn't realized just how much Fuuka shouted out things that were completely different from what he himself was feeling.

"Again? What nowww?" Fuuka cried petulantly, facing Sora on his left. He could tell it wasn't going to be anything good.

Sora knew how Fuuka felt about this man; they had left him behind years ago and never wanted to see him again. But he took the plunge and revealed the truth anyway.

"To tell you the truth, I saw Tamuramaro earlier this afternoon as well."

In the fourth-floor conference room of Daitokyo Bank's Mejiro branch, in a dark-gray suit, an attorney had irritated Sora with his display of superior composure. That attorney was, in fact, Tamuramaro himself.

"What?"

"And we met in court several times when I was a prosecutor." Sora hesitated to go back even further, but he continued. "...And we were in the same cohort at university, too."

He'd put down his chopsticks so that he could place his hands on his knees, and he sat upright, his legs folded underneath him. "I'm so sorry," he said as he bowed to Fuuka.

"Whaaat?! You went to that school every day for years—you mean you've been together with him constantly all that time?! And even today? What the heck?!" The emotion in Fuuka's voice was less anger and more sheer surprise.

Many long years had passed since Sora had last seen Tamuramaro, and he hadn't intended to face him ever again. But Sora had reunited with him at university thirteen years ago and had been running into him from time to time ever since.

"Not 'constantly.' I keep bumping into him, that's all. I've gotten so used to it that when the credit company told me the new lodger's name was Mr. Tamura, I just didn't connect the dots. I'm really, really sorry. Forgive me."

"Why didn't you tell me?!"

"I thought you'd get mad."

Sora's guess was spot-on. And given this information had been hidden for thirteen years, Fuuka was fuming so much his hair itself was bristling. It seemed nothing could mollify him.

"And you were just fine being with him this whole time?!"

"I haven't 'been with him,' and I'm not fine."

It had been a shock for Sora, too. After completing all the administrative procedures for applying to the university, studying for and passing the exams, and scraping together the entrance fee and the tuition, when he finally stepped onto the campus on day one, he was greeted by

Tamuramaro. "It's been a while," the man had said, looking totally at ease and apparently oblivious to Sora's discomfiture.

"But I just couldn't give up on law."

"You can do law all you want! That doesn't mean we should live with him!!"

"That's a different story. I really had no idea that the Mr. Tamura who'd passed the screening was Tamuramaro until I opened the front door. I don't have any intention of living with him, either."

When Sora glanced at Tamuramaro, who was sitting on his left, he was merely watching the brothers' exchange with a carefree, amused expression. He'd polished off the somen a while back.

"But, Sora, why didn't you even check his full name?!"

"I had his papers, but it was just so hectic until this evening, you see… I told you, the suspect's attorney is a real piece of work."

Sora finally had the chance to look through the documents, but it was too late. The credit company, to which Sora had already paid the commission fee, had finalized the contract with Tamuramaro.

"I'm a real piece of work, huh. You never were very endearing."

"I can't believe you're willing to defend a man who misappropriated an enormous amount of money and doesn't even show any sign of remorse."

"I'm not defending him. I'm only his representative, and he did what he did because he doesn't understand how law or documentation works. He just doesn't get the cause and effect. If he swindles a whole lot of money, he'll be suspected, and once the investigations begin, his crime will be exposed to the unsympathetic gaze of others. He doesn't understand that, and that's why he needs an attorney."

Tamuramaro delivered his spiel in his typical nonchalant manner. It was impossible to tell whether he was being serious or not.

"You should bring evildoers to justice."

The words flew out of Sora's mouth before he could even think about it. This was a familiar exchange for both Tamuramaro and himself, repeated countless times over the years.

"And they are brought to justice—under the law, at least. Besides, not every evildoer is a criminal, and good people can break the law, too. Everyone's human. Everyone's the same, but not equal."

"You and your twisted rhetoric…!"

Sora could tell Tamuramaro was trying to cloud his judgment, but he couldn't completely block out the man's words.

"No… It's too difficult for me. I can't handle it."

"Sora…" Tamuramaro's dark eyes widened. "So you do think it's difficult, then."

"I only meant what you say is difficult. I chose to work in *ritsuryo* because I believe criminals should be brought to justice! I believed that was the best way for me to face them…"

Sora's voice rose as the word *ritsuryo*, the man-made codes of law, came to him for the second time that day. He had strictly forbidden himself to let emotions get the better of him, though, so he let out a long, deep breath in an effort to release the indignation simmering underneath the surface. Even when he was investigating fraud, he never allowed himself to get emotional.

"I can't live with a lawyer who might represent any party under scrutiny in my work. How did I get into this mess? It's a conflict of interest."

He avoided Tamuramaro's eyes and started to review the tenancy contract once more, searching for a loophole to nullify the agreement.

"Only until Monday, though. Of course, I'm well aware of that, and I have it all figured out," said Tamuramaro.

"Don't give me that. I left the screening up to the company, just to keep some distance from the lodger. I didn't even do an interview. But now… How'd you find out about the rental anyway?!"

Only now did Sora's brain catch up to the fact that it couldn't have been a coincidence, and his voice rose again. Tamuramaro's close presence provoked him, and he was unusually agitated. He wanted this interloper to leave even more than Fuuka did.

"I didn't just 'find out.' I keep a close watch on you. That's why I even applied for the same department of the same university. That's how I became a lawyer. Digging up some info on a credit company and passing a screening? Easy as pie."

Already stretching out on the tatami floor as if he owned the place, propped up on his elbow, Tamuramaro announced all this without batting an eye.

"I'm going to terminate this contract," Sora declared, looking straight at Tamuramaro.

"Then I'll sue you, although it'll be a pain in the neck. You know I'm a young but extremely competent lawyer, don't you? Imagine the trial dragging on for decades as we live here. Together at home, together in court. I don't mind either way. Fuuka, you should make me this somen again sometime."

"Soraaaa! Can't you do something?! I'm not making my chili oil for Tamuramaro!"

The blend of clear sesame oil infused with fried garlic and cayenne pepper took some effort, and that effort was for Sora and Sora alone.

"It all depends on how you look at it, right? I mean, it's not the first time I've lived with you two. I'll never be late on rent, and if you have me as a lodger, Fuuka can stay in human form in the house anytime, even when I'm around."

"Well, when you put it like that…" Sora had no reply for that, and he looked at Fuuka.

His little brother must have been born a human, but at one point, he began to transform into a white dog in the presence of other people. Tamuramaro was the only one besides Sora who didn't trigger the transformation. Actually, Sora knew exactly why.

"Come on, Brother. I'm really not bothered about turning into a dog—you know that. As long as you turn on the AC for me before you leave, I'm comfy."

Whenever Sora left Fuuka by himself, he was content to wait at home, sometimes without even having the AC on. If he was by himself, he would wait in human shape, but sometimes in winter, he'd curl up in a ball as a dog to keep himself warm without turning on the heating.

"You always say that, but…"

Fuuka never complained to Sora about any inconveniences. Not even once.

But recently, Fuuka had begun to express his own feelings of dissatisfaction or distress outwardly, feelings that were only his. In the past, any discontent or pain or anger in Fuuka had always been a reflection of Sora's. They'd felt exactly the same, at the same time and place.

"I know you don't like Tamuramaro, Fuuka."

For a very long time, they had been a dissimilar but inseparable set, like a pair of black and white stones in Go. They were two in one, merged in a single life. But at some point, the younger brother had found anger that the elder didn't feel.

"But he's right—if you can stay in your human form as much as possible…"

If Fuuka was beginning to have emotions of his own, Sora hoped that more time in his human form would improve the chance that he would become a human being completely someday. Time probably wasn't what Fuuka needed for that, Sora knew, but he still hoped.

"I'll put in plenty of money for the food expenses, too. I'm a single lawyer, you know. I even donate to an NPO at the end of the year to cut back on my taxes—I pay the tuition for children who want to go on to higher education."

"Can you make up your mind if you're a bad person or not…?" Sora groaned at Tamuramaro being Tamuramaro.

"You have a troublesome habit of trying to judge whether something is good or bad right off the bat," said Tamuramaro with a wry grin. "You should do something about that."

As if to challenge his words, Sora snatched a cool can of beer from Tamuramaro's stash and cracked it open without asking.

"So have we come to an agreement?" Tamuramaro teased, raising his beer in a mock toast.

Just a few moments ago, Sora had wanted him to get out of his sight as soon as possible. Whenever Tamuramaro was with him, Sora couldn't keep his emotions to the low, steady line he normally did. Neither he nor Fuuka could stay the way they always were in Tamuramaro's presence.

"...I admit it *is* a good deal."

And Sora didn't think staying the way they were was a good idea.

"Could you still make that spicy oil for me, Fuuka? And I'll choose to give some of it to Tamuramaro. Think of it that way," he coaxed.

"I guess I could try, if I just remember he's beneath me..."

Fuuka was always cooperative when it came to his brother. He was still unhappy, but he gobbled up the rest of the somen and picked up a can of beer for himself.

"Fuuka, you shouldn't drink yet."

"You're a grown man, at least physically. Drink all you want," Tamuramaro interjected, apparently finding Sora overprotective. "Here's to living together again after a long break. Cheers."

When Tamuramaro lifted his can, Fuuka responded by reflex. "Cheers."

But Sora couldn't bring himself to say it. Instead, he said, "In honor of the dead."

"Are you saying that because it's Shimabara somen? That was a gruesome time."

"I seriously considered getting baptized as a Christian around then."

Shimabara somen called to mind the Shimabara Rebellion in the seventeenth century, when the now-famous Japanese Catholic Amakusa Shirou led an uprising against the local lords' oppression of Christians and others in present-day Nagasaki. Naturally, their talk turned to the early years of the Edo period.

"Poor Shirou...," Fuuka murmured sorrowfully and sipped his beer.

"How would you even get baptized, considering our roots?"

"Don't lump us together. We're completely different from you," said Sora, not about to let Tamuramaro off the hook.

"Hear! Hear! Brother's always right." Fuuka laughed.

Tamuramaro heaved a big sigh, much like an older man shaking his head at the naive youths.

"What is it?" asked Sora, irked by his attitude.

"You wanted to be all grown-up, but you haven't changed much, have you? Prove me wrong—I dare you."

"What's wrong with not changing?! Sora means everything to me, and if you even think about doing something to him again..."

"Don't growl so much, Fuuka. You're not actually a dog."

Fuuka bit down on his can and glowered at Tamuramaro.

"Tell me, have I ever done anything to harm your precious brother?" Tamuramaro stretched, his true feelings hidden under his usual relaxed grin.

"...You did once. I remember."

"Tamuramaro hasn't harmed me, Fuuka." Sora reached over to stroke his brother's silver hair to calm him down. Fuuka's glare was still fixed on Tamuramaro.

"Oh, are you sticking up for me, Sora? That's good to hear," said Tamuramaro, opening a second can.

"I'll never forget what you did," Sora answered. Unlike Fuuka, he didn't show any anger on the surface, but his eyes were boring into Tamuramaro. "I can't forget it, and I certainly can't forgive you."

Sora had voiced these words several times to Tamuramaro since they had first met.

"I know."

A somewhat lonely smile crossed Tamuramaro's face. At that, Sora felt his heart trying to catch up to his grown body, but he pushed it down and took a gulp from his beer.

Tamuramaro had moved into the house in front of the Shizukuishi bus stop on the second Friday of September, and in the late afternoon on Saturday the next day, Sora and Fuuka found themselves giving the new lodger a tour around the town.

"The town started with residential houses spreading here, some ways off from the train station, so it's like a little island with a shopping district of its own. You can get pretty much anything here, and if there's anything you can't find, it's usually stocked in the shops near the train station."

They stood at the entrance to the cozy little shopping street. Since it was the weekend, Sora was in his casual outfit: a T-shirt and jeans. He held Fuuka's red leash in his right hand, pointing to the other end of the street with his left as he explained.

"Is that it?" retorted Tamuramaro with a shrug, visibly dissatisfied. "So much for your new lodger who's gonna bring in money for the rent and food." He was in a T-shirt, loose cotton pants, and a pair of old-fashioned setta sandals, bamboo-lined and leather-soled.

"Grrrr." Fuuka snarled, annoyed at the prospect of having to spend the weekend walking with Tamuramaro. This was one of the few days he would normally spend entirely with his brother.

"There's nothing 'new' about you," countered Sora. "Fine. I'll go front to back, left to right, starting from the nearest shop. Japanese sweets, fruits and vegetables, deli, café, soba noodles, ramen, liquor, ramen, bar, drugstore, Italian, bicycles and motorcycles, real estate, dry cleaning, Western sweets, grocery store with meat and fish, bakery, café, sushi. If you step into a couple of backstreets, you'll find a calligraphy classroom, a cram school, a certified administrative procedures legal specialist and a judicial scrivener's office, a tax accountant's office, a hole-in-the-wall French restaurant, and so on."

Sora looked up at Tamuramaro with a deadpan expression, as if to say, "*Now* are you satisfied?"

"Why are there two ramen joints in a row? Ichirou and Tarou."

"They're run by twin brothers. Ever since they were little, they could never agree on which kind of soup base is the best for ramen, soy sauce or miso. A serious feud. Two years ago, their father retired from the stress, and the younger brother, Mr. Tarou, went independent in the shop next door. Ichirou serves ramen with soy-sauce-flavored soup, and Tarou serves miso."

Even the storefront curtains emblazoned with their names quarreled with each other: One was bright red, the other black.

"Do they have to compete side by side?"

"People say it's convenient; they can choose depending on what they feel like that day. And they both learned from their father, so their noodles are pretty much the same. Actually, I agree—"

Sora also ate ramen at both shops once in a while, but he stopped mid-sentence out of consideration for Fuuka, who had snuggled up to Sora's legs despite the hot weather. It wasn't just because he'd been keeping his ramen trips a secret.

"Coo?"

Since Fuuka transformed into a big white dog whenever someone else was around—anyone except Tamuramaro—he couldn't go into restaurants to eat. Out of all the cuisines offered in the food service industry, Sora secretly believed the most difficult dish to re-create at home in its full glory was ramen.

"I'm sorry, Fuuka."

A long, long time ago, Sora had discovered what ramen at a ramen shop was like, and ever since, he had been sneaking out every now and then to have some by himself. Truth be told, the presence of these two ramen shops was one of the reasons he'd wanted to live in this town. Ichirou's soy sauce style was his favorite.

"Let's go eat there sometime. I'm crazy about ramen," said Tamuramaro, eyeing the shops with interest.

Sora glanced over at him, but he didn't mention his own affinity for the stuff.

At any given moment, Sora had to look up at Tamuramaro. Normally, Sora never let anything trivial ruffle him, but when it came to Tamuramaro, he found the position humiliating.

"Oh, there they are. I wouldn't have guessed they're twins. They look nothing alike."

Just then, both Ichirou and Tarou stepped out of their shops and scowled at each other. Ichirou wore a bandanna wrapped around his shaved head, and Tarou wore a knit cap over his neatly tied bun.

"Mr. Ichirou and Mr. Tarou are brothers, but they're two totally disparate people. They're soy sauce and miso, after all."

Sora stared at the twins and sighed, thinking how different he and Fuuka's fraternal relationship was.

"Hey, are you all right, Sora? It's my first weekend here. Can't you be a little friendlier and give me a detailed tour? There are lots of new cafés here. Makes sense for a new town made up of an expanding residential neighborhood."

"No, all the new restaurants and cafés opened really recently."

Sora himself had witnessed the old shops closing and new ones opening up in the last two years.

"Ah, right. Pandemic," Tamuramaro said, quick to grasp the situation.

"Precisely. Some of the elderly shop owners thought it was high time they closed down, and new cafés popped up to take their place. Mr. Tarou, too—the shop that used to be there went out of business, so he stepped in."

Sora explained how the shopping street, which one would guess had been there for decades, came to be lined with newer storefronts. There were probably similar views wherever you were in the world: unnaturally new shops jostling against shops that were permanently shuttered.

"I hardly ever eat out. Fuuka is an amazing cook, and I like eating at home with him."

"How 'bout we go for a drink sometime? You can drink now, so we might as well… Ow!"

Since he wasn't allowed to bite humans, Fuuka head-butted Tamuramaro instead.

"Why not?" asked Tamuramaro. "Might do you both good to spend some time apart once in a while."

"Coo."

Fuuka looked up at Sora with a sad whimper, and Sora met his gaze, feeling puzzled. Apparently, Fuuka was livid at Tamuramaro's suggestion—but Sora himself was not angry at all.

"...We *have* been spending time apart ever since I started university. Even if that was necessary, I don't see why I should take the trouble to go out for a drink with you of all people." Sora sighed, kneeling down and ruffling Fuuka's neck with both hands.

Instinctively, he pressed his ear against Fuuka's body and listened to his heartbeat. Every time Sora noticed that he and his brother were beginning to harbor different emotions, he made sure Fuuka was still there.

"Come on—grow up. How long are you gonna stay there like that?" Tamuramaro cut in.

"The convenience store is on the way to the train station, along the road where the bus runs. That's all." With that, Sora wrapped up his tour of the town with as much warmth as a GPS.

"Hey there, Mr. Lawyer. You and your doggy are always so sweet together!"

A big, cheerful young man with wavy black hair stepped out onto the thoroughfare from the rather chic, black-walled fresh produce store on the right of the shopping street entrance.

Everyone in Shizukuishi greeted Sora like this, calling him "the lawyer who's in love with his dog." It was an apt moniker; even now, Sora had just been hugging Fuuka and pressing his ear against his fur.

"Whoops, is he a friend of yours? Sorry to butt in. I never see you hanging out with anyone." Noticing the tall figure glancing at Sora, the young man stopped in his tracks and scratched his head apologetically.

"Hello, Mr. Keita. No, he's not a friend. He's my lodger, Mr. Tamura."

Straightening up, Sora gestured to Tamuramaro on his right and introduced him to Keita Murakami, the son and heir of the vegetable grocer.

"Pleasure to meet you. I'm Tamura, his new lodger. I just moved in yesterday, actually. I look forward to getting to know you."

Tamuramaro bowed to Keita with a greeting that seemed oddly proper for someone not wearing a suit.

"Huh! Good for you, Mr. Lawyer. A nice, young lawyer like you living by yourself in that big house—you need something to fill the time."

"Woof, woof!" Fuuka protested at Keita's remark that Sora lived alone.

"Right, right—you got Fuuka with you. It's almost like you get everything I'm saying, Fuuka. Smart boy." Keita bent over and petted Fuuka's head.

"I don't have enough money. Or work," Sora explained in his mid-toned, monotonous voice. This living arrangement wasn't for fun, that was for damn sure.

"Come on, Mr. Lawyer. Don't be so depressing. So anyway, I'm having a family feud with my old man every day now. Oh, and here, take these veggies from the up-and-coming organic farmers; they're really good! And help me beat Pops!" Keita reeled this off in one breath, then jumped into the store.

"But, Mr. Keita, as I said before…"

Sora must've explained to the people of Shizukuishi at least a thousand times that he neither worked as an attorney, nor would he agree to represent them in return for organic vegetables.

"Don't they make your mouth water? Kamo eggplants, manganji peppers, mibuna leaves, and kintoki carrots!"

The vegetables that Keita brought out in a bamboo basket were the produce that he himself bought directly from the organic farmers. Keita's father, who wasn't retiring anytime soon, had allotted just ten square feet of the space in the shop for Keita to sell them. The vegetables really were a cut above the rest, but since they were too expensive to buy on a regular basis, even for an affluent neighborhood, his father's decision to limit their shelf space was wise.

"I wanna change the name of the shop, too."

"Greengrocer Oshichi[3]… Seems to me like your father has quite a sense of humor," said Tamuramaro, looking up at the sign on the store and admiring the wit of Keita's father. He pulled out a black case with

---

3. Traditional shops selling fruits and vegetables are called *yaoya* in Japanese, which literally means "eight hundred shop." The name is most likely a reference to the story of Yaoya Oshichi, a girl who was burned at the stake for an act of arson motivated by love; despite the magistrate's attempts to try her as a minor, she insisted she was sixteen (and therefore eligible for capital punishment).

his business cards and handed one to Keita with a smile. "I'm an attorney lawyer, by the way. If I can be of any help, please do get in touch."

"Wow! Two lawyers living together, huh." Keita studied the card, still convinced that Sora was the same kind of lawyer as Tamuramaro.

"Don't do your sales talk in this town. Get work where you're registered as a resident," Sora interjected in a whisper. He didn't want Tamuramaro to stick his nose into some dispute in the neighborhood, which Sora now saw as his own home.

"Is that a law?" retorted Tamuramaro without missing a beat.

Sora clenched his teeth, frustrated that he could only express his discontent in such childish words.

"...Of course, the best way to shut you up is bringing up the law. Typical, Sora." Tamuramaro gave the silent man a somewhat resigned smile. "Not to worry. I won't join in on a clearly losing battle."

Tamuramaro coolly surveyed the store and the current outcome of their family quarrel. However he looked at it, it was the father's management prowess that was holding up the business, at least for the time being.

"I see your office is in Ikebukuro. Pretty close. Mr. Tamura...maro?"

Keita cocked his head to one side, as if he'd heard the name somewhere before.

"Anyhow. Mr. Lawyer, you should be the one to do the divorce settlement between Ms. Tatsuko and Mr. Rokurou."

Keita wasn't kidding. Unfortunately, Sora was bad at giving ambiguous answers, so he couldn't react at all. He noticed Fuuka's tail flipping back and forth in a gesture of growing boredom, and he chose to change the subject. "Bean sprouts and scallions, please."

"Awww! What about our family feud?!"

"I'm not going to take those Kyoto vegetables as payment, and I doubt your quarrel has already reached the point of a legal dispute."

With this honest response, Sora pushed back the basket of organic vegetables.

Guessing what was for dinner, Fuuka peered into the store and rubbed his cheek against Sora's leg.

"And could we have the hakusai cabbage?"

"Shucks."

Keita, still wrapped up in his family competition, picked the vegetables for them. Sora paid and put them in his shopping bag.

"All right, then! See you around, Mr. Tamura!!"

"Just so you know, I'll take on any kind of case, from family disputes to divorces. No guarantees that I'll win, though," said Tamuramaro with a laugh.

Just as the three were leaving, they heard the lively voice of a woman. "Keita! Give me five pounds of kimchi!!" She was a brisk, neat, and tidy kind of woman, and Sora had caught sight of her on the shopping street a few times.

"Hey, Natsuki. Beer and kimchi are great, but how 'bout some Kyoto veggies?"

"They're too expensive. You better do the stocking once you've learned something about cost percentage and management!"

The woman named Natsuki seemed to be at least ten years older than Keita. She talked rough, but at the same time, her advice on management was warm and constructive.

"This town has a rather strong grasp of frugality," murmured Tamuramaro, voicing Sora's thoughts.

"Oh, Mr. Lawyer! Out shopping with Fuuka?" A few steps down from the grocers, the owner of the soba restaurant Kiriya called out to them brightly and splashed some water to clean the street in front of her place. "You're welcome to order some soba noodles from us; there's no minimum! If you help us with prepping the will, I'll make it free anytime, you know. Won't be long till Grandpa tips over!"

"Thank you. Maybe next time. Also, I'm not an administrative scrivener."

Apparently, everyone in town knew that Sora lived by himself in a big house, but they weren't concerned about remembering the specifics of his profession.

"I'm surprised. You're already part of the community here after just two years. But you've never stayed long in one place before," observed Tamuramaro, walking next to Sora and Fuuka. Knowing their past, he was genuinely impressed.

"Well, it was chance, really..."

There was a reason the townsfolk of Shizukuishi had welcomed him like this, but Sora didn't know how to explain it. As he scratched his head, that very reason came walking toward them from down the street.

"Fancy seeing you here, Mr. Lawyer!" The couple was waving at Sora and Fuuka.

"Coooo."

Fuuka noticed them first and wagged his tail with a happy croon.

"Oh, what's this? You have quite a handsome man with you today."

It was Mr. and Mrs. Kashiwagi, whom Sora usually ran into in Shakujii Park.

"Yes, and what a charmer he is."

With his sturdy build and honest face, which made him doubly attractive, anyone would quickly form a positive impression.

"He isn't handsome," Sora answered with a stony expression, inwardly disgruntled.

"Soraaa, come on."

"He isn't. He's a lodger who has been renting a room in our house since yesterday." Sora pointed at Tamuramaro. The childish sullenness on Sora's face was reminiscent of Fuuka when he was a human, in contrast to the tranquil smile that he usually wore whenever he saw the Kashiwagis.

"Hello, I'm Tamura. It's a pleasure to make your acquaintance." Tamuramaro courteously introduced himself in his deep, velvety voice.

Sora frowned.

"We're the Kashiwagis. Is that true? That's wonderful news. We were worried about you living by yourself—I mean, with Fuuka—in that big house of yours."

"Good to see your lodger is a tough man. It's too easy to break into that house, to be frank. It's mostly made of wood, and it's hidden behind bamboo, so we were anxious."

When they explained those specific reasons for their concern, Sora realized just how much the couple had been worried about the eccentric young man who had bought such a house and moved right in.

Apparently, Tamuramaro was as trustworthy as they come in the couple's opinion, and they had nothing negative to say about the new arrangement. He didn't like how highly the couple thought of Tamuramaro, but it gave him a surprising sense of peace to know that Rokurou and Tatsuko were looking out for him so much.

"Thank you for the somen yesterday. It was delicious. We ate it all up already."

"Oh, I had some of it as well," added Tamuramaro. "It was very tasty! Thank you."

Sora, Tamuramaro, and even Fuuka all bowed.

"You're eating together, too? That's nice," commented Rokurou.

"I hope *I* can eat alone before long," Tatsuko joked as usual, even though the pair looked and acted every bit the old married couple.

"Well, we'll see where it goes," Rokurou said gently with a sheepish smile, then turned to Sora and Tamuramaro. "There's some history to this neighborhood, but it's like a town made up of outsiders. I think you'll find it comfortable to live in."

"With the economic bubble bursting, the Lehman shock, and now the pandemic, the people here have come and gone. It might look like a residential neighborhood, but it's really more like a post town, where travelers can rest on their way. It's more welcoming to newcomers than you'd expect."

It certainly wasn't the sort of town to spurn strangers, Rokurou assured them.

"When we—er, when I moved here, Mr. Rokurou and Ms. Tatsuko

welcomed me like this," Sora explained to Tamuramaro. "They're both professional calligraphers, and they've been teaching calligraphy to the local kids for a long time. Many people here went to their classes growing up. Like Mr. Keita back there. They're like the parents of the whole neighborhood. And thanks to them, the people in town also treat me like a friend."

He spoke haltingly, revealing the reason why he had managed to become such a familiar face in Shizukuishi in just a couple of years.

"Wow, you really looked out for Sora and Fuuka..."

For a moment, Tamuramaro seemed to be on the verge of thanking the Kashiwagis, as if *he* were a parent—or at least, that was how it appeared to Sora.

"Of course, dear. That's why we want to ask him to settle our divorce."

"We have a lot of things around the house. It won't be easy to divide."

The couple laughed freely, discussing their divorce as usual.

"You seem very close, in my opinion, but if you ever need anything..."

As clever as the two were cheerful, Tamuramaro chimed in and handed one business card each to Rokurou and Tatsuko.

"Your new housemate's also a lawyer?"

"He's not a housemate; he's a lodger. Also, Mr. Tamura is an attorney, but I am not." Sora glared at Tamuramaro. "And this isn't the time to be shilling for your practice."

"Come on—I'm only introducing myself with a business card. I even enjoyed their somen, after all. Oh, actually..." Tamuramaro turned to the couple. "If it's not an inconvenience, please allow me to pay you a visit sometime. I'd love to get to know you better as your new neighbor."

"You're just renting out a room—no need for that!"

It was rare for Sora to become so animated in public. Rokurou and Tatsuko looked at him with surprise.

"Well, well, Mr. Lawyer. We were worried you only spent time with Fuuka, but it's good to see you do have a friend, too."

"This man isn't a friend! Not by a long shot!"

"You're even living together. You must be close. That sets our minds at rest a little."

The couple looked so genuinely relieved that Sora couldn't keep contradicting them anymore.

Tamuramaro joined in: "I'm sure we'll be quarreling and sharing meals every day from now on—ow!"

"Woof!" Fuuka rammed his head into Tamuramaro's knee in protest at his cheerful prediction.

"Are you all right? What's wrong, dear Fuuka?"

"Fuuka hates Mr. Tamura. You see? He can't even befriend a dog," muttered Sora with a sigh, and the Kashiwagis laughed even more.

"I don't know; it's rather sweet. You're acting like a little boy, Mr. Lawyer."

"He'll make a good housemate."

They seemed to think it was a good thing that Sora's usual composure was unraveled when he was with Tamuramaro. Meanwhile, Tamuramaro stood wearing his best "told you so" grin.

Sora knew he was reacting childishly, but he couldn't get his sulky face to behave.

"Oh, by the way," said Rokurou, smacking his hands together in sudden recollection. "You know that tax accountant's office over there? They said they had something to ask you, Mr. Lawyer."

"I can't defend them even if they helped me file my tax returns, and I do my tax returns myself."

"People in this town like to barter things for legal services… Maybe I'll be standing in the courtroom in exchange for some daikon radishes or bowls of ramen in the not-so-distant future."

Tamuramaro could already see that the locals tried to recruit Sora as their attorney every chance they got, even though he wasn't even a practicing attorney, with offers of goods and work.

"No, it was about that complicated job you always mention. They asked me if you really were in that line of work, since there aren't many people in Japan who do it. I couldn't say the exact title myself. What was it again?"

"Do you mean they're looking for a certified fraud examiner? At the tax accountant's office?"

"Yes, yes. That's it." Rokurou shrugged at the long, difficult name.

"That's great news, thank you. I'll get in touch with them." Sora bowed to them both and started walking away with Fuuka.

"Well, I hope to see you around!" Tamuramaro called out, waving at the couple.

Though Sora always tried to keep his cool, he was inwardly seething now.

"Of course, same to you, Mr.…Maro…Tamura?"

"Hmm? Or is it Mr. Tamura…maro?"

They heard the Kashiwagis' puzzled voices behind them as the couple tried to read his business card.

Apparently, this was nothing new for Tamuramaro, and he went on smiling without any sign of concern. His self-possessed bearing vexed Sora more than it had the day before—mainly because Rokurou and Tatsuko had been just as kind and caring to Tamuramaro as they were to him and Fuuka.

"Maybe the tax accountant needs a certified fraud examiner to look into some company. It'll be a big help."

After buying the rest of the ingredients in the grocery shop Araike, Sora was walking toward the Shizukuishi neighborhood bus stop a little way off from the shopping street, resigned to the prospect of going back home with Tamuramaro. Fuuka was still wearing his red leash.

"Are you really out of work?" asked Tamuramaro.

"There's not much demand for this profession." Sora was still furious, but when he consciously considered each reason for his anger, all of them were immature. He sighed.

"I never got around to asking you—why did you quit the Public Prosecutors' Office?"

It was a long overdue question. Sora had become a prosecutor straight out of university and quit two years later. And two years had already passed since then.

"...I used to think that I was cut out for work within the legal system, investigating and condemning evildoers and criminals," Sora began. He didn't want to hear that question, but as soon as Tamuramaro voiced it, he realized he had never been asked directly, even though there had been opportunities for it in the past two years.

"Knowing you, it must have been better than being an attorney. You'd have to defend criminals, too."

Despite being the one who had asked, Tamuramaro sounded as if he already understood why Sora had chosen the path he had.

A prosecutor probed into crimes within the logic of man-made law, rather than by the rule of force. Sora had believed such a role would befit his powerful conviction that evil should be punished. As a diligent, outstanding prosecutor, he thoroughly investigated numerous suspects during those two years, and, where appropriate, he had indicted the suspect with certainty. When he deemed it necessary, he pursued severe punishment for them.

"Did you think you went too far?" asked Tamuramaro. He had faced Sora in court several times as those suspects' attorney, and he had witnessed Sora corner them ruthlessly without batting an eye.

"Coo?"

As Sora's expression darkened, Fuuka whined and nuzzled up against him sympathetically. Sora stroked his brother's head.

"That's...what I couldn't bring myself to think," he confessed, meeting Tamuramaro's eyes. Even though he now knew that Tamuramaro thought he'd been too aggressive in the courtroom, he couldn't lie about his true feelings. "I kept thinking, over and over again, that the punishment should be harsher. I believed in my own indictment more than the court's judgment. And that's why I quit."

It wasn't because he didn't like the judges' rulings. He had quit because every time he believed that the suspect should be punished more, he had to admit he wasn't suitable as a prosecutor.

"I did have some hope that the legal system might help me be able to live with other people. But…" Sora had wondered whether the law would allow his extremely merciless judgment to coexist with the rest of humanity, but perhaps it wasn't meant to be.

"…I see." Tamuramaro sounded gentle for some reason. His tone called Rokurou and Tatsuko to Sora's mind—the way it felt when they worried over him.

"I also wanted to determine whether the codes of law, the *ritsuryo*, that your people brought in has really made people happy," murmured Sora.

"Happiness? Is that something so easy to see?" Tamuramaro didn't assert his view either way. "But I understand you're trying to engage with those around you, even if through those laws, Sora." He spoke softly, as if to himself. It really was like Rokurou and Tatsuko.

It was the first time Sora was attempting to be a part of people's lives, and perhaps he was succeeding now. Sora was aware of the fact that he was somehow trying, or at least struggling with, something he hadn't been doing for a long time—even if he was barely making it work.

"I'm no good at anything, but they're forgiving."

"You're too hard on yourself. Those people are kind to you, so you must be doing well." Tamuramaro seemed to be thinking of Rokurou and Tatsuko, too.

"Doing *what* well, exactly?"

"The sort of things people do. Expressing love, receiving love. If you can feel them forgive you, aren't you doing the same for them?"

Sora stopped in his tracks and looked at Tamuramaro, who was walking a few steps ahead.

Forgiveness. It was the most difficult act for Sora, and Tamuramaro knew it better than anyone else. Though Sora wanted to ask if Tamuramaro was trying to mess with him, he couldn't find the words.

Fuuka looked lonely, but Sora didn't notice.

"I'm getting hungry," said Tamuramaro, stretching his arms as they reached their house. He didn't seem to doubt for a second that the three of them would be eating together.

Sora was too tired to mull over Tamuramaro's true intentions. He passed through the gate with Fuuka, went up the little path through the garden, and unlocked their front door.

"You got the key to this house from the credit company?" Sora asked Tamuramaro as he stepped in.

"No, they'll give it to me the day after tomorrow. That's when our contract starts."

"…I forgot. Then why'd you come yesterday? You should've waited till I submitted the report on Monday, at least." The credit company had told him about the lodger's visit, but he'd seen the document with the start date. It was the same day his report for Daitokyo Bank was due.

"My domicile is registered at my office in Ikebukuro. Don't worry; I'm meticulous when it comes to those things."

"You haven't changed," grumbled Sora, clearly not impressed.

"What about you? I get the feeling you have," Tamuramaro remarked with a grin.

"See for yourself."

Sora looked down, starting to suspect that Tamuramaro wasn't, in fact, messing with him. He wanted to clarify what he'd meant by "doing well," but it was hard to put into words.

"Woof!" Fuuka barked, looking up at Sora.

"Fuuka? Why are you still…?"

They were in the house now, and the front door was shut, but Fuuka hadn't transformed back into his human shape. Sora followed Fuuka's gaze into the house.

"…Someone's already inside," Sora whispered. Every nerve of his body was on edge. Fuuka's white fur was already bristling. Sora gripped his leash tightly.

"Wait. Stay here, both of you."

Tamuramaro squeezed Sora's shoulder, stepping past him into the hallway. Without making a sound, he glided toward the office side of the house, which was connected to the living quarters by a door.

"You have a hunch?" Sora breathed out, stealing after him.

"Just...don't follow me. Stay back."

The office was silent.

Until the door banged open from the other side with a loud crash.

"...!"

The two intruders rushed out after kicking the door open. They must have hidden in the office once they heard the three come home. Apparently, they either hadn't found what they were looking for or had realized they would be caught.

"Sora, call the police! They're armed."

The men were very burly, wearing plain sweatshirts, hats, and masks, each holding an iron billy club and a boot knife.

"Take Fuuka and go!"

Tamuramaro estimated the reach of their knives at a glance, shoved Sora behind him, and charged at the men by himself. Sora knew Tamuramaro was tough in a fight, but he was still up against armed opponents. Even so, Tamuramaro lunged forward and kicked over one of the men before they could even attack.

Sora was about to finish dialing when the other man sprang at him, more agile than seemed possible from his heavy frame, and pushed the blade of his knife against Sora's throat.

"If I move my wrist, you'll be dead. Throw down the phone. We'll just get outta here; no need to make a fuss..."

Sora didn't mind dropping his phone or letting him draw the blade—what frightened him was another possibility. Something that should never, ever happen.

"Wait, Fuuka...!"

Sora was still gripping the red leash in his hand, and he felt a sharp tug from it as Fuuka leaped at the man with the knife.

"Whoa—a w-wolf?!"

The enormous man went down in a flash, and the blade flew out of his hand, nicking Fuuka's leg. But Fuuka wasn't about to let him off the hook for threatening his brother. Snarling, Fuuka moved to tear the man's windpipe apart without a moment's hesitation.

"Fuuka! No, stop!!" Sora shouted as he desperately dashed across the hallway. Just before the wolf's teeth met the man's throat, he froze.

"Leave what you stole and get out!" The deep rumble of Tamurama-ro's voice shocked the men out of their terrified paralysis, and they dropped the laptop before scrambling away.

They had likely been after the original copies of the evidence and, failing to find them, had attempted to take the whole laptop.

As soon as they were gone, Fuuka turned back from his wolf-dog form into a young man wearing a white silk robe.

"If it were me," said Sora, gently caressing Fuuka's cheek, "I wouldn't mind if you ripped me apart, Fuuka."

The white silk from the continent always looked pristine, and somehow, it had expanded in length and width as Fuuka's body had grown.

"You mustn't kill anyone else."

"But those men—they were trying to hurt you." Fuuka buried his face in Sora's shoulder and shook his head like a petulant child.

"I can protect myself."

As Fuuka pressed down on him, Sora realized how much his little brother had grown. He lay on the floor, unable to push himself up.

"Fuuka," he said again, his eyes clearing. He murmured into his brother's ear: "If you ever want to kill someone, kill me."

Lifting up a little, Fuuka looked at Sora's bright eyes. Just for a moment, a tangle of emotions flashed across Fuuka's face. There was a mournfulness in his expression, but there was also a knowing maturity as well.

"...Fuuka?" Sora wondered at these feelings that he'd never seen in his brother before.

"I don't wanna do anything like that," Fuuka proclaimed in his usual, childlike voice, and stood up.

"I wanted to intervene before it came to this, but if we call the police now, we'll be asked about our dog's behavioral issues," said

Tamuramaro, scratching his head at the brothers' long embrace and looking in the direction of the robbers' escape.

"Sent by Etou, you think?" asked Sora.

"Yeah. Well, just as you surmised, he was linked to a criminal organization and directing enormous amounts of money to them. Those groups don't leave much evidence, you see. I finally got hold of a scrap of it only yesterday. I doubted they would wait quietly for the report on Monday."

Tamuramaro had been concerned about Sora's safety over exposing the fraud, but he kept that part to himself. Instead, all he said was, "I'll accompany you until Etou's punishment is determined."

"I'm fine with that as long as my brother stays safe," chirped Fuuka cheerfully. The sadness in his expression was gone without a trace.

Sora was speechless. Just now, Fuuka had tried to kill a human being. And this wasn't the first time.

"I'm hungry, Fuuka. Could you make dinner?" Tamuramaro gave a light thump on Sora's back and picked up the shopping bag they'd dropped by the front door.

"I'm starving, too," said Fuuka, flexing into a full stretch. "Ah, can you both help out in the kitchen today?" His right arm had a bloody cut, but when he stroked it lightly with his left hand, the wound and the smeared blood disappeared completely.

Sora watched Fuuka head to the bathroom to change. Evidently, he wasn't even feeling any pain.

Sora stood rooted to the spot, unable to move.

"Hey, anything perishable, I'm gonna chuck in the fridge." Tamuramaro grabbed Sora's elbow and pulled him into the living room.

"You're still as strong as ever," Sora managed to say. Tamuramaro had, after all, knocked over one sturdy man with a single kick.

"Why, of course." Tamuramaro laughed, his eyes as calm as ever. "After all, I am none other than the former sei-i taishogun—the commander in chief—of the expeditionary force against the barbarians."

Only when he could hear Tamuramaro's voice clearly again did Sora realize that he had nearly slipped out of consciousness.

It was the third month of the lunar calendar in the twenty-second year of the Enryaku era, or AD 803.

Spring was drawing near in Heian-kyo, and Sora was crouching near the gate to the capital by the Tousandou path, in a place called Awataguchi. He was in his twelfth year, but he himself didn't know that. Clad in a white silk robe, he clutched a short, M-shaped bow in his hand.

"Aren't you sleepy, Brother? Aren't you hungry? Aren't you cold in these?"

His little brother, Fuuka, was beside him, with a short sword sheathed at his side. They'd left the north more than ten days ago, and they had brought their white silk robes with them.

It was a desolate path—barely a path, in fact—winding through the valley between the low mountains. The brothers were hidden under the shadows of the trees, where they'd taken up shelter as well. They'd been living on dried meat and nuts, but they'd already eaten the last of their supply several days ago.

"They say the people of the capital call us 'Emishi' and treat us as barbarians, just for the slight difference in our speech. We won't let them deride us any longer. As unpleasant as it is, we'll speak like they do and wear these robes that we gained from trade with the continent."

The white silk robes were given to them in the northern land. Sora wore his meticulously straight up to the collar, with the sash tied firmly around his stomach. The fabric spread out lightly under the sash, but it didn't get in the way of walking.

"It's really, really hard. But it's fine if you're not cold."

Sora's black hair was long, according to the tradition of the clan, and it was neatly tied back with a plaited vermilion cord and magatama stones shaped like curling teardrops. He drew vermilion lines out from the corners of his eyes. He had tidied up Fuuka, too, his hair flashing white in the dark. They needed to blend in among the people of Heian-kyo, including how he had told Fuuka to call him "Brother" in a formal manner.

This was a ritual. And a rite of politics.

"...Fuuka." Sora studied his brother, who was about the same height as him but whose features were still very childlike, and lowered his bow. "I still think you should go back to the north."

In fact, try as he might, Sora couldn't figure out why he had brought his little brother with him in the first place.

"How come?"

Fuuka probably didn't understand why they had journeyed across the wild trails on horseback all this way to Heian-kyo. He didn't know that his older brother was here to avenge his master, using arrows painted with deadly poison. Fuuka was innocent in all of it.

The people in the capital called Sora and Fuuka's home in the north "Ezochi"—the barbaric, or foreign, land. When the boys were born, the northern lands were already locked in fierce battle against the armies of the Yamato Imperial Court, and a formidable fortress, the Isawa Castle, had been built. The people were weary from the twenty-year conflict. Two clan leaders, Aterui and More, chose to surrender to end the fatigue of their people.

"I am here to assassinate the sei-i taishogun with this bow and arrow. His name is Sakanoue no Tamuramaro. I can do this on my own."

Aterui and More had met the commander and come to know him well before they decided to surrender. Sakanoue no Tamuramaro had convinced them that by surrendering, they could give their people a better, more peaceful life with means of farming, sericulture, and, most important of all, *ritsuryo*. Believing in him, they had accompanied him down to the capital.

"Why're you killing him?"

"He broke his promise. Aterui and More didn't return alive. I can't go back, Fuuka. You should go home on your own."

When the news came at the end of the summer that Aterui and More had been beheaded, the people of the north were devastated. They were no longer the strong band they once were, the Emishi whom the Imperial Court had seen as a force to be reckoned with. After long years of harsh conflict, the execution of Aterui—the pride of their people, their fiercest warrior—was their final undoing.

Awata-guchi was a site of execution, where the heads of the dead were left out in the open for all to see. The travelers pouring into the capital would stop here and observe the beheaded lawbreakers.

"Executing them was dirty enough. But to display them like criminals and use them as a warning..."

Sora was born clever and beautiful, and he was often chosen to perform dances for rituals. On the day his people fell back in the battle, there was even talk of offering Sora to the spirits of the forest.

Sora didn't mind. His people lived with the forests, the rivers, the mountains. He believed that the outsiders, who were trying to remold their way of life with the completely foreign logic of man-made law called *ritsuryo*, were the barbaric and contemptible ones. He felt no resistance to becoming a sacrifice if it would help fight back against their inhuman ways.

It was Aterui, his leader, who had refused the sacrifice. "Do you all think I am so weak as to need the life of a young boy?" he had demanded.

Aterui had made every important decision. His rule brought happiness to many people of the north—even in this surrender. In exchange for his own death, he brought peace and stability to his people.

Aterui's justice was the only thing in the world that Sora had ever trusted.

"Where is he?" Fuuka asked. "Where's the commander man?"

Aterui had been beheaded in the summer, and now spring was coming. Many among their people, once called Emishi, were now starting to engage with the Imperial Court in their daily lives.

"Tamuramaro has declared he will build another castle in the north."

There was no sign of a major resistance among Sora's people. The laws of government were swallowing them up. Their battle had come to a close with Aterui's death.

And so Sora made his way to Heian-kyo, where Sakanoue no Tamuramaro resided. Living among people who gave up the struggle, the women who had loved Aterui helped Sora prepare for his journey. "Come back safe," they told him. But Sora knew he would not.

"So he should be passing this way, on his way up north."

Sora and Fuuka had been lying in wait there for several days. They were used to hiding in the mountains. But they also had to stay awake at all times so as not to miss their opportunity to intercept the commander.

"Fuuka, go back home. Please."

With no food and barely any sleep, Sora was feeling dizzy. He had sworn to take vengeance, but he felt his life ebbing away.

"Everyone insisted that I take you with me, so I gave in, but ever since you were little…" He recalled the times when he had quarreled with his people over what was right and wrong. "You've always been the one to stop me when I fought with people. I don't know why they wanted you to be with me this time."

Sora could never forgive anyone when he witnessed them doing something unjust or wicked, whether they were children around his age or grown-ups, and he always confronted them head-on. When the argument reached the point that swords might be drawn, it was always Fuuka who wrapped his arms around him and tried to hold him back.

"I'm always with you, Big Brother. I'll protect you! Promise." Fuuka flashed a carefree grin, and Sora smiled weakly.

"But how?"

Fuuka had never even fought with anyone before, let alone wielded a weapon. Why *did* he bring his little brother? When? Sora could hardly think straight anymore.

"Where'd those kids come from?" The voice came from behind in the harsh accent of the capital. "Odd to find them in a place like this. Oddly dressed, too."

When Sora turned around at the deep voice, soldiers were already about to cross the path, wearing the familiar armor made of soft leather.

"Maybe they were brought here from the continent? I've seen the likes of them near the Imperial Palace. See, they tie the sash high up, like that."

This was Sora's first time seeing an army. The mass of soldiers under the command of Sakanoue no Tamuramaro, probably on their way to build the castle, was far beyond any horde he could have imagined.

"But all in white? That's peculiar. And their magatama stones are vermilion… I've seen those before. Could they be Emishi?" One of the soldiers who had fought in the northern battles apparently remembered the shape and arrangement of the tear-shaped stones.

"Aren't they pretending to be foreigners from the continent? This is where Aterui was executed, after all… Our commander said we should pray to the dead before we departed, but that's invited nothing but trouble. Seize them!"

Despite Sora and Fuuka's white silks, the soldiers quickly saw past the disguise, and the brothers were quickly grabbed by their arms and hemmed in by the massive crowd.

"Don't touch them! What is it? What happened?"

Beyond the wall of soldiers, a large man dismounted from his steed, suspicious of the break in his ranks.

Sora had never laid eyes on Sakanoue no Tamuramaro, but he knew who it was just from the way his feet hit the ground. There he was—the man who had fought against Aterui as an equal, and the man to whom Aterui had surrendered himself, believing the promise that he could bring more happiness to the people of the north.

"How could he believe in this coward, hiding his own weak conviction under sheets of armor?"

The people of the north didn't protect themselves with such full-body plates. They didn't wield iron swords embellished with ornaments. This man appeared stubborn and honest, but he had allowed Aterui's head to be displayed in the open.

Sora chose a slit in the armor to pierce with his arrow. Mustering all the strength he had, he flung aside the soldier's arm, grabbed the fortified grip of his bow, nocked an arrow, and pulled the string back till it was taut.

"...!"

Before the arrow could be released, Tamuramaro pushed aside Sora's arms.

"Brother!"

Speechless at the heavy, dull pain in his bones, Sora was immediately shoved down on the ground by the soldiers.

"How dare you...! You may be a child, but we cannot let you live. Off with his head at once!" shouted a soldier.

"He should be pleased to die in the same spot as Aterui!!" another one proclaimed.

As Sora heard their voices, his cheek pressed against the dirt, he felt exactly that—honored to die where Aterui had fallen.

From now on, the traces of Aterui, the single guiding light of justice in his world, would only grow more and more faint. Aterui's will was already beginning to disappear. Sora no longer had a home to return to. Even now, the people of the north were obeying a shapeless idea called "law" rather than a human being.

"I don't care if you kill me here and now. But my younger brother was just following me here. Take him north with you...please." Sora bit his lip and begged to the soldiers in a desperate attempt to save his brother's life.

"You don't use the tongue of the north." Tamuramaro crouched beside Sora.

That's right. This man talked at length with Aterui. He knows what our tongue sounds like. Sora glowered at him, his eyes as fiery as the red lines drawn from his eyelids.

"Don't glare like that. You're only a small boy." Tamuramaro stared at Sora with pity. When a soldier tried to pry the bow and arrow from Sora's hands, he intervened. "Wait. Be careful. There must be fatal poison on the arrowhead."

He knew full well how earnestly Sora had tried to kill him, yet he still pitied the boy.

"It's no wonder that an Emishi would loathe me," Tamuramaro said.

This man was incomprehensible.

"But, Commander, we all know how much you pleaded with the emperor to spare Aterui's and More's lives. The emperor was too determined not to 'let the tiger go out in the wild,' as he said, and he chose to kill them while they were still in our hands… How can a mere boy like him understand your pain, sir?"

For some reason, the young soldier who spoke had tears in his eyes.

"I gave them the promise. I was the one who couldn't keep it. It's only natural that they would despise me. Don't kill him. He's just a child."

"No, sir, I can't let him go! He tried to shoot you! Even if you may forgive him, our law does not!"

Could it be that this man is loved by the soldiers here, just as we once loved Aterui?

To Sora, his idea of the man who had tricked Aterui and put his head on display seemed completely incompatible with what he was hearing now.

"How can you tell anyone that your commander was nearly assassinated by a mere child?" said the man. "It's a disgrace. We shouldn't kill children. There's so much they don't understand yet."

As he listened to Tamuramaro's deep, calm voice, Sora heard Aterui's words in his ear: *"Do you all think I am so weak as to need the life of a young boy?"*

"We are about to build another castle in the north," said the soldier. "He may be a child, but anyone who draws an arrow on you now will surely plant the seeds of your ruin, Commander."

Seeing that none of the soldiers were backing down, Tamuramaro heaved a sigh.

Apparently, the long years of violent conflict with the north had left both the northern people and the Imperial soldiers with resentment.

Sora realized that they both held a grudge against each other for the deaths of their kind. There was no other way: He would be killed, then and there. If someone had aimed an arrow at Aterui, none of his people would have let the culprit live, either.

"Just spare my little brother, please."

Tamuramaro, still crouching, took Sora's chin and lifted his face.

"Your little brother… You want us to bring him to the north, eh? Will there be anyone to take care of him there?" asked Tamuramaro, studying Sora thoughtfully.

"Yes. There are women waiting there. Please take him back north. I beg you."

"Understood. I'll grant your wish. We'll take him." Tamuramaro gave a stern order to the soldiers, who looked doubtful. He straightened up, took one last look at Sora's face, and declared, "This child with the arrow not only speaks eloquently, but he is astoundingly beautiful. Offer him to the Imperial prince."

"To Prince Ate, sir?"

"He enjoys his sensual pleasures—he even sleeps with his wife's mother. He'll likely take in anyone who's beautiful. If the boy enters the Imperial Palace and gains the prince's favor, he won't be able to get out again. No likelihood of him returning to the north or coming after me."

Tamuramaro spoke without hesitation, and Sora understood what he meant.

"Fuuka. Go with that man. Don't worry about me."

Sora smiled at his brother. Once Fuuka was gone, out of sight, he would bite his tongue and end his own life.

His precious, innocent brother, who'd tagged along behind him his whole life. He should have left Fuuka behind, but he'd made the mistake of bringing him here.

With a child's purity, Fuuka believed in his brother above all else. Sora's heart swelled to know that at least he could return home safe and sound.

Sora didn't know when he and Fuuka had become so inseparable. Fuuka was a gentle, dutiful brother, sticking to Sora like his own shadow.

That was why he was still there with him on such a dangerous mission, but now Sora was simply glad they could part ways.

"If only Lord Aterui were still here…," murmured Sora. He had no regrets now, and the words escaped him as he felt his own death drawing near.

Perhaps the people of the north were on their way to building a peaceful, stable life. But Sora wasn't satisfied. Such a life was only possible with Aterui's genuine justice. But that honest leader had been beheaded, and to rub salt in the wound, his head had been left out here like that of a common criminal.

Sora could never forgive someone who broke a promise. Even if he died, even if he bit his own tongue, even if his soul was torn into shreds, he would keep his eyes wide-open and spend eternity seeking to mete out punishment.

"His virtue and justice were a beacon as bright as the sun itself. I'll never forgive those who betrayed him."

As Sora prepared himself to die, all he desired was justice.

"Brother?"

Tamuramaro was already gone, walking back to his steed. "He'll live," one of the soldiers was telling Fuuka. "Don't you worry."

"Then I'm going with you, Brother."

"No! Fuuka, you can't!!" For the first time in his life, Sora scolded his brother sharply.

"Why?"

"Your big brother's going to be a diversion for the Imperial prince. Be grateful he can keep his life."

"He isn't grateful. I can see it in his eyes." Fuuka suddenly drew a sword from the sheath on the soldier's waist. "It's going to kill his soul. He hates that his justice is dead. You're all liars."

With those words, Fuuka's eyes blazed a fiery vermilion red. He flung his arm without a moment's hesitation and slashed open the man's throat with the tip of the blade.

"…!"

"Fuuka…?"

He must have nicked a major blood vessel—Fuuka's white silk robe and skin were quickly drenched crimson. And when the next soldier rushed to stop him, not even a sigh or a hint of doubt escaped Fuuka as he thrust his sword into him.

"You little…!"

Now that two of their number were dead, all the soldiers readied their weapons.

Fuuka moved like the wind, dodging blades and striking back, discarding his own sword as soon as it dulled and taking up another from a dead soldier, until twenty men had been slaughtered. Fuuka himself only had slight cuts on his skin.

"What's going on?!"

When he heard Tamuramaro's voice from a distance, Sora became aware that all the soldiers who had been holding him down were dead.

It was as if a roaring flame were swirling, a flame that would not be extinguished for days on end, consuming everything it touched. Fuuka fought like a wildfire that slashed instead of burned.

The fierce fire raged on, as though fed by the wind, and it never wavered as it razed almost everyone around him to the ground. Only some of the men on horseback managed to escape.

It was only a fire burning—and burning was a fire's nature.

Before Tamuramaro could reach them, Fuuka had massacred another ten, then twenty, cutting them down as if it was as easy as breathing, sometimes picking up a spear to run his opponents through. While Sora held his breath, Fuuka was getting stained in blood before a growing mound of corpses.

"Are you all right, Brother?"

A fire didn't feel anything—it only burned.

When he saw that Sora was getting to his feet, Fuuka beamed, not a hint of brutality on his face.

Sora thought about his little brother, who had never even punched someone before.

"My men… It can't be. Just this one child?"

By the time Tamuramaro pushed his way through the corpses, they were long dead.

"Fuuka."

Before he had a chance to think, Sora clasped Fuuka's arm and started running. Fuuka had just been a fire, but his hand wasn't hot at all.

"So can we go back north, Brother? Together?"

Fuuka smiled artlessly, happy to hold hands with his brother again.

He was so innocent. There was not a trace of menace in Fuuka. Even though he had neither menace nor murderous intent, he slaughtered all those people as easy as breathing or drinking water.

Sora ran up the hill to the east. It was steep, but for the brothers, who had grown up in the narrow, craggy mountains and fields of the north, that was nothing.

"Fuuka."

They had played together in fields and mountains from when they were little, learning the art of archery and swordplay. They did everything together. The conflict with the Imperial Court had begun before they were born, but as far as Sora knew, they had never thought about killing anyone with their own hands as they were growing up.

"What is it, Sora?"

Sora, at least, had never imagined taking another person's life until Aterui's death. After that, he had considered murder for the first time.

It probably wasn't on Fuuka's mind, even now. All he did was love his brother and protect him.

"I was the one who broke the promise."

They heard Tamuramaro approaching from behind. When Sora turned back to him, he could see that the commander's whole being was brimming with an inescapable anger and grief, as if his blood were boiling too furiously to be contained.

The mound of corpses that Fuuka had thoughtlessly created was this man's soldiers. Sora had seen how they had admired their leader and the way they addressed him with respect.

"So kill me. Please let your revenge end there," Tamuramaro implored the brothers, whose white robes were drenched in blood.

"My brother…"

—might be a demon. The words almost escaped Sora, but he swallowed them. He couldn't let Fuuka hear that.

"I will take Fuuka. He comes with me." Sora took the sword in Fuuka's hand.

For the first time, Sora saw his brother as a fire that could cut down a multitude in a flash, even without any malice. If Fuuka thought nothing of killing, something could easily trigger him again to remorselessly take another multitude of lives.

Even if his fire was turned on enemies or used for revenge, Fuuka's truly unfaltering blade was not something that should exist within the reason of any human society. It had no place within the laws of government, either, which Sora was still resisting.

Sora loved his brother and cherished him dearly. But that was why he couldn't let him do this. He mattered to Sora more than anyone else.

"Let's go together. Right, Fuuka?"

"I'll go anywhere, if it's with you."

Sora looked at Fuuka, who was grinning as if they'd just been playing a game. Tamuramaro stood watching the pair, transfixed.

"Close your eyes, then."

"Okay."

Fuuka always obeyed his big brother, if no one else. He closed his eyes tightly, still smiling—still stained in the blood of countless people.

At least I can make it quick—no suffering—by my own hand. Sora gripped the hilt of the sword and pulled Fuuka into an embrace.

Tamuramaro couldn't say anything to stop him. He had just witnessed too many of his soldiers lose their lives in an instant.

"Fuuka." Sora said his brother's name one last time.

"Allll righty, then. Hold up, hold up. Don't be hasty, kids."

A voice rang out, androgynous and airy—not Tamuramaro's, not the soldiers', and definitely not fitting for the sordid air wafting from the execution ground.

Sora froze. He was still holding the hilt of the sword tightly, ready to die with Fuuka, but he couldn't move a muscle.

"Who was that?" Fuuka laughed. Perhaps he didn't understand that his brother had nearly killed him just then. As Tamuramaro had said, he was still a child, so there was much he couldn't comprehend.

Tamuramaro's blade remained sheathed as the commander stared hard at the vaguely familiar figure. They were neither like a man nor a woman, nor even a human being.

Sora was too overwhelmed to notice anyone else around him.

"Uhhh, I'm Miroku-bosatsu, or you might know me as Maitreya Buddha. Been around for a while, actually. Don't you know me?"

The figure was obscured from view, wreathed in a strange, white light. The middle finger and thumb on one of their hands touched to make a circle, and the rest of the fingers were held near their right cheek.

"How...long...have you been here?" Sora rasped, barely able to speak. He had misunderstood and thought they meant they had witnessed the whole massacre.

"From before this world began, I reckon. What do you think of this vestment? Looks good on me, doesn't it?"

Now that they mentioned it, speaking with otherworldly nonchalance, Sora noticed that they were wrapped in an ethereally beautiful robe made from a single layer of fabric.

"Yes...it does. But who are you?"

"...Miroku-bosatsu. Haven't you ever heard of me?"

"Don't argue," Tamuramaro whispered to Sora.

"No worries, no worries. I'm not the type to deal out divine retribution and punishment and whatnot."

"Then what do you do?" asked Fuuka openly.

Miroku-bosatsu kept smiling and gazing into Fuuka's eyes. "Well, you see, I take you humans to the Pure Land. My job is to help you pass and rest in peace. I suddenly found a lot of work to do here, so I just came flying over," they remarked lightly, looking back toward the valley.

"...Please guide them to the Pure Land, then. All of them." Tamuramaro bowed deeply for the sake of his fallen men. "Those soldiers are very dear to me. Many of them I trained up myself."

Sora listened to Tamuramaro's strained voice, unable to move.

"Then please take us with you as well," said Sora. He knew what it meant to pass into the Pure Land. In the north, the culture and religion of the Imperial side were already blending into their native belief of the forest. They were building shrines, seemingly overwriting their old beliefs.

"Certainly. I'll take care of the people in that valley. But you two are still alive... You can't just ask me to do that, you know."

"How can we go to the Pure Land, then?" Sora asked in all seriousness. The floating figure was clearly not of this world, however casual their manner was.

"Um, let's see. First of all, I'm born when the human life span becomes 84,000 years, and there's no more robbery, famine, and war in this world."

"Isn't that...impossible...?" Sora asked solemnly.

Whether they were joking or telling the truth, Miroku-bosatsu laughed.

"And preach the teachings of Buddha three times."

"Three times?! That's too much," cried Fuuka, shaking his head violently. That was far too long to listen to a preacher.

"And you'd also have to wait for 5,670,000,000 years."

"I can't wait that long for robbery, famine, and war to end," said Tamuramaro firmly.

"Well then, you go ahead without waiting," Miroku-bosatsu replied with a generous smile. "If anyone can do it, you can. Now, what shall we do about you...?"

In a moment, Miroko-bosatsu had drawn closer to the bloodstained brothers. They hummed, as if they were facing a conundrum, and peered at the boys intently.

"Sometimes it happens. A person who single-handedly kills a multitude is born into this world," they said with a sigh. "About one in a hundred years."

Sora gulped. "How many is a 'multitude'?" He couldn't help asking, though he thought the people Fuuka had just killed in a matter of seconds were already a "multitude" enough.

"A whole village, for example, or a city, or a nation, or a race. Or all who follow a different religion."

Miroku-bosatsu's voice was gentle, but Sora was horrified to imagine the scale of the "multitude" he was describing.

"Easily a hundred times more people than those killed today. You probably can't even imagine it. Once in a long while, someone comes along who can do such a thing. They might be called different names, like Asura, or Yaksha, or the Devil, but they all do the same thing."

Miroku-bosatsu watched closely as the red faded from Fuuka's eyes, then turned to Sora.

"That kind of person will end many lives, working all alone. The numbers are truly extreme, so it can't be easily overlooked," they went on, never ceasing to smile.

"Alone...?"

"Yes. There will likely be more to come in the future, too."

"But why is that? Does the power come from bad karma? If it does, could you absolve it?" asked Sora.

"You don't need *power* to kill. You need intention. To will and to believe."

"What...what belief guides them to kill?" Sora felt like he was clutching at straws—perhaps Fuuka wouldn't do anything like that again if he could only dispel the source of that belief.

"That power of belief is no small matter. If you'd like to call it karma, the force of their belief is the weight of their karma. They were born with the fate of holding a fierce belief."

Miroku-bosatsu looked at Sora with a gentle expression. Then, meeting Fuuka's eyes, they tilted their head to one side.

"Fuuka, is it? Is that really your true name?"

"Mm-hmm. I'm Sora's little brother, Fuuka."

Sora felt a pang in his heart to hear Fuuka's innocent voice. *Could it be me Fuuka believes in so much?*

"In that case..."

We have no choice but to leave this world, fate and all, Sora thought.

"Now, now, don't be rash, I tell you. Do you mean to end your life here, boy, and waste your wisdom and intelligence?"

It took some time for Sora to register that Miroku-bosatsu's words were meant for him.

"Are you going to stay like that?"

"What...do you mean?" Sora wasn't following at all.

"Actually, I don't usually see those who kill multitudes in the first place. What a peculiar encounter we're having." Miroku-bosatsu's fingers still formed that circle. "Now, is this nothingness,[4] or infinity? Or, in fact, a beginning? Or perhaps—"

Instead of finishing the sentence, they unfurled their fingers, opening the circle.

"Wha...? Huh?! F-Fuuka?!"

Their finger was pointing to where Fuuka had been standing just a moment ago—except now a little puppy with sleek, white fur sat plump on the ground.

"Coo?"

"He can't kill a multitude if he's a dog. As long as he turns into a dog in front of other people—problem solved. That's that, then," Miroku-bosatsu announced brightly, and took a good, long stretch.

"Wait a second. But...please let us die as humans, at least!!" Sora begged, rushing toward Miroku-bosatsu before they could take off.

"Who said you could die? To die is to pass into the Pure Land. You're

---

4. Nothingness, or *mu*, is a central kōan, or point of meditation, in Zen Buddhism. In the kōan, it is the answer given to the question "Has a dog the Buddha nature or not?"

far from ready for that, very far. You better stay on your journey until you find an answer."

"An answer for what?!"

"Now, I wonder. Will there be an answer? Of course, death would come as a relief for you. However…"

Miroku-bosatsu turned his gaze toward the mound of corpses at the bottom of the steep hill, the people Fuuka had razed like a blazing fire.

"Don't think you can die so easily."

"Is this…a punishment?"

"It's a journey. If you find what you need to find, you might be able to die as a human being. Maybe."

Miroku-bosatsu didn't even tell him what he was supposed to be looking for.

Something warm snuggled up at Sora's feet—Fuuka. Even as a puppy, he still loved and depended on his older brother.

"Coo." He let out a soft murmur.

"Fuuka…"

There was no blood on Fuuka's pure-white fur. Did this mean he could start over with a clean slate? Or did this mean everything had been returned to nothing?

"Just one thing. Don't tell anyone about Emishi or Aterui, okay?"

"Why not…?" Even in his state of extreme confusion, when Miroku-bosatsu had hardly given him any answers, Sora couldn't help but ask this.

"Because even I can't fathom how long your journey will be. This is *your* journey; remember that. Those who lose are wiped from history. It's an honor to be remembered by posterity. That's the way it goes, you see, so don't let the cat out of the bag."

"Miroku-bosatsu…!" Sora shouted, but the figure had disappeared. He hugged the puppy Fuuka close.

"Whoopsie-daisy, I almost forgot." Miroku-bosatsu reappeared the next moment, then turned to Tamuramaro, who had been staring intently at the otherworldly scene. "Mr. Tamuramaro, you still have some stuff to do yourself. Well, if you feel like calling me up on your deathbed, just say my name, and I'll hop right over again. After all, we're acquainted now."

"Miroku-…bosatsu…" Tamuramaro, who knew this entity, murmured their name just a little dubiously.

"As for the soldiers down in the valley, I'll take them to the Pure Land, so rest easy."

With that, a celestial light swelled from Miroku-bosatsu.

The light washed over people, mountains, trees, and rocks, obliterating all distinction between them, and Sora began sprinting away with the puppy Fuuka before they could be seen again. That was the last time Tamuramaro saw them for some time.

As Miroku-bosatsu had predicted, this revolt at Awata-guchi was never recorded in any of the officially commissioned historical records—neither *Shoku Nihongi* nor *Nihon Kouki*—and was forgotten without a trace in the annals of history.

More than 1,200 years had gone by since then.

"The sei-i taishogun at the time, Sakanoue no Tamuramaro, donated his own residence in his lifetime, and that became what we now know as Kiyomizu Temple."

The TV screen showed Tamuramaro's abode from 1,200 years ago.

"How could we ever have defeated a man who lived in a place like that…?" Sora grumbled at the solemn, magnificent facade of Kiyomizu Temple as he sat at the dining table with Tamuramaro, wrapping gyoza dumplings together.

"Not that I had much time to live there. I had a lot to do. More like a fortress than a home, really." Tamuramaro looked at his own donation, now a mainstream tourist attraction, and shrugged.

"Still wrapping, guys?" Fuuka called out from the kitchen. He was cleaning up the dishes from the authentic-style ramen they'd eaten after the thugs had gone.

"Still going," replied Sora.

"This is a first for me, making gyoza. I'm finally getting the hang of it now," Tamuramaro chimed in.

When they were walking down the Shizukuishi shopping street, Sora had bought fresh noodles to have ramen and gyoza for dinner at home. The scuffle with the burglars had made them all hungry, so they'd decided to whip up the ramen first. Tamuramaro proposed drinks, and they all took a bath and relaxed in front of the TV. Sora and Tamuramaro were wrapping the filling in the thin gyoza skins.

From their experience, this was something they simply had to do that night—to drink and do something completely nonviolent. Regardless of the opponent, a serious battle stirred the blood, and they had to calm it down by doing something else.

"I like wrapping gyoza. It's pretty fun once you pick it up," said Sora.

The small, repetitive motions were perfect for cooling down, and at the end of it all, they had something to eat, so what was not to like? Sora went on, methodically folding the wrappers.

"You're right; I'm starting to enjoy it. The shape's getting neater, too."

There was hardly anything Tamuramaro couldn't do if he tried. Even with his lack of experience, he was making well-formed gyoza in no time.

"What are you gonna do with all that gyoza? Freeze them? You don't have to make so many. I'll do it by myself when I'm home during the day." For Fuuka, who was kneading salt into chopped hakusai cabbage for the filling, there was no need to do anything to calm himself down. In his case, his state of mind in battle was comparable to that of his ordinary life.

At first, Sora thought this was because of Fuuka's innate potential to kill a multitude. But this kind of incident was also nothing new for Sora and Tamuramaro in their 1,200 years. If this had just been a fight with thugs, they would only have needed to wrap a few gyoza to cool down again. What concerned Sora, however, was not the scuffle itself, but the fact that Fuuka had tried to kill their attackers.

"And of course I'd have the data of the evidence backed up to the cloud.

You would've thought it was obvious." Sora sighed at the criminal organization's pathetic attempt to thwart his investigation.

"I'd say it's more a threat than anything else. It's not elegant, but the suspect must be desperate," said Tamuramaro, picturing his client driven into a corner. "Simply put, he snapped."

"He must've had some awareness of his own actions, at the very least, or of the damage he's caused. He's far too unreasonable."

Tamuramaro smiled wryly. "Imagine being quietly interrogated and admonished with valid arguments when you know deep down that you've done something harmful and deserve the punishment. Of course he's angry." He went on softly: "If you can, try toning it down next time. Otherwise, it won't be the last time this kind of thing happens to you."

"Well, I'm trying—"

Sora had been trying to mend his ways for a long time now. He'd been working on it for more than forty years. But his nature wasn't so easy to change.

The TV show was still going on about Tamuramaro. *"Legends of Sakanoue no Tamuramaro live on in many shrines across Japan. Even after his death, he was placed in an upright position in a casket, wearing his armor and holding his sword. He was buried facing the east, as a guardian of the capital in Kyoto. Now he is widely known as a god of martial arts."*

"Ugh, 'god' this, 'god' that. Shut up about 'gods' already," Sora grumbled at the narrator, who was singing Tamuramaro's praises ad nauseam.

"Music to my ears, whenever I hear it. But being buried upright? Man, that boss of mine, Emperor Saga—talk about working you into the ground. If he were alive now, he'd get in trouble with the Labor Standards Bureau in a second."

Now a modern man through and through, Tamuramaro shrugged, thinking back to the four emperors he had served under.

"It's a gigantic place… Kiyomizu Temple, I mean," Sora remarked as he watched the students horsing around on a field trip. Its formidable structure would certainly pass as a fortress. "Did you build it in memory of those who were forgotten by history?"

Whether or not it was meant to be a fortress, it was a fact that the sei-i taishogun had left behind and donated as a temple a site that would survive for 1,200 years. Sora also knew from history that Tamuramaro had worked tirelessly during his lifetime.

"It's for everyone."

Tamuramaro grinned, putting down a wrapped gyoza on a tray dusted with potato starch powder. He knew Sora was thinking of the soldiers Fuuka had massacred that day in Awata-guchi.

"Two sides of the same coin. Back then, we counted heads to determine the winner. That's just the way it was. When you were little, I carried out a large-scale operation of suppression in the north. Four hundred fifty-seven beheaded, one hundred fifty captured, and seventy-five villages burned down. Even then, they said that wasn't enough."

Carefully recounting the numbers, Tamuramaro picked up another wrapper.

"One Kiyomizu Temple isn't enough to honor them all. Right, Sora?" he asked quietly. "You were born in a well of hatred, but somehow you survived…and grew up like this."

After Tamuramaro's death, the three of them had encountered one another countless times as history wore on. In the beginning, Sora could only feel contempt for the man. But as far as Sora remembered, Tamuramaro never showed a hint of hatred toward them. Instead, he always talked to them as a caring grown-up would talk to children. Perhaps even on that day at Awata-guchi, he had spoken to the brothers like that.

"We've both killed many. It was an age when the number of deaths was the axis around which the world of politics revolved. That's why the emperor hid the fact that an Emishi child took down so many soldiers. It's not in any of the records," Tamuramaro explained. The sight of his old fortress had apparently inspired a wave of memories.

"What happened that day…," Sora began. It was the first time in a long while that he had talked face-to-face with Tamuramaro and spoken of Awata-guchi. He gazed at Fuuka, who was making the gyoza filling in the kitchen. "What Fuuka did was also fueled by my anger. I had the same rage inside me. In fact…"

Sora had been stunned by the way Fuuka had stormed through the soldiers like wildfire—but he also remembered vividly that the one who had longed for death to befall them in that moment was none other than himself.

"In fact, that rage was mine and mine alone."

How did Fuuka become Sora's hands and feet, mindlessly enacting what Sora felt? These days, Fuuka's body and thoughts were so clearly distinct from his own that Sora couldn't help but wonder.

"That's only natural," said Tamuramaro.

Sora braced himself for the inevitable mention of Aterui.

"You knew that your beloved master was killed there. And besides, if I could do it all over again now, I'd save your life in a different way."

In the last 1,200 years, Tamuramaro had rarely mentioned Aterui to Sora. But he hadn't forgotten his orders that day to offer Sora as a new attendant to the lustful Imperial prince, who later became Emperor Heizei.

"But if I were to go back in time, that would still be the only way to save you."

As he listened, Sora realized that Tamuramaro walked through from one age to the next with his feet on the ground, fully recognizing the ways of each period without letting them drag him down. Sora wasn't very good at adapting to the logic of the times.

"Either way, I would have died," said Sora. Even if he had been thrown into the prince's bed before he could kill himself, his soul would have been dead.

"Do you still have a grudge against me?" Tamuramaro gave a resigned smile.

At the direct question, Sora thought over it again. Even though he couldn't readjust his own logic, he understood by now that Tamuramaro had been trying to save his life at Awata-guchi. But it was hard to put any of that into words.

"Just now...," he began, switching the subject to the present day. "My feelings weren't the same as Fuuka's. I wasn't angry, but Fuuka was."

"Oh? Can I kill Tamuramaro now?" Fuuka appeared with a bowl of gyoza filling and plopped down behind Sora.

"None of us can die, remember? No one can kill us. You can munchy-munchy him, but keep it at that."

"It's thanks to Miroku-bosatsu. We're all on a journey through eternity," added Tamuramaro.

Fuuka could never remember this fact, and whenever he thought his brother's life was threatened, he nearly killed the one responsible. And in the past, he *had* killed them at times.

"Hey, Tamuramaro, why aren't you more like an old dude?" Fuuka grumbled. He set down the bowl with the filling next to Sora—it was full of salted hakusai cabbage, ground meat, ooba leaves, and a generous amount of scallions kneaded together.

"What's gotten into you? You've never asked me anything like that before." Tamuramaro's eyebrows rose.

Fuuka pointed at the TV without a word.

"Sakanoue no Tamuramaro, who died from a disease at fifty-four years old..."

The program was still delving into the history of Kiyomizu Temple, and the narrator was just mentioning Tamuramaro's age at death.

"I called to Miroku-bosatsu on my deathbed, and they popped up. So I asked them to put me in my body when I was at my strongest and most active."

"What the...? You could ask for *that*? And that sloppy Miroku-bosatsu granted your wish?"

Sora was dumbfounded, hearing for the first time why Tamuramaro's current body was younger than the age he died, or even when they had crossed paths at Awata-guchi.

"It's probably 'cause they're so laid-back. Why so surprised?"

"But—*we* didn't get any older for more than a thousand years!"

"Exactly," Fuuka complained, his silver hair tied in a ponytail and his torso wrapped in an apron. "We couldn't drink much, either!" He cracked open a beer can, as though to make up for all the years he couldn't drink.

"Wait till we fry the gyoza, Fuuka," said Sora.

"No, let's drink and cook together," Tamuramaro cut in, taking two of the cans that Fuuka had brought over and handing one to Sora. "Don't know why, but…this is nice. Making gyoza."

After they clinked the cans together, Tamuramaro was lost in the gyoza-wrapping process again.

"Yeah. Gyoza is good," Sora replied, popping open his own can. He'd always liked making these.

"Who knew you two were getting on so well, living like this," said Tamuramaro thoughtfully.

"Hey! This is weird!" Fuuka broke in, looking back and forth between the two men.

"What is?"

"I dunno! You're acting more like friends now! You haven't been hanging out together without me, have you?!"

Fuuka had been turning into a white dog in the presence of other people for the last 1,200 years, and it was only with his brother, and occasionally Tamuramaro, that he could be in human form. Which meant for all that time, he had rarely been in the company of anyone but his brother.

"No, listen, Fuuka. We were in the same year at university. We took the national bar exam at the same time. Of course, we went to the same get-togethers a few times—"

"Mixers, you mean. Blind date drinking parties." Tamuramaro sniggered, dashing Sora's attempt to mollify Fuuka.

"Ugh! Sora!"

"Well, well. I'm guessing you've never been with a woman, Fuuka?" asked Tamuramaro, more serious now. He himself had had a wife and children during his lifetime.

"How can I when I turn into a dog every time?!"

"Good point. No way around that."

"What about you, Sora?!" Fuuka turned to his brother. "I know what those parties are like!"

"Don't believe whatever he says! I haven't been to any of those parties, and besides…!"

Sora was always doing his best to live his life with as much composure as he could muster, but right now it was spinning out of control, thanks to gyoza, beer, Kiyomizu Temple, and Tamuramaro.

"I've been too busy worrying about other things. That hasn't changed in twelve hundred years," he concluded.

"It's a long time, that," Tamuramaro remarked in a pensive tone, which got on Sora's nerves even more.

"I mean, we looked like children for so long. I wish we would've had a choice."

"Was there a choice? It's one thing to turn back time you've already lived, but another to fast-forward to a nonexistent future, don't you think? Seems reasonable to me."

"You think there's any form of order to what that Miroku-bosatsu does?"

The "sloppy Miroku-bosatsu" had reappeared before Sora and Fuuka several times over the centuries, but they were always as insouciant as ever. There wasn't a single occasion when they had not been irresponsible.

"'Order,' huh. Well, we've already veered off course from the laws of nature, if it comes to that. Wonder how our bodies work? We never die, but we get hungry. We can get injured, too. But…" Tamuramaro looked at the brothers, suddenly more solemn than usual. "Last time I saw you in the Showa period, around the 1960s, both of you still looked like children, just as you had back when I first met you. Now you're all grown-up. What happened?"

It was a question that Sora had puzzled over for a long time, and Tamuramaro threw it on the table so matter-of-factly.

"Tamuramaro," Sora began, turning to face him properly. It was now or never. "You fed us when we were still 'children' in the Showa years, but we left without saying anything to you. I am sorry."

Sora bowed to Tamuramaro in an earnest apology, although he didn't press his starch-and-gyoza-filling-covered hands to the floor. The resulting palms-up pose was rather funny-looking.

"What's this? It's not like you to apologize to me. We'll see pigs flying tomorrow."

"I'd give anyone a sincere apology for discourtesy," Sora retorted, turning away.

Fuuka peered at his face inquisitively.

"I missed you guys when you suddenly disappeared, but I wasn't worried. I knew you wouldn't die. Did you leave because you grew up?"

"We noticed our bodies growing older after we left your house."

The brothers had lived as children for more than a thousand years, but after living with Tamuramaro in the time of rapid economic growth in the Showa period, their bodies had unexpectedly begun to develop. When he reflected on that time, Sora could identify a certain trigger.

"Was that what happened?" Fuuka piped up.

"Yes. Especially you, Fuuka—you shot up all of a sudden. I was surprised."

Fuuka looked back at him with wide eyes. Sora wanted to pet his brother's head, but of course he still had potato starch on his hands.

"We'd slept under the same roof a few times before then, too, in the Edo period and Meiji era. But sometime after World War II, society changed, and it got harder for kids to live on their own. That's why I took you in," Tamuramaro reminisced aloud, summing up his reasoning in plain words.

"We even got pulled into an institution for war orphans by the GHQ one time. Though we escaped almost immediately."

Sora heaved a sigh, remembering their hard times before, during, and after the war, despite their immortal bodies. But come to think of it, that marked the end of an era when the number of deaths made the world of politics go round in Japan.

"A society that doesn't let kids live on their own isn't a bad thing. In fact, it was a step in the right direction, in my opinion," Tamuramaro said, perhaps thinking along the same lines as Sora. "The world does change a lot in twelve hundred years. How'd you get your family register?"

"Once we started looking like adults, I worked by the day, drifting from town to town, and bought it."

"It was lucky for both of us, getting the registration right before everything went electronic. Nowadays, it wouldn't be so easy."

Apparently, Tamuramaro had bought his family register around the same time as Sora. Sora guessed that was when he changed his name as well.

"Why did you pick Maro Tamura, of all names?"

Whenever someone heard his full name, they did a double take. After all, Sakanoue no Tamuramaro was a famous historical figure whose old fortress and such were still featured on TV.

"We're well into the twenty-first century now. I figured I could pass by saying my parents were big fans of the sei-i taishogun, or something like that."

"Was it a joke?"

"I got my name back. Same goes for you, doesn't it?"

Sora was speechless, and he wasn't sure how much Tamuramaro meant what he said.

"Sora's your childhood name, isn't it? It's rather short," Tamuramaro remarked. The subject was trivial, but it snagged on Sora's mind.

Sora tried to explain what it meant, but for some reason, he couldn't utter a word.

"This is so boring," Fuuka blurted out, pouting. "I'm gonna go grill some gyoza. You wrap the next batch."

Fuuka was used to having Sora all to himself, and he found it frustrating to see the way Sora talked differently when he was with Tamuramaro.

"Is he hitting that rebellious age? That's proof he's growing up," Tamuramaro murmured, looking at Fuuka's back as he returned to the kitchen with the wrapped gyoza. Then he turned to Sora. "You're really not giving up?"

For 1,200 years, Sora and Fuuka had been on a journey they'd never asked for. They had nowhere to return to. They couldn't go back to the north now, since it was a completely different place. No one was there to welcome them home.

"I'll find a way to turn Fuuka back into a human."

Against all odds, Sora wasn't about to let that go. Turning Fuuka back meant liberating him from his fate of becoming, as Miroku-bosatsu put it, "one who single-handedly kills a multitude."

"You saw how he tried to tear that thug's throat open back there. How would you go about doing that?"

"I wonder...if he still has the same belief inside him."

"You don't need power *to kill. You need intention. To will and to believe."*

That's what Miroku-bosatsu had said. They never told Sora what exactly it was that Fuuka believed in that made him kill people. But after all these years, Sora finally had an inkling of what that belief was. Yet he still feared looking directly at the truth.

"If only that Miroku-bosatsu had never appeared...," mumbled Sora.

"Then you would've died at the age of twelve, before you even got to know anyone. Is that it?" Tamuramaro smiled with an air of resignation.

"Why did they appear only for us anyway? Once in a hundred years or so, someone *did* appear who would slaughter people en masse. But many of them were initially overlooked, weren't they? ...Like Hitler."

Sora didn't want to put Fuuka's fateful burden together with Adolf Hitler, one of the most famous representatives of genocide in history, but the discrepancy still bothered him.

"Remember what Miroku-bosatsu said."

"What?"

"You could see them. Those too relentless in their belief wouldn't have been able to do that, even if Miroku-bosatsu was right in front of them. That's how they are."

Sora pondered over this for a long time, trying to understand Tamuramaro's reasoning.

"How they are, huh."

The phrase was very vague. Before now, that kind of ambiguity would have been completely lost on Sora.

"And Buddha isn't there to dole out punishments," Tamuramaro went on. "They appear before those who need them."

"But I didn't even know Miroku-bosatsu back then."

Even as he spoke, Sora grasped that this was probably the way it was. He could at least somewhat understand that gods and Buddhas didn't work according to a set of laws, not like the legal system.

"Hey! It's time for episode two!! Change the channel!" A wet towel came flying out of the kitchen with Fuuka's shout, amid the juicy sizzling of gyoza.

"What's that?" Tamuramaro asked.

The two of them wiped their hands with the towel.

"It's the crime drama series that Fuuka's hooked on. He's a fan of the informant, one of the side characters. He wants to dress up like him."

Fuuka was obviously fed up with seeing Kiyomizu Temple on the screen, and he'd grabbed the remote to change the channel. A trailer for the crime drama was already running.

"That *is* a nice outfit. Want me to get it for you? To celebrate our new life together."

"You know only you and I will see Fuuka in this outfit, right?"

The informant's costume was rather idiosyncratic, like an indigo samue that Japanese Buddhist monks wear as work clothes, except embellished with vermilion embroidery. Sora couldn't even begin to guess where he'd go to buy such a thing.

"...Aterui had—"

"Shut up."

Sora cut Tamuramaro off, but he knew what he was about to say.

Aterui had worn something similar, although the resemblance wasn't strong. Sora wasn't sure whether Fuuka had any recollection of it, but ever since Sora had noticed this similarity, he found himself thinking about Aterui more often.

"Miroku-bosatsu told me never to speak of it, but Aterui's name did leave a mark on history," Sora observed. Countless times, he'd almost asked Tamuramaro whether that had been his doing, but he could never say it out loud.

History remembered Aterui as a wise, resilient leader of the north—which wasn't in keeping with how the revolt at Awata-guchi was erased from all records. So many things about Tamuramaro, or Sora's image of Tamuramaro, perplexed him. Things didn't match up between the history the winners had written about Tamuramaro and what Sora saw of the Tamuramaro who sat right in front of him.

"In your case...," Sora began. He gazed at the man who must have betrayed and executed his lord Aterui, who was like a father to him, and left his head exposed in the open. He knew from the soldiers' words at Awata-guchi as well as from historical texts like *Nihon Kiryaku* that Tamuramaro had begged the emperor to spare Aterui's life.

"Your appearance matches your age that's on the register, Tamuramaro. You look older than you did when you were at university, like a normal person. It makes sense that they could turn back time, but not the other way round."

"I don't have as much control over it as you think. I'm just getting along in years, you know." Tamuramaro shook his head and drank some beer. The aging of his body wasn't something he'd wished for.

"But for me, at this rate..." Sora paused.

Forty years ago, after he had left Tamuramaro's house, Sora had suddenly become an adult. A desire had sprung up in him to study and get involved in law—the legal system that developed as an extension of the old *ritsuryo*—so he sought to set up his family register. His life as Sora Oushuu began with applying for university. But even now, he hardly looked older than his late twenties.

"At this rate…what?" asked Tamuramaro, though he'd seemed like he wasn't paying much attention. "You don't want to say it? It's a good town here."

Tamuramaro always spoke in a way that kept some space open—not for himself, but for the one he was speaking to. Even after 1,200 years, this was still an impossibly difficult thing for Sora to handle.

"Gyoza's ready! Right in time for the show!!"

Fuuka rushed in, putting down a tray with two plates of golden, crispy gyoza arranged like a disc on the table.

"Looking good!"

"The ones with ooba leaves are best with just vinegar and soy sauce."

He laid out chopsticks and more beer cans for all of them, his eyes already fixed on the TV.

"Thanks, Fuuka." Tamuramaro crammed his mouth full of gyoza filled with ooba. "Mmm, good stuff! Ow, hot!"

They clunked their cans together again—they just felt like it.

The ooba came from Keita at the fresh produce store. He'd apparently deduced from their other groceries that they were having gyoza for dinner, and he had wrapped some ooba with the hakusai cabbage for free.

"Thanks, Fuuka. So good! Whoa, it *is* hot!" Sora cried out in pleasure, savoring the steaming-hot juice squirting out of the wrap.

Keita had been generous with his gift, and the ooba's subtle, fresh scent made the gyoza irresistible. The three couldn't stop wolfing them down until every single dumpling was gone.

If their bodies continued to stay still in time, never growing any older, they would eventually have to move on from this town, away from the people they'd come to know. It was only a matter of time, several more years at best, until the townspeople would start to grow suspicious of Sora's apparent youth.

I've never felt like this before, thought Sora.

Sooner or later, they wouldn't be able to stay in Shizukuishi. When he thought about that prospect, it weighed down on his heart like lead.

He didn't remember anything about his parents, and perhaps as a consequence, he'd never felt attached to any particular person or town. As far as he could recall, he'd never formed a good relationship with anyone, really. The brothers had held each other close, supporting each other to survive. All Sora needed was Fuuka.

At least, that's how the two of them had been living for the last 1,200 years.

The next day, on Sunday, Tamuramaro went off somewhere on his own, just as the credit company had promised, and was gone for the whole day.

On the Monday of the third week of September, Sora and Tamuramaro were scheduled to meet at Daitokyo Bank to look over the report, but when Sora arrived at the Mejiro branch in his suit and tie, the prosecutors were already there, carrying out documents.

"I do apologize for not discussing this with you beforehand," Nakategawa explained to Sora, bowing again and again. "Considering the scale of the embezzlement and where the money had gone, we thought it would be even more damaging for our bank to try to deal with the matter internally. So we alerted the prosecutors immediately."

The prosecutors' team moved with alacrity, and although he had called them in himself, Nakategawa seemed shaken by it.

"I believe it was a wise decision," said Sora.

"Of course, we will pay you the fee that we agreed on initially. By the way, I heard some gang members even came to your residence, Mr. Oushuu—I hope you didn't suffer any injuries. Are you safe?"

"Oh? Yes, I'm fine."

Judging from the question, Sora surmised that Tamuramaro had tipped them off with the necessary information to begin the investigation. He recalled Tamuramaro saying he'd gotten hold of a scrap of evidence, too.

"This is the first time something like this has happened since I became the general manager, so to be honest with you, I was at quite a loss as to how to handle the situation," Nakategawa went on, sheepish and apologetic.

"Daitokyo Bank has a policy manual, don't they?"

When he began his investigation, Sora himself had seen the manual, which specified what to do when an employee commits some act of dishonesty.

"Well..." Nakategawa sighed, a troubled look on his face. "I made the decision myself to put a stop to this before you are harmed. I have no regrets. I am so sorry, Mr. Oushuu."

At Nakategawa's sincere words, Sora understood that the manual he had seen was just for show.

"Then what about you?"

"I'll be fine. It's an immense issue, and we have the receipts," he said, looking over at someone on the same floor with confidence.

No doubt it was Tamuramaro who had obtained those "receipts."

"We'll manage somehow," Nakategawa assured him.

Nakategawa had handled the situation in the best way he could, going above and beyond his own capacity and discretion. Sora realized that Nakategawa was a bigger man than he'd imagined.

"...I should apologize to you as well. I'm very sorry."

"What do you mean? Please raise your head."

Of course, Nakategawa had no idea why Sora had just bowed to him.

"Um, Mr. Oushuu. We did receive a tip-off from someone else, but it was because of you that I could make the decision to report it to the prosecutors." Naturally, Nakategawa kept the informant unnamed, but he spoke earnestly.

"Oh?" Sora looked up, confused.

"How can I put it...? I'm ashamed to admit it, but when I thought about the future of the Mejiro branch and the bank itself, I did try to find ways to evade the whole problem without exposure. Many times, in fact. But..."

Nakategawa studied Sora's black eyes with some kind of awe. Sora could grasp, just barely, that he was being recognized and admired.

"But it was impossible to resist your influence. As Etou himself said, you are irrefutably right, Mr. Oushuu."

Sora couldn't answer. His fingers curled into his shirt over his chest.

"You know, it's the first time I've seen prosecutors at work up close like this. It makes me wonder, weren't you much more suited for this job than your current one? I'd feel confident if I knew you were one of them, Mr. Oushuu. No criminal would stand a chance. I can just picture it."

"That's—"

—*not true*, he was about to say, but that would have been a lie.

"Well, I'll leave you for now, Mr. Oushuu. We'll speak later."

Nakategawa rushed off, busy with his responsibilities as the general manager.

Sora had judged Nakategawa earlier—he simply couldn't comprehend why anyone would even consider covering up the crime. But now he realized that Nakategawa had been struggling inside, and despite the internal conflict, he had reached the right decision.

Sora hadn't sensed any of that inner turmoil, even though he'd been sitting right next to him. People were so difficult to figure out. Was it the core inside him—that burning flame—that got in the way again? Had he not quenched it after all?

"It was impossible to resist."

There were some people in whom Sora couldn't see goodness, and they had even cowered under Sora's gaze.

"But that's exactly why I quit the Public Prosecutors' Office." He couldn't make himself lift his face, and he heaved a deep sigh. He recalled his own words to Etou during their last hearing.

"Did you ever stop to imagine how your own greed might lead to someone's death?"

"No wonder I scare them."

Still looking down, Sora felt like an empty shell, hollowed out in his pursuit of justice. He heard an icy, distant voice ask, *"What's wrong with being right?"*

After a long interval, Sora realized it was his own voice. He was still rooted to the ground.

"Hey, Oushuu!"

A familiar voice called to him out of nowhere, and he noticed he'd been holding his breath.

"Fujiwara."

It was his old colleague, an assistant prosecutor named Fuhito Fujiwara. He raised his right hand at Sora without so much as a smile.

"It's been a while. How are you?" Sora asked. As expressionless as Fujiwara was, Sora felt something stir in him to see his acquaintance. He hadn't wanted to run into Fujiwara here and now, but he'd wanted to talk to him again before long.

"Skip the small talk. You're the investigator on this case, right? I have some questions to ask for the report."

Though he was only an assistant, Fujiwara never showed Sora any sign of courtesy or cordiality.

"Of course. I've just prepared my own report. I'll assist your investigation as much as I can," Sora answered deferentially.

Fujiwara shot him a dark look, then turned away to get on with his work.

Someone put a hand on Sora's shoulder. "You know what kind of response aggressors want from their victims? Normally, it's shrieking or crying."

It was Tamuramaro. This time, Sora could breathe out a long, deep sigh.

"No need to show an aggressor the reaction they're looking for." Tamuramaro shrugged, looking at Fujiwara's back.

"Fujiwara isn't an aggressor," Sora murmured, shaking his head.

He wasn't an aggressor, but he certainly was a difficult person to communicate with. Sora found him even more of an enigma than people usually were to him.

"Don't let him get to you every time."

"Is that how you let everything pass by you without actually dealing with it?"

Tamuramaro was right. Sora always gave reasonable answers to

Fujiwara's rude treatment, and sometimes it had sparked serious trouble. But Sora remembered that on one of those occasions, the trouble had been necessary.

"Not everything," said Tamuramaro breezily. "I leaked some intel this time, didn't I? Since the embezzled money went to an organization that could put people's lives at risk, I stepped in. That's breach of confidentiality—I could lose trust as an attorney."

As always, Tamuramaro's conduct in his interactions with other people took Sora off guard.

"What, you mean…?"

"I can handle it. I'll play it smooth. As for the branch manager, his strong move now will help him gain back his credibility in time. And I've got a grueling session of questioning waiting for me as the attorney of the suspect, of course. Here it comes. See you later."

With a laugh, Tamuramaro walked off toward the assistant prosecutor who had gestured at him to come over.

Sora watched him amble away, with a mixture of frustration and humiliation. "That's what I don't like about you."

Tamuramaro had been a military officer and a strategist. With the full trust of the emperor, he had led the campaign to conquer the north, and even after his death, he was buried upright, tasked with the duty to guard over the nation as a war god, the honorable commander in chief. At some point, Sora had learned that knowing how to fight and being strong were two different things.

"Well, it's not that I don't like it. It's that there are people who lose because you're strong."

Their people, and he himself, had lost to the commander. Evidently, good did not always triumph over evil. Once it was clear that a violent organization was involved in the embezzlement, this case became one to be judged and punished in the public sphere. Many lives would be saved this way. Tamuramaro won, and a good deed was done—but following a different route from the one Sora had believed to be right.

Once again, Sora found himself thinking about his master from

1,200 years ago—the one whom he had loved and believed in like his own father, and the one who had surrendered to Tamuramaro in order to save many people.

"I'm different from him, too."

Aterui was broad-minded, and Sora was nothing of the sort. In fact, Aterui had been concerned for him.

For a long time, Sora had been tracing the very same path that Aterui had worried he would, hand in hand with Fuuka.

"What's wrong with being right?"

He heard his own voice again—a voice that resonated as if it came from some omniscient being, like a god or demon.

But that voice seemed to come from a long way away.

For some time now, Sora had been trying desperately to distance himself from that voice—and from the one who had cursed a multitude of lives to avenge his master and desired to mete out punishment with the self-appointed authority of a god. From himself.

He wanted to believe that the icy voice he heard was a mere distant echo.

Since Sora had already nearly finalized the evidence and documents on the embezzlement, the prosecutor's questioning didn't last long. He would likely be called back later, but Nakategawa backed him up by explaining to the investigators that he had received advice from two legal practitioners to treat the matter as a criminal case while also reporting it to the Financial Services Agency.

"If they'd brought it up to the Public Prosecutors' Office much earlier, they would've been spared some of the pressure they're getting now," Sora murmured.

He didn't have much choice but to go home with Tamuramaro, and they were walking through Shakujii Park in the early afternoon, still in their suits. The soft green of the bald cypress trees colored the scene, and dappled light fell through the leaves of the zelkova.

"If things were that straightforward, nobody would have a hard time."

Tamuramaro walked on Sora's right by the lake. He stretched his arms and breathed in deep the air of the thick forest.

Sora sighed. *Does he have to be so good at everything, even deep breathing?*

"I found out today that there'd been some conflict inside Mr. Nakategawa. I should've noticed. I was sorry I never realized."

He was also somewhat appalled at Daitokyo Bank for having a confidential manual just for insiders.

"But isn't it true that the more you go in the wrong direction, the more you end up wasting your energy on things that gain you nothing? Why do they always take the roundabout way? I just don't get it."

"Nothing to gain, huh." Tamuramaro paused and glanced at Sora, choosing his words carefully. "Well, that's what people do, after all. It's human to do useless and roundabout things."

"I don't get it."

That was why he wanted to ask why they did the things they did. On second thought, he decided *useless* wasn't a good word choice. He said it was useless because when people engaged in useless activities, it led to exhaustion. And extreme fatigue often coincided with unhappiness.

Sora felt disappointed. The part of himself that he thought he'd left behind was still lodged firmly inside him.

"Fujiwara isn't an aggressor." If he hadn't changed, he had to make sure Tamuramaro heard this.

"Are you defending a guy who always takes it out on you like that? He's unreasonable—that's what he is."

Sora noticed that Tamuramaro had been watching Fujiwara's interactions with him during their encounters in the courtroom. That was how he'd judged him to be an aggressor.

"Not quite. Fujiwara has reasons to doubt me."

Sora breathed out, steeling himself to reveal a story Tamuramaro didn't know.

"Just before I quit the Public Prosecutors' Office, the verdict of the first trial came out, on the murder of a family of five. There were children among the victims."

"I remember well. The perpetrator was brainwashed by a conspiracy theory website and believed the family of immigrants were secret agents. The defense argued that since the conspiracy theory was a delusion, no criminal responsibility could be found in the culprit. In the first trial, the jury decided on a life sentence."

It was a high-profile case in the news, so Tamuramaro remembered all the details, even though he hadn't been involved in it.

"Even if the delusion was planted by the website, the murderous intent and the act of murder itself are the responsibility of the individual. The defendant deserves capital punishment."

Sora had made the same declaration back then, and he tried to deliver it again in the same tone and pace. He could still hear it, even now—cold and devoid of emotion.

"That was my argument, and I criticized the jury system itself. I thought trial by jury gave too much weight to sentiment and didn't guarantee impartial justice. The Supreme Court will pass the final judgment, but the jury trial, which can be swayed by emotions, is useless. When I said that, Fujiwara got angry with me—he said the judicial system exists for every single citizen."

That wasn't the first time he and Fujiwara had clashed in that kind of argument, but that was the moment when Fujiwara's words pierced his heart.

"So Fujiwara isn't an aggressor. What he said made me quit prosecution work. I realized I couldn't understand. And without understanding, I couldn't stay in a position that gave me opportunities to demand capital punishment."

After Sora's confession, Tamuramaro silently watched him for a long time.

"Sora," he said eventually. His voice was gentle. "When the thugs attacked, you told Fuuka that you wouldn't mind if he tore you apart." Now there was a hint of rebuke in his tone. "According to your judgment, do you deserve capital punishment as well? Do you deserve to die?"

"That time..." It was true—Sora did say that to Fuuka.

"If it were me...I wouldn't mind if you ripped me apart."

It wasn't impulse that made him say it. He had a distinct reason for that wish.

"Don't say things like that, all right? You're intelligent, so maybe not understanding is painful to you. As for the jury trial, you were affected by it because you saw that Fujiwara's argument was valid, right? He happened to make the right point then, but he's always been treating you that way, hasn't he?"

Come to think of it, he remembered that his assistant had always lashed out at him, over anything.

"That's true. I wonder why?"

"Maybe he just hates how aloof you are. If he's constantly acting that way for no reason, that's called aggression."

Sora realized that aggressor or not, Fujiwara's attitude had never bothered him at all until the argument about the jury system. He simply hadn't cared enough for it to have an impact. Perhaps Fujiwara had sensed this, that Sora wasn't interacting with him as another human being. Maybe that was the root of his irritation.

"...Fujiwara's behavior was probably my fault. I'm sure it was."

"Don't overthink it. You really do make things difficult for yourself! Remember how Miroku-bosatsu said that you have wisdom and intelligence?" said Tamuramaro, shifting his tone.

"If I were wise, I wouldn't be here."

It was unlike Sora to say anything so down-to-earth. Tamuramaro's tone must've pulled it out of him, and he found it a little amusing.

"That's true." Tamuramaro agreed so thoughtfully that Sora almost laughed.

Maybe "being human," as Tamuramaro called it, had something to do with this feeling of bumbling through life however you could. Maybe that was the thread to some kind of answer. Sora let out a short breath.

"By the way, when you were a young boy, you had this surreal beauty about you that seemed almost divine, but now you don't have that other-worldly aura. How did that change?" Tamuramaro grinned. Apparently, the memory of Miroku-bosatsu's words called to mind Sora's previous appearance. He'd had such an exquisite appearance that he would've been made into an offering for the gods anywhere, but now he wasn't that striking.

"Isn't that what happens when you grow up? It's made things much easier for me now. Back when I lived in the north, people used to find every reason to try to float me down a lake or a river, or bury me in the forest..."

In fact, in places similar to this very Shakujii Park, Sora had almost been turned into a sacrifice every time there was some natural disaster or calamity. Now he'd grown up into a normal person, looking just a little more refined than average, and Sora couldn't be happier about that.

"They tried to sacrifice you?" Breaking his usual composure, Tamuramaro looked around in surprise.

"Surely that wasn't so uncommon back then? They talked about it quite a few times."

For Sora, growing up in the north, it had made perfect sense for him to go through with it, if that was what everyone had decided. Whenever Sora was in danger of becoming a sacrifice, it was Aterui who cast aside the idea. Nevertheless, the people of the north had kept on trying to offer Sora to nature—almost as if they wanted to *return* him to nature. Sora remembered that at times, there was pain on Aterui's face as he rebuked the others.

"Sora's your childhood name, isn't it? It's rather short."

Sora recalled what Tamuramaro had said the day before, and he got half of what it meant. For names of that period, both "Sora" and "Fuuka" were short, but it wasn't unheard of. The fact was, the brothers didn't have any parents. They were two of the children who were raised by the clan of Aterui. As far as they knew, they weren't from the kind of family that would have long names.

"Too much is as bad as too little. It's a good thing you grew up to be like this."

Sora looked up as Tamuramaro's voice pulled him out of his tangle of doubt. Tamuramaro was smiling at him with a warm, tender gaze. Sora had survived his childhood as the kind of woeful, beautiful child destined for some kind of tragedy, and he'd grown up to be an adult who could blend into society well enough.

Needing protection meant being a weakling. Sora wondered whether Tamuramaro might know something more about who had protected him and why, but he wanted to steer clear of that bewildering thought and changed the subject.

"...I'm glad the case went up to the District Public Prosecutors' Office, but doesn't that mean you lost out on your contingency fee?"

"I already had a hunch there might be trouble when the client approached me, so I had my fee paid up front. Besides, I still have work to do as the suspect's defense lawyer."

Tamuramaro said it like it was nothing, but Sora was stunned.

"Why? How?"

"I'd already agreed to represent him. The only difference is that I'll be visiting him in jail instead of the bank. This part is when the client really needs a defense lawyer."

"How is there any scope for a defense?"

Since they had been having hearings for half a month, Sora himself had talked to Etou a number of times. It was the job of a certified fraud examiner to hold interviews with the suspect, with their consent, based on the evidential documents. Unlike an interrogation, the strategy was to go in on the pretext of lining up the facts, and in the process ascertain the missing piece that would make the case. Sora had found the missing piece immediately, but he couldn't detect any signs of regret, repentance, or guilt in Etou.

"A lot more than you think. First off, we've got to start with making the suspect himself understand why he's going to be judged."

Sora had wanted to point out that that was exactly why Etou hadn't thought twice about connecting with a criminal organization, but he'd stopped himself. Then Tamuramaro casually went on to say something along the same lines. He was planning to teach Etou.

Sora stared at the weeds growing at his feet. "I could never do a job like that."

He noticed the lack of biting sarcasm in his own voice.

The protector and the protected, the right and the wrong, the strong and the weak. All the borders between those people had dissolved into obscurity, and he even lost track of where he stood himself.

That confusion was why he had tried to get away from the version of himself who spoke in the icy voice, who judged others to mete out punishments. Even now, it was vivid in his memory: the very moment when he began to feel lost. Sora felt the urge to share this recollection with Tamuramaro.

"Forty years ago, before we left your place, there was that incident, the synchronized guerrilla attacks on the National Rail," he began hesitantly. He was referring to the incident around the end of the period when Tamuramaro had taken care of them.

"It was 1985. If I remember correctly, it was an act of terrorism by the Japan Revolutionary Communist League and the labor union to oppose the privatization of the National Rail."

"I was in your apartment, taking in the news from the newspapers and the TV, and I was sympathetic to the ideas of the union. Except for the violence, of course."

"When you were basically twelve." Tamuramaro groaned, but he wasn't surprised. He knew Sora well.

"I was of the opinion that the laborers were being exploited, and they should bring about a revolution. It was like economic war back then."

Although he'd had the appearance of a child, Sora had been learning from the world every day. After 1,200 years of learning, his obstinate belief in what was just and right gradually weakened. The more he learned, the less certain he became. Especially when he was living with Tamuramaro.

"The next day, the old lady living next door was found dead," Sora went on.

"I remember it was her daughter who lived in the neighboring city who found her unconscious—we heard her scream. It was in the early evening. We called the ambulance, but…" It was Tamuramaro who had supported the wailing daughter and immediately dialed emergency services.

"She said she was supposed to have come the day before. She cried and told us she couldn't come because the trains weren't moving. If only she could've come earlier…"

Sora had stood by, listening to her cries of regret. It felt like her voice was coming from a great distance, looming nearer and nearer as he listened.

"Back then, I thought the laborers were right, but…"

The elderly woman next door lived modestly by herself, and she was kind to Sora, a child who didn't go to school, and Fuuka, the little puppy living in their no-pets apartment.

"She wasn't even counted as one of the victims."

She'd worried over them and talked to them often. Sora hadn't let his guard down, but she always gave him a warm smile.

Over the last 1,200 years, Sora and Fuuka had interacted with more and more other people, little by little, sometimes living with Tamuramaro. At that moment, though, Sora had felt a different world opening up to him. It was like he'd spent all this time looking in just one direction through the eye of a needle, but now enormous curtains had been flung aside.

"I just realized why Fujiwara always treated me that way. For two years, I hadn't been *looking* at Fujiwara, nor at people."

Ever since this journey began, Sora was discovering more and more questions instead of answers.

"There's so much I don't understand, and it's only increasing. It makes me anxious."

He didn't mean to tell Tamuramaro how he felt, but the words tumbled out of him. He only realized he'd said it out loud upon hearing his own lonely voice, and his head snapped up. Sora couldn't make out the other man's expression in the bright dappled light.

"You're starting to see the world, I think," said Tamuramaro mildly, leaving much unspoken, as always. "Maybe it's a good thing."

If Sora was beginning to see a world that he hadn't been seeing before, and if he was encountering more and more things that he didn't understand, then all these worries made sense.

"That old lady, our neighbor—she didn't die, Sora." The question Sora had never dared to ask, Tamuramaro answered without hesitation. "She was hospitalized for a while, and when she was discharged, she wasn't all back to her old self, but still. When she got out, she popped by to say hello to me on the way to her daughter. She missed you."

Sora was holding his breath, listening intently.

"She gave me a bar of chocolate to give to you. I was waiting for you to come home for a while, but..."

By then, Sora and Fuuka had already run away from Tamuramaro's apartment, never to return. They couldn't go back.

"Sorry. I ate it." Tamuramaro laughed.

"It was forty years ago. I don't blame you." Emboldened by Tamuramaro's joke, Sora chuckled along.

"Anyway, we got off work awfully early. Come on—let's go eat ramen," Tamuramaro announced brightly, changing the subject.

"Then you go to Tarou. I'll go to Ichirou."

Though Sora knew this man was several steps ahead of him in life, it still got on his nerves, so he said that just out of spite.

"Now, now, go easy on me." Tamuramaro leaned closer to Sora, and Sora dug his elbow into Tamuramaro's ribs.

Just then, they heard Rokurou's voice from the bench ahead of them. "Oh, if it isn't Mr. Lawyer and Mr. Tamura."

Sora's face creased into a smile. "Hello there."

Rokurou was enjoying the breeze blowing through the leaves of the dogwood tree overhanging Sanpouji Lake.

"Hello. Are you taking a break from calligraphy class today?" Tamuramaro asked cheerfully. They were starting to see children running in the park on their way home from elementary school.

"It's Ms. Tatsuko's class today," Sora explained, overly defensive.

"We take turns according to the days of the week. I teach fifth and sixth graders, and today she's teaching the third graders," said Rokurou good-naturedly.

"I see. Perhaps younger kids like having a female teacher."

"Ms. Tatsuko is strict, you know. I'm too soft, so maybe that's why she took the younger ones. After so many decades, I don't remember how it started anymore." He laughed.

"That makes sense, too."

Tamuramaro's suave manner made Sora even more disgruntled. "Don't just say whatever pops into your head, Tamurama—Tamura."

"It's nice to see you like this," Rokurou remarked in an easy tone.

It took a moment for Sora to realize who Rokurou was referring to.

"Do you mean me?"

"Oh yes. You're always so quiet and collected for such a young man. I thought that was how you were by nature, but it seems I was wrong about that. When you're with Mr. Tamura, you act more like a child. It looks like you're having fun."

"I'm not a child!" Sora blurted out, more indignantly than he'd intended.

"See?" Rokurou chortled. "Very nice. Ah, by the way, Mr. Lawyer, if you're already done with work for the day, how about paying that tax accountant a visit? It's called the Kouichi Koudera Tax Accountant Office."

"Oh!" Sora remembered that Rokurou had mentioned the accountant on Saturday, when they'd met on the shopping street. "I'm sorry! I completely forgot…!!"

Sora had planned to get in touch with the office on a weekday, but the whole commotion that morning had pushed it out of his mind.

"Not to worry, not to worry. If it were really urgent, they would've come to you themselves. We're all adults, after all. I was just being a busybody," said Rokurou, waving his hand.

"...Thank you so much." Sora bowed deeply, despite Rokurou's assurances.

"Ms. Tatsuko's thinking of calling on you later with a moving-in gift for Mr. Tamura. Brace yourselves." Rokurou waved to both of them with a mischievous grin.

"But I was going to pay *you* a visit!" Tamuramaro replied. "Wonder what she has in store. I'll be looking forward to it."

"You're really cheeky, you know that?"

Elbowing each other again, Sora and Tamuramaro bowed to Rokurou, then headed to the west exit of the park and toward the shopping street.

"Why do they want to get divorced anyway? Mr. and Mrs. Kashiwagi, I mean," Tamuramaro asked when they were outside the park. He sounded earnest, more puzzled than merely curious.

"I'm never gonna tell *you*."

"Ha. He's right—you're more childish than you've ever been in twelve hundred years."

Sora huffed at his remark and glanced at him, but he found Tamuramaro wearing a completely different expression than what he expected. Now that they were out of the forest, he could see his face clearly now. There wasn't even a trace of mockery in his expression, nor was he trying to tease him.

The same question circled round and round in Sora's mind again: What was the difference between the protector and the protected, the right and the wrong?

For a long time, Sora had only believed in one answer, but now the world was extremely complicated.

"...Knowing you, you're bound to hear about it from someone in town soon enough. Everyone here knows."

The look on Tamuramaro's face perplexed Sora. He didn't know what to make of it. And back when they had lived together forty years ago, he had seen this expression many, many times.

"Nothing beats soy sauce!"

Tamuramaro groaned in pleasure as he eagerly slurped up the ramen noodles in Ichirou, the third building on the Shizukuishi shopping street. A red shop curtain hung in front of its sliding doors.

"I bet you'd say the same thing about miso if you went to eat next door," Sora retorted, rolling his eyes and wolfing down his own soy sauce ramen with the same vigor.

The soup at Ichirou was rich, with the stock taken from small dried fish, but it didn't smell fishy. The full flavors of the soy sauce soup formed a perfect match with the fresh, curly noodles. The succulent, slow-cooked char siu pork, thinly sliced on purpose, was so tender that it melted in your mouth.

"Can't promise I won't."

There were perfect rings of oil on the surface of the clear, golden soup, proving its supreme quality. Without another word, Sora and Tamuramaro both slurped up the noodles and drank the soup.

"Whatever it is, ramen is the best! A fantastic invention."

In no time, Tamuramaro devoured the flavored soft-boiled egg with the runny, orange yolk spreading out in his mouth, then put down his chopsticks.

Sora had called the tax accountant's office from outside the park and set up an appointment for the next day. Tamuramaro, who had been listening to his call, had given a mischievous grin, and now here they were, eating ramen together at the counter.

"How can you look so worried after eating this amazing ramen? What are you, an old hina doll?"

"Hina dolls don't look worried; they just look pale… I always feel so guilty eating at ramen shops, but I can't give it up."

Sora sipped his soup, wanting it to last longer. He put down his porcelain spoon with an expression of genuine distress.

"Ah, right, 'cause Fuuka can't have it. The ramen we had on Saturday was pretty authentic, though."

Unusually for him, Tamuramaro's face fell. He'd realized that Fuuka would never be able to have ramen at a proper shop like this as long as he turned into a dog in front of other people.

"But it's not the real thing, is it?" Sora muttered.

"Well, true. It's impossible to re-create at home."

"Exactly! We've ordered delivery before, too, but it's nothing like the freshly made noodles!!" Sora grew uncharacteristically heated and slammed a hand on the counter. "At this rate, Fuuka will never get to taste this."

"Yeah... I can see why you're so desperate to make him human. I get it."

Stone-faced, they both drank the rest of their soups and stared at the bottom of their empty bowls, where they could now see the word ICHIROU.

"Flavors...disappear, you know," Sora murmured.

This place was open all day long, and at three thirty in the afternoon, midway between lunch and dinner, the eatery was empty except for them. They didn't feel like leaving yet, and they drank water as they talked.

"Disappear?" asked Tamuramaro.

"Yeah. The first time I had gyoza and ramen was in Manchuria."

"Ah, I remember."

The owner, Ichirou, whom they had already greeted, came over to offer them free glasses of barley tea. "Your first ramen was at Manchuria?" He thought Sora was talking about the familiar chain restaurant. The bandanna wrapped around his shaved head was the same red as the shop curtain outside.

"Well, um..."

"Oh, yes, there was one nearby where we grew up." Tamuramaro cut in with a laugh. Sora was bad at lying on the spot. "But your soy sauce ramen. It was brilliant. You use noodles with high water content, I see?"

"Hey, you know your ramen! The noodles are important, too, but you've got to have fresh, clear water to boil them. Pops made a water purifier with pebbles that works like magic. My bro and I've been fighting over it… If I ever kill him by accident, I'm counting on you to defend me. I'll give you coupons!" Ichirou nodded, jabbing a thumb in Tarou's direction next door, then went back in the kitchen.

"Well, you would get a lighter sentence for accidental manslaughter, but please try not to kill him at all. If you killed Mr. Tarou, we wouldn't be able to use your coupons… And we wouldn't have Mr. Tarou's ramen to enjoy, either." His voice lowered to something like a whisper—or a curse. "There's nothing but misery there." He turned back to Sora. "Now that you say it," he went on, "the gyoza and ramen we had in Manchuria were totally different from the ones we're having now. Gyoza was boiled, not pan-fried. Takes me back to those days."

Instead of the chain restaurant, they were talking about the country that no longer existed, where they had been about eighty years ago.

"They've completely changed."

Both of them had wandered over to Manchuria at some point during the war, and now they were both reliving the first taste of Chinese food they'd ever had.

"…You're right. Flavors do disappear." Tamuramaro knew exactly what Sora had meant, and he tensed up. "Makes me shudder."

"These days, you can look up a recipe for anything you want to make, and if you're willing to bend over backward, there's no ingredient or seasoning you can't get your hands on. Once Fuuka got big enough to use the kitchen, he said he had too much free time and volunteered to cook. He's been cooking for decades now, so he's honed his skills."

"I'm impressed by his work. It's homey but also as good as a restaurant's. Even better, in fact. Yeah, I see now. It's hard to use a kitchen if you're not tall enough or your arms are too short. Makes sense."

Tamuramaro put together why Fuuka had cultivated this new habit after the three had last lived under the same roof.

"I don't know why, but Fuuka shot up so much. He got so big that when we moved into our house two years ago, we even renovated the kitchen to make it taller."

"He's grown a lot. I was surprised. I've seen you now and then since university, but it was the first time in about forty years that I've seen Fuuka in human form."

When they'd lived together forty years ago, Fuuka was also still in the body of a child, just like Sora.

"My little brother outgrew me," he mumbled to himself.

"It's like you're two separate people," said Tamuramaro with uncharacteristic gravity. "Sora, do you remember when Fuuka was born?"

"You ask me that sometimes."

Sora didn't remember when it started, but Tamuramaro had been posing the same question to him once in a while.

"He's only one year younger than me. So I don't remember when he was born."

"Right, now I remember."

Sora found it hard to believe that Tamuramaro would have forgotten this, given how many times he had asked the same thing in the past. Every time he asked it, Sora wondered why he brought it up, but now he was beginning to suspect the reason. Whatever it was lay hidden in the same place at the bottom of his heart where he repressed his doubts.

"Something's changed about Fuuka," Tamuramaro said brightly, trying to cheer up Sora before he sank into the gloom again.

Something. Sora felt strangely soothed by his vagueness.

Tamuramaro always left some space open when he talked. He never made dogmatic assertions. He never passed judgment on people. In the past, Sora had found it an untrustworthy trait. But the way Sora looked at things had changed considerably—although he couldn't say when.

"Once I started attending university, we spent most of the day apart for the first time." Though Fuuka's transformation was still puzzling, Sora knew what had triggered it. "He changed. He developed his own thoughts and feelings, different from mine."

Now that he could see the space in Tamuramaro's way of talking, he also saw that there was no space like that in his own words. Though he still couldn't do anything about it, he hadn't even noticed the difference before.

"Maybe it's because I changed… Back then, Fuuka didn't think anything at all," Sora murmured softly, recalling Awata-guchi again.

Tamuramaro could have asked why Fuuka had burned all those soldiers' lives to the ground then—but he didn't. Perhaps he knew the answer already.

"You people were right about me. I was barbaric—just me, not the rest of my people in the north. In the end, everyone accepted the agriculture and sericulture you brought in, and they obeyed you. Their lives probably got easier than when they were living with nature… And they needed the laws of government, too."

Sora had been adamant in rejecting the period of integration between the Imperial Court and the north.

"I never thought you were barbaric—not you, nor the rest of your people. If you were just a barbarian, then the Imperial Court wouldn't have been so afraid of you. Barbarism doesn't make you strong in war." Tamuramaro talked about strength like a true warrior and commander, and Sora understood what the word meant to a man like him.

"It's because he was there to guide us." He thought of his master, the kind of leader who could surrender himself to the enemy to save everyone else.

"Sometimes, even as a young man, I would get in a quarrel with the people of my clan, trying to achieve fairness, justice, or equality."

He knew now that he had only been a child too small for battle.

"I felt those emotions before I knew what to call them."

Tamuramaro listened in silence as Sora tried to make sense of the feelings inside him.

"It was always him, our lord, who would caution me when I cornered others. He would persuade me to accept that some things had to be what they were, because we were all just living, getting through our lives."

Sora thought Tamuramaro was much bigger than himself, reporting the case at Daitokyo Bank to the prosecutors while also looking ahead at the consequences.

"For me, it's impossible to get a sense of that. It's always been that way. Even now."

Tamuramaro's words from the other night came back to him as an echo. *"Imagine being quietly interrogated and admonished with valid arguments when you know deep down that you've done something harmful and deserve the punishment. Of course he's angry. If you can, try toning it down next time."*

"I never doubted him. He was my guide to justice back in those days. I lost the person I depended on most."

He wanted to demand whether Tamuramaro could possibly understand how unsettling that was for him. But he knew he shouldn't. The question was meant for someone else.

"Forty years ago, too, I believed in the revolution for the laborers. I supported them."

Tamuramaro had just assured him that the old lady next door hadn't fallen victim to the revolution. Back then, when he believed in what he thought was the right path, when he was sympathetic to that voice of revolution, Sora had felt uplifted, burning with a passion that built his conviction that he could see far-reaching consequences. He had believed in the future.

But when he learned about the pain experienced by his neighbor—someone whose voice he'd heard, whose warmth he'd felt—he suddenly found himself knocked off his feet, realizing that his passion lacked a firm foundation.

"It's no different now. I'm surprised at myself. Even now, I can't live well among other people. Fujiwara's words, too—all I can do is keep thinking about them. If I lost Fuuka, I'd be all alone."

He was tired of harping on the same string.

"But you *are* living among people. And if you get a chance, you should let Fujiwara know you've been thinking about what he said."

"I don't have any answers. Look at this case. All I know is that if you'd been the one to investigate it from the very beginning, things would've gone very differently. If I follow what I believe is just, I stray from the path of humanity. It's because I—"

"That's because you wish to bring happiness to a multitude."

This time, Tamuramaro got to the heart of the matter, without leaving things open.

"Why do you pursue justice the way you do? It's because you believe justice can save people from cruel misfortune, isn't it?"

Sora listened to his words in a daze, his eyes wide-open.

"How…?"

Tamuramaro put into words the sense of justice that lay hidden deep inside Sora's heart—this belief that Sora took out of its hiding place once in a while and studied closely. He never knew what to do with it, but he was never able to let it go.

Was this also how Tamuramaro had understood Sora when he'd talked about doing pointless things earlier that day?

"As a child, you probably witnessed many things that were inhuman—merciless cruelties and deaths. I'm partly responsible for that."

Sora just listened.

He had only been able to have a real conversation about what happened 1,200 years ago during the time they had lived together. Sora had come to realize that even when he got agitated, Tamuramaro stayed calm. Over time, Tamuramaro's words had come to mean more, to carry more convincing weight, and that scared him. He'd shut out Tamuramaro's voice and turned to newspapers and books to know more about the world.

"Sometimes the path of justice that you see leads you along a path you can walk with others, and sometimes it doesn't. That's normal. If what happened today was one of those times when it doesn't, there will be other days—tomorrow, or the day after tomorrow—when it does align," Tamuramaro said lightly, and Sora looked up again.

Just as Sora kept on ruminating over those questions, he did the same with Tamuramaro's words, too. Once in a while, he pulled them from a memory and mulled them over. He wondered if anything in himself had changed from one day to another.

"What's wrong with being right?"

He could believe with certainty now that the voice had become more distant than before.

"...What do you want for dinner?" asked Sora. He felt like thanking Tamuramaro somehow. "I'm the one who goes shopping, so I usually choose the menu."

"The season for somen's coming to an end, so I'd love to have the same thing we had the other day while we've got the chance. Now, that was amazing," said Tamuramaro, trying to keep alive the memory of the flavors.

"You're not as greedy as you look. Fuuka's good at dan dan noodles, too, with somen flavored with ground sesame sauce. And a heap of seasoned ground meat on top."

"Let's go with that," Tamuramaro replied immediately.

"Oh." When Sora stood up, he remembered that Tatsuko was planning to drop by with a gift for Tamuramaro. "On second thought, let's keep it modest."

"How come?"

They paid their bills separately at the cash register.

"I have a hunch..."

Living in Shizukuishi had taught Sora that there were no limits for a parent who cared about filling up a child's stomach.

They both thanked Ichirou for their meal and stepped out of the ramen shop, passing under the red curtain. Unfortunately, maybe since it was the time of day when business was slow, they got caught by Tarou, who was sprinkling water in front of his black shop curtain.

"Next time, we'll go for miso!" Tamuramaro called out cheerfully, and Tarou's frown quickly brightened. Sora wasn't good at smooth talk at times like this.

"They look totally different from a distance, but up close, their eyes are the same. They really are twins," said Tamuramaro casually. After all, Ichirou shaved his hair and wore a bandanna, and Tarou wore his hair in a bun covered with a knit cap.

"Eyes, huh." Sora remembered his brother's crimson eyes and wondered whether his own bore any resemblance, too.

"When I say Fuuka's changed, it means that now I notice he's there, too," Tamuramaro remarked as they walked down the shopping street, bowing to the passersby in greeting.

"That's what I'm saying—he's starting to form his own self," said Sora.

"No, that's not what I mean."

Sora could sense where he was going with this and steeled himself.

"That day at Awata-guchi, I couldn't see Fuuka clearly."

Sora stopped in his tracks, and Tamuramaro stopped with him.

"You thought you were going to die, and you were begging for your brother's life, so I listened. The soldiers seemed to think there was another child with you, but… What about Miroku-bosatsu?" Tamuramaro murmured quietly. "You were on the brink of death, so I didn't argue with what you said, but for a long time, I never knew for sure whether Fuuka really existed—"

Tamuramaro paused. He noticed that Sora was holding his breath next to him.

"I couldn't really tell before, but now I can. That's what I'm saying," he concluded, lightening up and giving Sora's back a pat.

Sora breathed again. "How can you say that when all I have is Fuuka…?" he hissed. He was regretting any gratitude he'd felt just a few minutes ago.

"Sora." Tamuramaro's steps came to a halt again. "I knew that incident with the National Rail and our neighbor was what made you leave." His voice was as relaxed as usual, with no strain. "I always knew that, Sora."

He looked at Sora with compassionate eyes—eyes that seemed to say he also knew how lonesome it felt to lose the pillar of justice you'd depended on.

"Here, let's take another way home," he said.

If I'm starting to walk down a different path…if I can keep walking that way… where will Fuuka walk, then?

With the question hovering in his mind, Sora could only stare at his feet.

As expected, the doorbell at Oushuu Law Firm rang at four thirty, just before the three of them started getting ready for dinner. It was Tatsuko, who had wrapped up her calligraphy class.

"Thank you for coming. I hope I didn't make you feel obliged to come by after I promised to pay you a visit."

Tamuramaro was standing tall in the middle of the entrance hall, still wearing a dark suit that was almost black. It rankled Sora to see him greet Tatsuko as if she were *his* guest. Like a master of the house who cut an annoyingly good figure in a well-fitted suit.

Like him, Sora was also in his work clothes, except for his suit jacket.

"Woof!"

Before he could say anything snarky, a big white dog thwacked Tamuramaro's chest with both forepaws.

"Watch out, Fuuka!"

The push wasn't enough to knock down Tamuramaro, since he had a strong core, but he still backed up against the wall and wrapped Fuuka in his arms.

"Oh, I see you've already made friends with dear Fuuka, Mr. Tamura."

Tatsuko was in her late seventies, her white hair tied back in a neat bun, and she was still strikingly beautiful.

"Woof, woof!"

Fuuka barked furiously as he pummeled Tamuramaro's chest. To the men, it was obvious this was a vehement no.

"Oh, we're inseparable now!" Tamuramaro grinned.

"Of course. Fuuka just loves him with all his heart," Sora added. "Ms. Tatsuko, thank you so much for coming. Mr. Rokurou told us at the park that we might see you later, and I've been looking forward to it very much."

Leaving Tamuramaro and Fuuka to their scuffle, Sora knelt down on the raised hallway. Tatsuko was still standing in the lower entryway, so this brought him closer to her eye level. Tamuramaro was taken aback a little to see Sora being so openly affectionate, and just as he smiled, Fuuka head-butted him again.

"You look so lively together. Isn't it lovely you can play with Mr. Tamura, Fuuka, sweetie? Here, I brought you some soup. If you don't mind having something homemade."

"Everything you cook is so delicious. If Tamurama—er, Mr. Tamura—er, Tamura! If he says he doesn't want it, I'll be more than happy to have it all by myself."

"Hey, come on."

Tamuramaro got up, holding Fuuka's big white body with his right arm in a tremendous show of strength. Fuuka was so fierce that if Tamuramaro wasn't so burly, anyone would've thought he was being attacked.

"Of course I'd never say that. Wow, did you make it for me? Thank you very much."

"Woof!"

Fuuka tried to take a bite out of Tamuramaro's throat, but Sora pulled him back.

"No, Fuuka. You're getting a little too friendly with Mr. Tamura."

Tamuramaro knew full well that Fuuka had almost gone for his throat. Still grinning, he held out his right elbow, offering to let Fuuka bite that instead. "Go easy on the munching, all right?"

"Coo, coo."

Though he whined at being held at bay, Fuuka was soon happy in his brother's forceful embrace and hugged him back.

Sora held him close and, once again, listened for the thumping of his heart. It was a habit he couldn't give up. This time, the urge to listen was particularly strong.

"It's a chicken hot pot. When that man and I went to Kyoto some time ago, he said there was a restaurant he wanted to treat us to—not like him at all, you know. And the chicken hot pot we had there was just fantastic."

Rokurou was apparently "that man," rather than a husband or spouse.

"He got excited because it was a dish that Sakamoto Ryoma liked, though I wasn't interested in that. Men always like Sakamoto Ryoma, don't they?"

Sora did think it would be rare for a man to pick a specific restaurant on a trip, but when he heard the reason, he wasn't surprised.

"Ah-ha, we do indeed. He's every man's dream! Sakamoto Ryoma!!" Tamuramaro declared with a proud grin.

"Seriously, does anything shut you up?" grumbled Sora, still holding on to Fuuka.

"Oh." Tatsuko was looking at Sora with a warm smile. Noticing her gaze, he pursed his lips, though he couldn't wipe away his sulky pout.

"Anyway, all that aside, the hot pot was delicious," she went on. "I'm trying out all these different ways to re-create the same flavors. I've made a big batch today, so if you'd like, please give it a try."

Tatsuko held up a big cooler bag. Inside, there was a white chicken-stock broth in a plastic bottle and some ingredients for the hot pot.

"I can tell from one look at the soup that it's going to be amazing," said Tamuramaro. "I'm excited! Can't wait to try it."

"For the stock, I simmered chicken bones with fresh ginger and the green part of scallions. I think the chicken was a good one this time, so this turned out quite well. Hope you enjoy it with the chicken meat and some of these Kyoto vegetables that Keita is so proud of."

All the ingredients were in the bag, and they could see some vibrant, well-shaped mibuna leaves, kujou scallions, and kintoki carrots.

"Wow, what a feast… You're too kind," said Sora apologetically. He knew the produce's price range, and he felt it was too generous a welcome gift for Tamuramaro.

"Don't worry; I just couldn't leave them to rot in the shop! I can see why Keita loves them so much. He told me he's close with the farmers who grow them. Once you see their farms in person, no wonder he wants people to try them."

When he was in elementary school, Keita used to take the Kashiwagis' classes. Now he wrote the labels for the Kyoto vegetables by hand with a calligraphy brush on rice paper.

"I see. So you're pampering Mr. Keita, and we're reaping the benefits," said Sora.

In contrast to his casual manners and talk, Keita's penmanship was surprisingly impressive, and perhaps it was also a pleasure for Tatsuko and Rokurou to see the good results of their teaching.

"You know I like to pamper you, too, Mr. Lawyer," teased Tatsuko good-naturedly.

"Oh yes, that's true."

Her tender tone was one he'd never heard before he met her—it must be how a mother sounds when talking to her child.

"And let's not forget you, Mr. Tamura. If I were thirty years younger, I'd try harder. You're like a handsome actor in one of those movies from overseas. Hope you'll like my cooking and stay in Shizukuishi for many years."

"No need to take away thirty years. You're charming just as you— Ow!"

As Tamuramaro's velvety baritone deepened even more, Sora and Fuuka both gave him a good kick to his leg before he could finish his sentence.

"Take it easy, you two! We're not in a wrestling match!"

"Who do you think you are, talking like that to Ms. Tatsuko! It's disrespectful to Mr. Rokurou, too!!"

"Woof, woof, woof, woof!"

Forgetting their supposed maturity, Sora and Fuuka lit into Tamuramaro, who was rubbing his shin.

Tatsuko let out a soft giggle, which sounded oddly gentle in all the ruckus, and Sora snapped his mouth shut.

"You really do change into a different person, Mr. Lawyer, when you're around Mr. Tamura."

Sora had noticed many changes in himself as well, now that he was living with Tamuramaro for the first time in a long while. If Tatsuko was mentioning it, too, then maybe he really was undergoing some kind of metamorphosis.

"He's my father's archenemy," he explained sulkily.

"Now you're pulling my leg. You know, I was worried that you were so quiet all the time. You looked hardly alive. You're so much better now."

Her eyes were filled with a gentle warmth. Sora had come to know, to understand, and to feel what this warmth meant.

"Do you think so?"

It was something he couldn't learn until he had received it himself. It had taken him a very long time to learn to feel it.

"I really do," she replied. With a cheerful good-bye, she moved to the door. Sora stood up to escort her, but she waved him aside.

"Thank you again!" Tamuramaro called out, bowing deeply.

"Don't mention it." Tatsuko smiled, sliding shut the front door before walking off.

Opening Tatsuko's bag in the living room, the three of them admired the rich, white color of the broth, the plump freshness of the pink chicken meat, and the beautiful sheen of the Kyoto vegetables.

"This broth looks so good; I can just taste it," said Fuuka, back in his human form and his white silk robe. "Can you ask her for the recipe next time, Sora?"

The broth was white, but not because it was cloudy. They could see that she had taken care to scoop out the foamy scum, leaving behind a mouthwateringly clear soup.

"You don't have to work so hard in the kitchen, Fuuka."

"It's fun to cook, and this looks super yummy."

The precious ingredients packed into the bag all looked so succulent that the mere sight of them was entrancing.

"What a wonderful gift. I'm so grateful," said Tamuramaro, nodding wholeheartedly.

When Sora thought about how Tatsuko had prepared all this for Tamuramaro, his lips twisted into a disapproving frown. Although, if he was honest, it was less disapproval than childish envy.

"You really never change, do you? Wherever you are, whoever you talk to. *Of course* you were favored by four emperors, no less."

"Well, I didn't get along with the former emperor Heizei, though, so when Emperor Saga ordered me to capture his Heijo-kyo, I didn't waste any time. The Kusuko Incident required speed."

Tamuramaro mentioned an event, long referred to in history as the Kusuko Incident, as if it had taken place only a day ago.

"That former emperor Heizei..."

Sora had learned from historical records that were later compiled that this Heizei was the very same Imperial Prince Ate, the libertine, to whom he would've been offered had Tamuramaro's orders at Awata-guchi been carried out.

But he didn't want to mention Awata-guchi in front of Fuuka.

"This is overdue, but let me just say this," said Tamuramaro, guessing what was on Sora's mind. "It was a well-known fact back then that Imperial Prince Ate liked older women. He took a young girl as his wife, but he spent lavishly on her mother, Kusuko, which eventually led to his ruin. I did know he had no interest in children."

Tamuramaro couldn't have been sure what would happen to Sora, but he'd believed it would have been better than death. Sora could understand that now, though he couldn't put it into words very well.

"Long, long overdue. By twelve hundred years."

"If you hadn't been as beautiful as you were, my excuse wouldn't have convinced the soldiers at all."

Tamuramaro had said earlier that it was fortunate that Sora had grown up to be less conspicuous. Even Sora understood that social values and political strategies had changed over time.

"Awata-guchi… Imperial Prince Ate? Sora, I wanna do munchy-munchy on Tamuramaro!! Can I do it now?!"

Though Fuuka didn't get the full meaning, he had a rough idea of what they were talking about and suddenly shifted into a white dog, baring his teeth.

"Wait, Fuuka!" Sora scrambled to wrap his arms around Fuuka's neck and hold him back.

For a split second, Sora felt relief wash over him.

"That day at Awata-guchi, I couldn't see Fuuka clearly."

Even before Tamuramaro had mentioned it, Sora sometimes had the feeling that Fuuka had no recollection of that day. Sometimes he felt an overwhelming rush of fear, wondering whether Fuuka had really been there at Awata-guchi as a human.

"I should be held accountable for making up a cute name for it like 'munchy-munchy,'" said Sora. "It's trivializing the act of biting someone's throat."

Fuuka transformed back into a human at his brother's words.

Here's proof that he existed. Fuuka is definitely aware of Tamuramaro's presence.

"Can you explain it so I can understand?"

Sora realized he had been too relieved to express his thoughts clearly, and he cast about for the right words.

"…We used to share the same feelings without even having to talk." Sora sighed. "We were one, whatever came our way."

With his right palm, he caressed Fuuka's cheek, which was currently puffed up in a pout. He felt the difference in body temperature between them.

It must have been because they were so close together, bound as one, that Fuuka's individual presence had felt ambiguous to Sora as well. *That must be it*, he told himself.

"Fuuka."

Sora was aware that Tamuramaro was observing them again.

"Tamuramaro saved me today. Remember those thugs who came here with knives the other day? The prosecutors and the police are dealing with the higher-up people who gave them orders. And that's thanks to Tamuramaro," he explained slowly, looking straight into Fuuka's eyes. The red fire that was burning there gradually faded away. "You shouldn't—"

—tear apart Tamuramaro's throat. Sora wanted to finish the sentence, but try as he might, he couldn't bring himself to say it. Tamuramaro had betrayed the one person Sora had believed in. It wasn't so easy.

Just a moment ago, he could believe that the icy voice had receded somewhere far away, but now... Was he born with such a cold heart that he couldn't believe in anything unless he knew whether it was good or evil?

"Fuuka, I'm begging you. Don't kill anyone else, please."

For 1,200 years, that was the one thing Sora had prayed for from Fuuka.

And that wish extended even to the immortal Tamuramaro's life.

"...I got in trouble again," mumbled Fuuka with an abashed smile, shrinking like a dog with downturned ears and hanging his head.

The doorbell rang out in the quiet.

"That's probably for me," said Tamuramaro in his usual, easy tone, which sounded out of place in the tense atmosphere. He stood up to answer the intercom. "Hello. Yes, this is Tamura."

He hung up and flashed a mischievous grin at the brothers as he went to the front door. "Thank you. I'll sign for it by hand, if that's okay."

They heard him receive the delivery. Sora assumed it might be some of Tamuramaro's belongings. It had been a few days since he'd moved in, but all he'd brought so far were some clothes and documents. Perhaps he was also wandering from one apartment to another, just like Sora and Fuuka had been before they bought this house.

But when Tamuramaro came back, he put down a small cardboard box on the table in front of Fuuka.

"To celebrate the start of our life together again..."

"What is it?"

"Well, open it. I can't guarantee you'll like it, though."

Since Tamuramaro wouldn't give it away, Fuuka was too curious not to look inside.

"Ooh!"

He pulled out a set of clothes that looked like a samue but included a haori jacket for the top, made with indigo cotton fabric. Big, whirling patterns were embroidered onto the sleeves and around the collar in vermilion thread.

"It's the informant's outfit!"

The set looked just like the costume of the character in the crime series that Fuuka was obsessed with.

"How did you find it?" asked Sora, surprised at the close resemblance.

"I searched online with the title of the show, the character's name, costume, and mail order. They came lightning fast, huh?"

"You sure have adapted well to the modern age…Sei-i Taishogun," Sora muttered, dumbfounded.

Meanwhile, Fuuka was so excited he'd already changed into the costume. "Sora! What do you think? Does it look good on me?!"

There wasn't a trace of sadness anymore on his glowing face.

Sora looked at Fuuka in the indigo outfit with mixed feelings.

…Aterui.

Aterui had worn something similar when he was alive. It closely resembled what was now known as the native clothes of the Ainu people. There were modern theories that the Emishi were the Ainu, but Sora didn't know the real truth. The northern lands, far away from the Imperial Court, had consisted of numerous clans living in various regions, and their cultures and languages blended into one another in subtle gradations. From what Sora remembered, they were neither clearly divided into separate nations nor united as one.

"You look great, Fuuka. Come on, now—you have to say thank you for the gift."

Aterui had been the foremost leader of them all, guiding the many clans through the battle against the Imperial Court for over twenty years. There had been days when he would don indigo-blue attire with beautiful patterns embroidered in red. It was his garb for battle and for rituals. A ceremonial robe for politics and rites.

"...Thanks. Tamuramaro," Fuuka choked out, struggling over every syllable.

"Consider it my thanks for your good food," Tamuramaro replied breezily.

"All right, I'm gonna get the hot pot ready!"

Fuuka leaped up eagerly and hurried off to the kitchen with Tatsuko's gift, in his new indigo outfit. Sora watched him go, still surprised by how tall he'd grown.

"He's starting to look like him," murmured Tamuramaro, almost to himself.

Sora's heart skipped a beat, as he was thinking the exact same thing.

He saw it, too, as clear as day. His grown-up brother was beginning to look just like Aterui.

It was Monday evening in the third week of September, when the night air was turning chilly.

In total silence, the three of them were hungrily sipping the steaming-hot chicken soup.

"I can't stop! It's too good." Fuuka looked at the soup left in his bowl, wishing it would never end.

Fuuka had chopped all the Kyoto vegetables into neat shapes, and the thick, juicy shiitake mushrooms were prepared with incisions crossing the top that made them look like flower petals.

"No kidding... What is this soup? It looks thick, but it's only lightly salted, but the chicken flavor is so rich... It hits the spot in all the right places!" Tamuramaro groaned at the sheer umami. "The chicken is so soft and tender," he went on. "And all the vegetables, like the mibuna and carrots—they all have their own flavors, but they blend perfectly into the soup. Now I know why Keita is so passionate about them. I'd crave these, too, at least once a year...but only cooked in this hot pot."

Though the vegetables didn't stand out too much, each one of the sweet kintoki carrots, the mibuna leaves, and the kujou scallions mingled in harmony with the carefully prepared broth.

Sora was chewing on a sweet, star-shaped piece of kintoki carrot and relishing every bite.

"Look, she gave us some white rice and eggs, too. With red shells," said Fuuka.

"Time to finish it off with the rice!" cheered Tamuramaro.

"We're counting on you, Fuuka."

Fuuka jumped up at their eager request and rushed off to the kitchen with the pot.

"Man, you two are really living the good life here."

"Once in a while, Ms. Tatsuko gives us something truly special. It's thanks to you today." Sora could admit to this much, and he gave Tamuramaro a slight bow.

They were so intent on eating the hot pot that they'd completely forgotten about their beer. Now each of them lifted his slightly lukewarm glass to his lips.

"You, thanking me? It's gonna hail tomorrow," Tamuramaro quipped. "Anyway, on the same note—about Etou and the organization he was linked to. Really, no need to worry about it anymore."

Sora had been worried because they already knew his address, but Tamuramaro assured him everything was all right.

"What did you do?"

"Watch the headlines this week—there's gonna be a big magazine article on how gang members broke into the investigator's house. It'll include as much specific information as possible on the culprits. The organization wouldn't take meaningless risks just to get revenge on you. They're criminals, but they're also a business, and they wouldn't feel any sense of duty to follow up on Etou."

Listening to this explanation, Sora could understand why he would be safe, but not what steps Tamuramaro had actually taken.

"I've been a lawyer for a while now. I have a few cards up my sleeve," Tamuramaro said, patting his right arm.

"You look like you fit in with the modern world, but you still gesture like a shogun from the Heian period. A musty Heian old-timer."

"Say what you want," Tamuramaro said with a laugh, not at all bothered by Sora's snide remarks.

Sora could see now that Tamuramaro adjusted well to every period, but he was always a military man. Even if he wasn't holding a weapon or wielding a sword, he was strong.

Strong and just.

As Tamuramaro had pointed out, seeing more of the world had introduced many contradictions to Sora, and it made his footing precarious.

"I thought he was pretty strong, too…but who knows? Maybe he'd had too much to drink," said Sora, changing the subject to the man who, according to Tatsuko, had been a fan of this hot pot. He would have had a sword and a pistol.

"Ryoma, you mean? He must have had days when he let his guard down. It's impossible to stay alert all the time," murmured Tamuramaro. He could say the same about himself.

After the leaders of the Emishi were killed, Sakanoue no Tamuramaro's mission in the north had changed from waging war to building friendships. Sora knew this, too. They built castles, worshipped gods and Buddhas, and, under the order of the *ritsuryo* legal codes, learned other methods of agriculture and sericulture, and their lives settled down into peace.

"I was the one who broke the promise. So kill me. Please let your revenge end there."

There was a thought that would cross Sora's mind from time to time: That day, when the Imperial force had been on its way to build a new castle, the age of war might have already been over in Tamuramaro's eyes. And perhaps, for this man, there was never enough time to form any grudges.

"They say when he died, he was waiting for the chicken to come. To be honest, it wasn't nearly as good as this hot pot, though," Tamuramaro mused.

"Didn't he treat us to a simple hot pot one time? He thought you might be a man from some samurai family."

More than 150 years ago, as the long rule of the Edo shogunate was coming to an end, Sora and Fuuka had been living with Tamuramaro. Looking back now, Sora noticed that Tamuramaro showed up out of nowhere whenever the world became volatile.

"I wasn't great at hiding my military background back then. All the hot-blooded men were taking up arms right and left. Ryoma was from a rich family, so maybe grabbing whoever stood out to him and treating them to a meal—connecting to people—was his way of moving ahead."

Perhaps that was how the secret Satsuma–Choshu Alliance had come about—where Sakamoto Ryoma had helped unite two of the strongest Imperialist domains, who had once been irreconcilable enemies.[5] It had been a decisive event in the Meiji Restoration—but in the present-day world, the real details were lost to history, not just to Tamuramaro.

"He was a show-off, that Ryoma!"

Fuuka's word choice was simple, but not necessarily inaccurate as he returned to the living room with the pot in his hands, carefully holding it with pot holders.

"Show-off, huh. Even Ryoma's losing face."

"All right! Five more seconds!! Five, four, three, two, one!" Fuuka lifted the lid.

"Wow…"

"Oh…!"

Inside the pot, soft shreds of egg spilled over the white rice while fluffy, plump bits of melty yolk glistened in the chicken broth.

---

5. In 1866, the Satsuma and Choshu feudal domains joined forces in the movement to overthrow the Tokugawa shogunate and restore Imperial rule, which eventually found success. The following period is known as the Meiji Restoration.

“I chopped up the leftover kujou scallions into tiny pieces. And drizzled some ponzu sauce over it.”

“I can’t wait to dig in!”

“Thank you, Fuuka!”

Both Tamuramaro and Sora snatched up their porcelain spoons and empty bowls without a moment’s delay to help themselves. Any care for etiquette went out the window as each of them scooped up a spoonful of zosui rice porridge with the plump pieces of egg, blew on it to cool it down a little, and scarfed it down.

They all sighed contentedly.

“Now, this…this is paradise…” Tamuramaro sighed.

“For once, I agree with you completely,” murmured Sora.

“Wish Ryoma was here to taste this, too!” chirped Fuuka.

They savored every moment the subtle, rich flavors of the broth lingered in their mouths.

“We were just saying that the chicken hot pot that *he* liked was pretty different,” explained Tamuramaro, filling in what Fuuka missed when he was in the kitchen.

“As long as war doesn’t break out, I think food only gets better and better,” Sora remarked. “If we want a simple flavor, Fuuka can make that, too. Apparently, they can calculate the sugar content in grains and fruits now. It’s scientific progress.”

“Still, that chicken hot pot Ryoma treated us to *was* really yummy.” Fuuka smiled. It was the most luxurious meal they’d had around that time, and he remembered it well, as if it were yesterday.

“True. I couldn’t believe something so good existed. It felt extravagant.”

“You’re right. It really was tasty in its own way,” Tamuramaro agreed. “Funny, isn’t it? At the time, we thought it was a splendid meal in a fancy restaurant in Kyoto, but when we look back at it now, it seems so simple.” He scratched his head in slight frustration.

“Same name, changing flavors.” Sora sighed. Even though the dish was becoming more delicious, he still felt a little melancholy—but this in itself was a luxury.

"You know what you said about flavors disappearing? It's scary to think about it. Ryoma really did love that hot pot. My guess is that he shared it with anyone he wanted to talk to especially," said Tamuramaro. It was so long ago, he couldn't remember clearly anymore.

"You might be onto something. He liked it, and it was an extravagant meal. He was well-off, so he had the means to treat people he wanted to get close to before anything else. Maybe that was a key to the restoration that he worked toward." As he finished up his zosui and put down his bowl, Sora decided Tamuramaro's theory had some merit.

"Who knows what really went down in the Satsuma–Choshu Alliance, though. I heard some talk a few years ago that Ryoma's name might be taken out of history textbooks."

"Why?"

For Sora, when official accounts of history changed, it also meant they were rewriting the path of his own life.

"Apparently, they judged that there wasn't enough evidence to prove that he was a leading figure in the alliance. And besides, Ryoma was assassinated in 1867, but it was only during the Russo-Japanese War, in the early 1900s, that people started talking about him like a legend."

"I saw his name in the newspapers… That he appeared in the empress's dream," Sora said with a little snort. It was a strange piece of news to be printed in the Meiji era.

"They held him up like a symbolic figure to boost the country's morale during the war. To be fair, he did seem like a good-natured trader and a strategist."

"…I couldn't keep up with anything in those turbulent times," Sora admitted. "I didn't even notice the Tokugawa shogunate was coming to an end until it did. I'd thought a lasting era of peace had finally arrived. But I guess you must've known earlier that it would collapse."

When he looked back at the time Tamuramaro had invited them

to live together, he realized it was before Ryoma was even born. Tamuramaro must have already sensed some impending upheaval at that point.

"The shogunate had been ruling for two hundred sixty-five years. It's only natural to expect it to keep going." Tamuramaro laughed.

Even so, he must have noticed its end approaching. That was why he'd come to Sora and Fuuka.

"I keep a close watch on you."

That's what he told Sora. It was probably true, if not in the exact sense of the phrase.

"I suppose that's the mark of an able strategist in war—to notice those unguarded moments when they arise," Sora observed.

"Or the mark of a terrorist. Most things are judged based on the end result, at least in the history books."

"But..." Sora fell silent, unable to go on.

When he was studying for his university entrance exams, Sora found that Aterui was sometimes mentioned in textbooks. Of course, Tamuramaro always was. While history textbooks might make judgments according to the result, they didn't dictate which of the two had been right.

Neither of them had been wrong. But Tamuramaro lived, and Aterui died.

"Stories and history books want to line things up and string together a narrative, but it's impossible to balance those accounts while we're still living. That's not why we're on this earth anyway," Tamuramaro murmured.

"Is that really true?"

Just then, it seemed to Sora that Aterui and Tamuramaro had each fulfilled their duties, both in the records of history and in his personal memories.

"Maybe some people can live consistently, and others just can't."

And maybe I'm the latter, thought Sora, looking back on his long journey.

Sora was trying to believe in something that he could never believe in before, and the effort left him on wildly unsteady ground. He vacillated from one side to the other, and his wavering vision made it very difficult for him to make out the world that he might be just beginning to see.

I can't do it. Sora was starting to believe it was impossible.

"Brother," Fuuka called out suddenly. He had finished his bowl of zosui and had been listening quietly.

"What's up?" asked Sora in a gentle tone. He'd been so wrapped up in the conversation that he'd left his brother behind. Even though Fuuka was all grown-up now, Sora's voice always softened when he talked to him, as if he was talking to a little child.

"I wanna study."

His words startled Sora. It was the first time in 1,200 years that Fuuka had said anything like this.

"...What do you want to learn?" asked Sora, swallowing back the other question that almost slipped out of him. *What for?*

"I dunno exactly. I dunno what I don't know, listening to you guys talk. But I want to understand," muttered Fuuka, pulling a sulky face.

"Can you read?" Tamuramaro asked while Sora was still remembering to breathe.

"I can read hiragana. There's a lot of kanji I don't know."

"Then I'll teach you."

Tamuramaro's voice was gentle, too, but to Sora, it sounded like he was speaking to Fuuka as an equal. That wasn't how Sora usually treated him.

"That's my responsibility, Tamuramaro."

"Why?"

"Because I'm his big brother."

"Sora." Tamuramaro spoke soothingly, but there was a hint of firmness in his voice. "It's not the brother's job to teach a child how to read and write. I know it's hard to take in, but it's important. It's a job for adults." Turning to Fuuka, he asked, "Can you write your own name, Fuuka?"

"I can write mine and Sora's!"

"Then you should learn how to write mine, too. That way, you can put a curse on me," Tamuramaro joked. "Bring some paper and a pen."

"Ooh, I can curse you!" chirped Fuuka, taking the pot back to the kitchen.

Sora wasn't used to helping with the cleaning, so he simply sat back, dazed, and watched Fuuka deftly clear the table.

All this time, Sora had been focused on turning Fuuka back into a human for good. That was all he ever thought about. But gradually, he was beginning to discover what it really meant to return Fuuka to his human form. He didn't want to think that he'd fully realized it already. But what Fuuka said just now made it clear to him that he'd been running away from admitting to that discovery.

"We can keep 'Aterui' for last. The kanji in his name are the hardest, and besides, those characters were only chosen by the Yamato Imperial Court to go with the sound of his name."

Tamuramaro mulled over how to teach his lesson as he watched Fuuka wash the dishes. He acted like an adult—and a real parent.

When they'd lived together in the Showa period, he'd pretended to be the brothers' father in front of the neighbors, and that became the acceptable explanation in those times. Eventually, he had naturally fallen into playing the part of a father inside the home as well.

"On Friday evening, when I came here…," Tamuramaro began. Sora was still too tense to speak. "You said you could never forgive me, Sora."

He was smiling, as usual.

"But before, you used to say you *wouldn't* forgive me."

Sora understood what Tamuramaro meant.

"I'll never forget what you did. I can't forget it, and I certainly can't forgive you."

That's what he had said, slowly, truthfully, making sure there wasn't a lie in those words.

"We seem to never change, but maybe time is passing for us, too, don't you think? After all, you look grown-up now."

Tamuramaro had carried himself like their parent, and now he was treating Sora like a full-fledged adult.

Things were different before.

After they'd lived together several times in the Showa period, Sora realized that was what parents did—though it wasn't the first time he'd noticed this tendency in Tamuramaro. He'd discovered what it felt like to have a parent look after him and protect him from day to day. He'd never known anything like it before, but perhaps Tamuramaro had taught him to recognize it over their many years together.

And so, when he moved to Shizukuishi, he was quick to comprehend what Rokurou and Tatsuko wanted to give him. Sora was showered in their love, the kind of love that constantly worried over how well he was eating, the kind of love that came from a father and a mother. He had finally learned how to receive such affection. Somewhere in his heart, he had known.

He'd been taught, and he'd remembered.

"I'm gonna write down your name and curse you forever!"

Fuuka skipped over with a pen and a scrap of paper. Looking closely, Sora saw it was some flyer Tatsuko had used to wrap the ingredients, now soggy with moisture.

"My name's simple. Perfect for the first lesson." Tamuramaro moved closer to Fuuka on his left.

By the time they'd gone to Awata-guchi, Sora had already learned some things about the world. In the interest of knowing his enemy, he'd learned about the culture of the Yamato Imperial Court, and he'd already begun to study literature from the Tang dynasty traders who visited his people.

Even so, there was more and more he didn't understand, and every time they lived together, Tamuramaro helped fill in the gaps. It wasn't only book learning that he didn't understand, but also people. Living with them and understanding their hearts. What hatred led to. Though Sora couldn't bring himself to swallow it back then, he had seen that they were there: the different kinds of justice that existed in the world outside of himself.

Now there was no going back to that blissful ignorance. Although he still didn't know where he was headed, Sora was facing forward, taking one step at a time—walking on a path that was surely different from before.

"*Ta* as in *tanbo*, the rice field. Picture it in your head—the kanji looks like a square rice field, see? That's how you get a kanji…mostly. Easy, right?"

"Yeah. *Ta* for rice field—got it!"

Even though Sora had been desperate to turn Fuuka back into a full human being, he hadn't even considered teaching him anything before.

"I'll get a notebook for you tomorrow, Fuuka."

That was all he could say for the moment.

"Thank you, Sora."

Fuuka's voice sounded more mature than ever before. And there was a blue tint in his eyes that followed the letters on the paper, a color that wasn't normally there.

Sora could only gaze at him and the hue he vividly remembered: the blue as clear as a lake.

Staring up at the ceiling, Sora lay in his futon in the tatami-floored room. He was wearing a yukata that served as his pajamas. Upstairs, Tamuramaro was organizing his clothes and work equipment, and Sora could hear him shuffling around.

"Are you asleep, Sora?"

Fuuka slid open the door, wearing his white robe. He had just finished prepping the rice and dashi broth for breakfast the next morning.

"I'm awake."

Since it was a very old habit, the brothers still slept together in one futon. They had slept under eaves without a futon before, and when they were at Awata-guchi, they had huddled close together in their hiding place in the mountain for days.

At least, he was pretty sure they did.

"Let's get another futon for you, Fuuka," said Sora as Fuuka snuggled down next to him as a matter of course.

"How come? We don't need that."

"But..." Sora couldn't help reaching over and stroking Fuuka's cheek and hair, like one might do to a small child. After all, Sora had always viewed Fuuka only as his little brother. "You're a grown man now. You've gotten much bigger than me."

"Want me to turn into a dog? It's getting a bit chilly," Fuuka said with a cheery laugh, not heeding his brother's words.

"It's only September. The nights are getting chilly, but it's not that cold yet."

"But, Sora, you look kinda sad." Fuuka didn't even have to think to know how his brother was feeling. "I was worried you might be crying."

They had never questioned the way they could share the same emotions. Sora had convinced himself that was just due to their fraternal bond.

"I've never cried in my life."

"I know. Me neither."

But brothers were still separate people, and these days, Sora had been unable to sense Fuuka's feelings more and more often.

"And I'll do the dishes starting tomorrow. I've left all the chores in the kitchen up to you till now—I'm a horrible brother."

"Don't worry. I've got nothing else to do! Did Tamuramaro say you're a bad brother?!"

"Tamuramaro wouldn't say something like that. He's even teaching you to write. From now on, I'll clean up in the kitchen while you're studying. I'm sorry."

Before Sora got to his apology, Fuuka transformed into a big white dog. He curled up into a fluffy ball and nuzzled his head against Sora's chest. Sora hugged him close and felt the warmth from his body, a distinct contrast to the cool night air.

When Sora caressed his soft, furry cheek, Fuuka was already fast asleep.

"Fuuka…do you—"

—*want to become human again?*

He couldn't say the question out loud, not even when Fuuka was asleep. Perhaps he had never asked him directly before.

Why did he want to return Fuuka to human form? And when that happened, what would he do? What would happen to them? At some point, he had lost sight of his true motive.

"If the day comes when you can live as a human, you'll need to be able to write."

Until now, he hadn't even thought of this simple fact.

"Why do you feel my sadness?"

They'd always been living together as one being, but dog or human, Fuuka had a separate body and a separate temperature.

"Fuuka."

Even in his sleep, Fuuka was obedient—his curled tail shifted in response.

In their long, long lives, they had huddled close together to survive. They didn't need futons to stay warm while he could nestle against Fuuka as a dog. They'd had fun on their journey, too. They were fortunate.

That night, during Tamuramaro's lesson, Sora had seen Fuuka's eyes turn blue for the first time.

Although none of the historical records mentioned it, Aterui had silver-white hair and deep-blue eyes. He was superhuman in his sturdy build, and young Sora had looked up to him in pure admiration—the strong, honest, and kind leader.

Sora had wished to grow up like Aterui. Now, barely out of boyhood in appearance, his body had become that of an average young man.

"Who are you really?" The words slipped out before he knew it.

All these changes seemed to be as unstoppable as the passage of time itself. Sora shut his eyes tightly and buried his face in Fuuka's chest.

II

The Lawyer Is Thrown into the Client's Game

Sleep is impartial, visiting all equally and bringing a new day not quite like any before.

Fuuka, whose presence was uncertain, began to study writing and reading. And for Sora, it was just possible that here in Shizukuishi, he was beginning to live and coexist with other people for the first time in his life.

Sora was thinking about what Tatsuko—who brought them her delicious chicken hot pot the day before—had said that day at the park.

"They say wolves and dogs used to be the same kind of animals. One lives together with humans; the other can tear them apart. Maybe that's the only difference, and we humans give them different names for our own selfish reasons."

At some point, without realizing it himself, Sora had come to long for a steady life with the people of this town, to live in harmony with them. And to that end, he needed to work hard to earn his keep.

At this moment, he was having a glass of barley tea in the reception space at the Kouichi Koudera Tax Accountant Office, nestled in a side alley next to the Shizukuishi shopping street.

The tax accountant Natsuki Koudera was smiling broadly at him in such a puzzlingly brazen manner that Sora bowed instinctively. "Thank you for making the time to meet," he said, despite being the one who'd had to accommodate her schedule because she had been too busy for an appointment the previous day.

If he remembered correctly, the woman in the blue-gray pantsuit sitting in front of him was the one with a keen sense of finance. She liked her beer with two kilograms of kimchi. Sora wondered where Kouichi Koudera was.

"Thank *you*. I'm so glad you came."

Her lecturing Keita on the cost percentage and management of his vegetable business made sense to him now, considering she was a tax accountant.

"You seemed to be quite busy. Was today a good time for you?"

Sora was simply excited that someone in Shizukuishi might be in need of the rather specialized services of a certified fraud examiner. In his own way, he was eager to make the best impression.

"Oh, no, I just happened to be out on a routine audit for a client company yesterday—I have way too much time on my hands around this time of year. *Way* too much, let me tell you. Work is so, so slow. My calendar's so blank, I even went out for drinks after the audit," she said, waving her hands vigorously.

She was a little hungover, though she gave the impression of a neat and tidy woman in her midthirties. Her hair was clipped in a straight bob just above her shoulders.

"I see..."

After he quit the Public Prosecutors' Office, Sora had only worked with stuffy, older men in internal audit offices who wore their ties stiff and straight. He wasn't used to being in the presence of a woman, let alone having a conversation with her. He glanced toward the back of the office, anticipating the moment when Kouichi Koudera would swap places with Natsuki. At the moment, the fifty-something man in the back, who looked exactly like how he'd expect a tax accountant to look, was busy filing away some receipts at his desk.

"January, February, and March are hell. The rest of the time, I'm pretty free. I wish everyone handed in their receipts every month! If I could keep a monthly register, I wouldn't have to work myself to death in the busy season."

Sora was well aware that tax accountants sometimes helped manage a company's accounts, but their real battle came when it was time to file tax returns. For a certified fraud examiner, how a company did their accounting, kept their records, filed their tax returns, and paid taxes were all crucial details.

"I want to renovate this office, you see," said Natsuki, looking around the room with eyes defined with sharp, clean eyeliner. She sighed.

Sora had hoped she might finally broach the real subject of their meeting, but it was not to be. "Now that you mention it, the office is a little..." He trailed off. Slightly overly keen to land a new project to stay in this town, he was trying his best to keep the conversation going, though he was very perplexed by the abrupt change in topic.

"It's old, right?! Doesn't it look like some tax office from the '50s or something?" She looked over her shoulder. "Hear that, Mr. Hiraga? He thinks it looks ancient, too!"

The fifty-something man in black-rimmed glasses was apparently not Kouichi Koudera.

"Oh, no, I never said that! Not in the least!" Sora blurted out, almost rising to his feet in a fluster. He wasn't used to trying to talk about something he didn't understand just to be agreeable, and now he'd put his foot in his mouth.

"Ms. Natsuki's always going on about it," said Hiraga, smiling gently. He himself looked like he'd stepped right out of some '50s TV show, wearing a white shirt, holding a calculator and receipts.

"You know we don't have time for that, boss." A woman chimed in from near the door, twirling her smartly curled hair around her finger. Her name tag read KAWAGUCHI. She appeared to be in her twenties, apparently doing some minor clerical work, and she clearly didn't care about mincing words. "Renovation means hauling all our papers and computers outside till it's over, right? Fat chance. Literally impossible. I'd quit."

"Awww, Mikuuu. I'd die if you quit. Ummm, anyway, I should introduce us. I'm the chief here, and Mr. Hiraga is my firm partner. Ms. Miku Kawaguchi here is the best assistant ever. My father set up this office to do taxes for the people on the shopping street and things like that, but we lost him ten years ago. He died so young," she concluded lightly, drinking her barley tea.

"I see. My condo—" Sora paused, unsure whether it would be appropriate to offer his condolences for someone who was still there in the name of the office, even after ten years.

"And then I asked Mr. Hiraga, who was my father's firm partner, if he could take over. But he said he couldn't keep it up if he wasn't a partner, so… We're a corporation, you know, so we need two tax accountants to make it work. I used to do this work in-house for a company, so that's how I came back to Shizukuishi."

Natsuki praised Hiraga's wisdom, and Sora had to agree in spite of himself. He had set up his own firm all by himself, and now he was beset with struggles.

"I don't mind being back, though," she went on. "I never cared much for those high-rise tower blocks. The only thing is, that shopping street is around half a century old, and my father's clients are getting on in years. Some of them are even older than he was. Sooner or later, they're gonna start kicking the bucket, too, you know?"

Sora was always calm, except when he was with Tamuramaro, but now he choked on his tea as she brought death into the conversation again.

"…!"

Evidently, his prospective client for this important occasion—his very first project here in Shizukuishi—was to be this Natsuki, who was sitting right in front of him. For Sora, it seemed like a test of his emotional endurance to prove that a harmonious life with the townspeople was even possible for him.

"You okay? Aren't you too young to have things going down the wrong way? Take care. You know Keita, the grocer? Ugh, that kid. He has the gall to say he'll manage his accounts on an app. If the tax office kicks down his door, he'll deserve it. Anyway, to put it in a nutshell, we want to expand our clientele, you know? We're trying to think of the future twenty years from now."

This whole spiel was apparently Natsuki's introduction of the company, and she positively beamed as she finished.

"That's…very important," Sora managed to say, though they were off on dubious footing.

"It really is! We're putting to use whatever business acumen we've got, and we're also a consultant for Odajima Construction."

Sitting up straight and staying collected, Sora listened to Natsuki's unstoppable talk.

"Ah, the one near Nerima Station."

Sora had seen their large, impressive sign—just the kind of sign a major construction company would put up—every time he went somewhere by train. It was only one stop away from Shizukuishi on the express lines, and four stops away on the local ones.

"The sign's hanging at Nerima, but the home office is at Takanodai Station. It's faster on foot. They built their company back when there was a lot of land to spare around here, so it's too big for them. Now they're hemmed in by drugstores and home improvement stores. They might as well sell it off. But they're the go-to company for major general contractors."

Though Sora struggled to keep up with Natsuki's flow of logic, at least he managed to grasp that Odajima Construction at Takanodai in Nerima was a fairly large company that functioned as a subcontractor for general contractors.

"When I came back and realized my father's clients didn't have much longer to live—"

"Um, you can skip that part. I've heard enough about that."

"Really? But it's important, you know. We're all in the same boat—my father's clients, me, and you, Mr. Oushuu—everyone dies eventually. And society lives on. So we have to prepare for the future," said Natsuki simply, glancing at her younger employee, Miku.

"Everyone dies eventually," she'd said. But even more than Natsuki's constructive view on the matter, Sora wished he could die just like everyone else: to walk down the passage of time, as a normal human being, until it ended for him and Fuuka together.

"Who said you could die? To die is to pass into the Pure Land. You're far from ready for that, very far. You better stay on your journey until you find an answer."

When Miroku-bosatsu had told him just that, Sora had had no idea that such a journey would sever him so much from the lives of other people. Sora never wanted to part with this town—and especially not with Fuuka, who was growing and becoming more mature as they lived here.

"...I want to die properly."

"What?! Not in here, please!"

"Oh, no, I was talking about resting in peace in the Pure Land. I'm sorry."

"A young man like you, choking on tea and wanting to 'rest in peace'—what's going on here? By the way, I don't want to be rude, but you do look young for this line of work. I expected someone a bit older. How old are you?"

Sora snapped his mouth shut. This question hit him square in his weakest spot.

"I...have a massive complex about that. I'm thirty-one."

"Massive, huh. Sorry I mentioned it! Forget I ever asked. Let's get back on track. We've been a consultant for a subsidiary company of Odajima Construction for eight years, but things have been odd these past two years."

Sensing that the conversation was finally turning to the main reason for their meeting, Sora put down his tea on the table.

"What do you mean by 'odd'?"

"Back when I started with them, there was a post-disaster special demand for the construction industry. It's not a phrase you love to hear, but there we are. Mr. Odajima turned their old subcontractor into a subsidiary company after it collapsed in the disaster, and they were doing well."

Sora listened silently, jotting down notes in a notepad.

"Ah, I should mention that the company I'm a consultant for is just that subsidiary company in the area affected by the disaster, that's all. So, long story short, what's odd is that their income and expenses don't balance out. In the last two years, they paid fifty-five percent tax for unspecified expenditures. They say they're fine with that. But that's a big sum, you know?"

As a tax accountant, Natsuki would be feeling an itch to balance the books, but for Sora, the biggest problem was that something that hadn't happened for six years was now happening in the past two.

"Is there anything missing in the account books?"

"Sometimes there's a transaction, but the sales would be zero. When I ask him, 'Isn't there something missing here?' he brings over a wad of bills from his safe and asks me how much there should be..." Natsuki flopped back on the sofa with a distant look in her eyes. "He's never been the type to look at his accounts. He hasn't had to do much real work for a while."

"I've seen many like him. They're surprisingly common among senior management."

In his work as a certified fraud examiner, Sora had encountered similar situations several times, where a potential case of fraud turned out simply to be sloppy bookkeeping, as some presidents of small-to-medium-sized companies didn't even want to look at numbers. In those cases, he only had to take care of the inadvertent omission in the tax return filing, and the matter would close without turning into a criminal case. Those were the best-case scenarios, but Sora was shocked by the number of business managers who never looked over their accounts.

"Managing a business and managing accounts are two separate things, I guess—and apparently, in the old days, they did just fine going by ball-park figures and slapdash bookkeeping. Mr. Odajima probably has decades' worth of savings stashed away, and the company's doing well with multiple departments. They didn't drop out of the race even after the bubble burst and the Lehman shock happened. But now, *this* is something else." Natsuki sighed.

After all that, Sora had a big question. "Wait a moment, Ms. Koudera. Then who is going to be my client? Aren't you a third-party accountant for the subsidiary company owned by the chairman?"

"Just 'Natsuki.' Everyone in this town calls me by my first name. Yes, and there's the rub." Natsuki folded her arms in contemplation as Sora wondered what she meant by that. A few moments later, she said, "I'll hire you. How much do you charge?"

This was a twist Sora hadn't expected.

"I don't think it's reasonable or profitable for you to hire me. I've never dealt with a case like this before."

Almost always, some internal personnel of a company would hire Sora as an independent third party. In a situation like this with Odajima Construction, the internal audit office of the company itself would usually be the one to call him in, either because they couldn't handle the issue themselves or because they couldn't investigate the chairman internally.

"I don't want Mr. Odajima to get arrested or anything! I'd pay you a million yen if you could clean up the mess before it gets out."

"I can't just step in and 'clean up the mess'! I'm not a jack-of-all-trades." Sora's voice rose in disbelief. To prevent an arrest for a million yen? He'd never heard of such a haphazard request.

Apparently familiar with Natsuki's ways, Hiraga and Miku went on with their work as usual, not even looking up from their desks.

"I know that," Natsuki answered, her face suddenly serious. "Mr. Oushuu, you're a professional. A certified fraud examiner. If there was anything fishy going on, you could pin down the evidence and make him come to his senses. Please!"

Natsuki clearly had an accurate understanding of what Sora did for a living, even though the work of a certified fraud examiner wasn't common knowledge.

"If I found evidence of a significant collusion, I'd need to report it to the District Public Prosecutors' Office—otherwise, it would amount to a cover-up."

"Collusions are run-of-the-mill for the industry, more or less. Odajima is the go-to company for general contractors, after all, so I could tell that something or other was going on in the past, too. That's normal. But now it's become sort of chaotic. I don't have a clue what they're up to… I'm worried for them."

Natsuki's fierce gaze met Sora's. Despite her unwavering determination, Sora could sense that she was truly anxious.

"I'm not a good candidate for this case."

Sora let out a heavy sigh when he realized that Natsuki wanted to protect Chairman Odajima. Sora had been ready to take a step forward, brimming with a desire to live in harmony with the people of Shizukuishi, but the reality hit him. Just one night's sleep wasn't enough to change who he was.

"How so?"

"I'm very uncomfortable with gray zones. I chose to follow the path of law because laws can judge people's actions rationally and punish criminals properly for their misdeeds. I'm sorry to disappoint you, but that's who I am at heart."

Though he himself was disappointed by this turn of events, especially since he'd felt so inspired to build a new life with these people, Sora thought it was best for both sides if he declined this offer.

"That's a heavy burden to bear."

"I agree completely, but it's not easy for me to change. If the law says something is a crime, then I have to—"

"Mr. Oushuu, what's your first name?"

"Hmm? It's Sora."

He tilted his head in confusion at the abrupt question. He'd been offering this earnest confession for both their sakes, so why was she interrupting?

"How do you write it? Can you show me?"

She handed him two pieces of paper, and Sora wrote down the kanji characters, thinking of his brother, who was just beginning to learn how to write.

"It's a slightly unusual combination. The kanji for *so* is the same as *kara*, or *emptiness*... Oh!"

Someone grabbed his right hand from behind, and before he knew it, Miku had dabbed a red ink pad onto his thumb, pressed his thumb down on the paper, and returned back to her desk as if nothing happened.

"It might be old-fashioned to make use of thumbprints and stamps in a contract, but we're grateful for your agreement."

"What are you doing?! Please give me back my thumbprint!!"

"Now, now. I'm not as ruthless as you think. Could you hear me out, at least? Please!"

After her bold move, which not even a yakuza member would do nowadays, Natsuki clapped her hands in front of her face in entreaty. Sora sensed the weight of her desperation, and a deep sigh escaped him, not just because of the thumbprint.

He'd confessed his true character to Natsuki because he didn't think he could do it. But she didn't stop to listen.

"I'll listen to your story, but that's all I'm going to do..."

At the same time, he also thought this might be part of learning to coexist with people—to finally learn to accept the things that couldn't be changed. Now that he was living in Shizukuishi with a somewhat parental figure, he could feel himself changing more rapidly than ever before. His iron grip on his ideals of righteousness and justice was beginning to loosen.

"That's settled, then. We'll pick a day and go have a chat with Mr. Odajima. I'll take you as my assistant of sorts. I'll deal with that somehow, with some begging and pushing."

"Do you mean you'll force me in?"

Whether it was good or bad that this job with Natsuki was his first step toward coexistence, Sora couldn't tell. It was so beyond the familiar bounds of his experience that he couldn't make any guess as to the future. Even if he could change a little, he found it hard to believe he could ever adapt to the gray zones as much as people wanted him to.

"By the way, I hope you're going to take care of Ms. Tatsuko's divorce," Natsuki remarked, suddenly switching her tone and subject to something far less ambiguous. "I know you're not that kind of lawyer, but you can do it, can't you?"

Since she understood what a certified fraud examiner's work entailed, she also knew it wasn't impossible for him to assist in divorce proceedings, even though he wasn't an attorney.

"Are you in favor of them getting a divorce?" asked Sora, relieved to see that Natsuki had a thorough understanding of how things worked in society.

"Of course I am. I learned calligraphy from them, too, you know," she said coolly as she flipped through her schedule book to choose a date. "Didn't you choose the path of law so you could judge rationally and punish appropriately? Do them a favor and make a clean cut of it. I'll deal with all the tax business." There was no hesitation in her voice.

Those who knew how matters stood thought that if Tatsuko wanted a divorce, that was how it should be, and Sora could understand why.

"So you did hear what I said, even while you forced me to give you my thumbprint… And I see calligraphy and penmanship are two separate things," Sora observed, his eyes on Natsuki's notebook.

"I'm well aware of how messy my handwriting is, thank you very much!" she retorted. They left the matter of the divorce unresolved.

Deep down, Sora noticed that it was he himself who let the subject drop. Not long ago, he would never have allowed something to remain so vague.

Sora turned in a different direction than usual and went to the shopping street in front of the train station to buy a notebook for Fuuka.

"I'm back."

It was still early, since his appointment with Natsuki had been just a chat, but he'd taken no less than an hour to pick out a notebook.

"Welcome back, Sora!" Fuuka came bounding out to greet him, as he always did.

For some reason, Sora felt a rush of relief to see his brother and his usual affectionate hello, but he had mixed feelings about the outfit. He was wearing the blue costume that Tamuramaro had given him.

"Here, this is for you, Fuuka."

As he loosened his tie, Sora handed the paper bag to Fuuka, whose arms were wrapped around his waist.

"What is it?"

"Go ahead—open it," said Sora, taking off his jacket.

Fuuka opened the bag eagerly. "A notebook?!"

"That's right. Hope it's useful for your studies."

This was the conundrum Sora had puzzled over for an hour. He himself had already known how to read and write by the time they'd begun this long journey, so he didn't know where to start when it came to finding a notebook that was suitable for learning kanji. In the end, he resorted to asking the staff and chose a kanji practice notebook lined with big squares, intended for students in the lower grades of elementary school.

"Looks perfect!" Fuuka appeared delighted, flipping through the notebook at the dining table.

"Glad you like it," Sora said quietly with a sigh of relief.

"But it's frustrating to have to learn from Tamuramaro. Why can't you teach me, Sora?" Fuuka pleaded.

"Of course, I can teach you anytime. But..."

Sora thought of Tamuramaro, who was still busy with the Daitokyo Bank case. He would be presenting himself at the Public Prosecutors' Office, meeting with Etou, who was now ousted from his position, and so on.

"It's not the brother's job to teach a child how to read and write."

Those were his firm words to Sora from the day before.

"Maybe being frustrated means you'll learn faster from Tamuramaro."

Back when they lived together in the Showa period, Sora had learned countless things from Tamuramaro. Not just for school, but also about society, about human beings. Though he didn't like to admit it, he knew Tamuramaro had cared for him and raised him as a child.

"Do you still hate him that much?" asked Sora, suddenly curious why.

Sora himself harbored feelings about Tamuramaro that tugged in opposite directions. With the incidents from 1,200 years ago and all that had happened since, he couldn't sum up how he felt about Tamuramaro in one word.

"I *hate* him!" Fuuka cried, sticking out his tongue.

Sora didn't share Fuuka's animosity toward Tamuramaro. His own feelings were far more troublesome.

"Why's that?"

"When you're with him, you change so much… It's happened before," said Fuuka, his gaze turning lonely.

It was true that over the centuries, Tamuramaro nurtured Sora's young and stubborn heart. Sora had feared this change in himself, and that was what had made him run away from home forty years ago. He was startled that Fuuka could read his feelings so well, even if only by instinct.

"That might be true."

Both of them had grown up to be adults, probably thanks to Tamuramaro's efforts to raise them.

"Ugh! He's horrible!" Fuuka puffed out his cheeks like a sulky little boy, and he was still nothing but endearing.

"Have you been curious about studying for a long time?" asked Sora. He felt ashamed for not noticing such an important wish in his younger brother.

"Nope. There's nothing I wanna do. Ever," said Fuuka quietly. All trace of his childishness was gone in a blink.

"Really?"

"As long as you're smiling, and as long as you're eating yummy food, I'm happy."

There had been times in the past when Fuuka would talk like this. Sora had listened to him without questioning it, as natural as the rustle of the wind.

"As long as you're happy, that's all I want," Fuuka declared.

"Fuuka," Sora cut in, unable to let the words pass this time. "You wanted to learn how to read and write. Isn't that true?"

"Yup."

"The other day, when the burglar drew his knife, you tried to tear out his throat, didn't you?"

"Yup."

Sora wanted to explain that Fuuka had wanted to do those things of his own accord, not by Sora's will. But he couldn't find the right words.

The brothers had been like two people sharing one soul. They were only a year apart. But why had Sora already received some education at twelve, while Fuuka hadn't?

"Once you know your letters, what do you want to write?"

"Do you remember when Fuuka was born?"

At some point in their 1,200-year journey, Tamuramaro had raised this question to Sora. As he pondered the question over and over again, Sora realized it wasn't just that he didn't remember Fuuka's birth because they were born a year apart. For a long time, he'd seen Fuuka as his other half—a piece that matched up perfectly with himself.

"I wanna put a curse on Tamuramaro," Fuuka replied.

Now things were different. Fuuka absolutely lived outside of Sora's existence. Sora had never noticed until Fuuka himself existed. Fuuka was an independent, separate life from Sora.

"Don't be so hard on him."

For a long time before that, Sora hadn't been able to distinguish Fuuka from himself. They were one pair without any boundaries.

"I really, really hate him!"

But it was clear that Fuuka—with his deep, lake-blue eyes, shining silver hair, and tall, sturdy build—was completely different from Sora now.

"Don't you go killing him, okay? I know he can't die, but still. Let's go for a walk, Fuuka. Sanpouji Lake."

"Whoo-hoo!"

For centuries, Sora had accepted Fuuka's words without question: that he lived only for his older brother, was devoted only to Sora, and was happy to wait by himself at home. Now, however, Sora couldn't just accept what Fuuka told him. He had learned more with Tamuramaro and come to have second thoughts about things he had so resolutely believed in; he could see more of the world.

"It's nice out today. How about a lap around Shakujii Park?"

"Yippee!"

"You really have grown into a fine, full-fledged man."

When Fuuka stood up, he had the appearance of a tribal leader—a strong, sturdy core that no one could shatter, with a heart to match; a sinewy body, solid yet supple; a long, dignified mane of flowing hair; and deep-blue eyes like the water of a lake.

"Sorry I can't turn into a little puppy, Sora."

"Huh?" Sora looked up from his seat on the tatami floor in surprise as Fuuka touched on something that was hidden deep inside him.

"In the beginning, I could stay young like you. Maybe that's the way you want me to be. I dunno." Fuuka tilted his head. "I could've disappeared, too. Sorry. I could've, but I didn't."

"What are you saying?" Sora raised his voice, getting up on one knee.

"You tried to kill me, didn't you?" Fuuka said with a troubled look. He didn't usually seem to remember Awata-guchi.

"Fuuka, that time…" Sora could hardly breathe, but he pressed on. "I was going to die with you."

"The other day, you said you wouldn't mind if I killed you. I bet your life would be easier if I wasn't here." Fuuka spoke casually, neither serious nor accusatory.

"That's not true!" cried Sora. "Definitely not! You're...you're all I have, Fuuka. If you weren't here, I'd...!"

Sora groped for the words in vain. He was so flustered that he could only shout, "No," over and over again, shaking his head. He felt like his throat would rupture.

"I'm sorry," Fuuka said, for the third time, and knelt down to hug Sora. "That's not what I meant." He pulled Sora close with arms as wide as a father's. "In the old days, I could stay a puppy, and I could make myself disappear if I'd wanted to."

"You...could?"

"Yeah. I knew I could, but I guess you didn't. I just never told you 'cause I didn't think it was anything important at first. I didn't know it was special," Fuuka explained anxiously. "And as time went on, I wanted to stay more and more—to stay with you, Sora. So I couldn't break it to you."

Fuuka loosened his embrace and peered closely into Sora's eyes. "And then I got big. I don't have any control of myself anymore. I can't go back to being little. Looks like I can't disappear, either."

"You don't have to! Don't!!"

"These days you talk about me getting bigger a lot, so I thought you didn't like it." Fuuka was taken aback by Sora's unusual burst of agitation, and he stroked Sora's hair with his large hand as Sora always did to him.

"Of course I do. I'm really impressed by you, growing up so tall and strong. Now you're even learning to write."

"Then I'm happy. I just thought you might be sad."

"I'm not sad at all."

Fuuka beamed and transformed into a big white dog. Nudging his head against Sora's cheek, he coaxed Sora to head on their walk.

"You're strong and beautiful. I'm proud of you, Fuuka."

"Coo?" Fuuka whined adorably, his eyes round.

"Let's go. Come on." Sora took Fuuka's red leash and made for the door.

If Fuuka had been able to stay in the form his brother expected to see, perhaps that meant he didn't have a will of his own back then. From the day Sora had begun to doubt Fuuka's words, his existence, perhaps the brothers were no longer an inseparable pair, and each of their bodies started to grow in their own ways.

"That day at Awata-guchi, I couldn't see Fuuka clearly."

Tamuramaro's unforgettable words were still haunting Sora. According to him, he hadn't even fully grasped Fuuka's presence. He'd suspected that Fuuka had never been there in the first place. What's more, he'd clearly stated that this was no longer the case. Even if Fuuka had never existed in the beginning, he was certainly alive and present now. He was starting to breathe on his own.

"I don't have any control of myself anymore. I can't go back to being little. Looks like I can't disappear, either."

Fuuka had no control of his own life—that in itself was proof of his existence.

"Don't you want to become a human being, Fuuka?" asked Sora for the first time, when they stepped out of the house with the leash tied, even though Fuuka couldn't talk anymore.

There were things he wanted Fuuka to have now that he'd grown up and begun to learn, fully present in his own life.

"Coo." Fuuka whined as he tilted his head to one side. It almost looked as though his mind was blank.

But no. Sora had only assumed that Fuuka never had any desires of his own. And when Sora's refusal to think otherwise as they lived together plunged him into doubt and anxiety, he had left Tamuramaro's home. He had been frightened of discovering what might have lain beyond his field of vision—of realizing that the world he had been focusing on was just one small part of it. Meanwhile, a wider, unknown world containing multiple forms of righteousness and justice unfolded just outside it.

"Fuuka."

They were, indeed, a pair. Fuuka must have been there since they were little, repressing Sora's nature, but even his presence had become uncertain. Why did Fuuka suddenly turn into a killer that time at Awata-guchi?

One reason why Sora was able to accept Tamuramaro in their home, forty years after their last parting, was because he could be certain that he heard heartbeats inside Fuuka.

Fuuka was there, alive.

"I want to interact with people and to understand *ritsuryo*, so I'm sure you'll also..."

So Fuuka, too, would find a way to live. If he turned into a human being for good, Fuuka would have his own interactions with others. As his brother, Sora could only hope for this with all his heart.

"Coo?" Fuuka whined gently.

Sora found himself clinging to Fuuka's neck just outside their front door. He was listening to his brother's heartbeat again. Fuuka's body was sounding a steady rhythm. He was alive.

"Fuuka."

For 1,200 years, Sora had thought of Fuuka as his little brother, and he had been running away from thinking about his presence because he couldn't bear even the possibility that Fuuka might not actually exist. Outwardly, he'd been saying that he wanted to find a way to turn his brother back into a human, but some days, Sora merely wished to hold his breath and keep living together with him—just as he had done in the valley at Awata-guchi. Even though Fuuka might not have been present back then.

Now, for the first time, Fuuka had admitted to Sora the uncertainty of his own existence, and how that ability to disappear seemed to be gone now.

"I love you, Fuuka."

In the end, more than anything else, Sora wished to stay as close as they were now. He wanted to live as they had when they were little, just the two of them together. He wanted to leave everything behind—the house, the town, even Tamuramaro.

"Coo," Fuuka murmured softly.

For Sora, Fuuka was the only warmth in the world. They were brothers who had nothing but each other.

"I love you, Fuuka."

His voice wavered as he tried to force a laugh. He tried to stand up, but his legs wouldn't cooperate. He looked at the sky.

"Woof."

The sky was clear. He stared into the blue past the leaves of the low trees. From this height, he wouldn't be able to look straight into people's eyes. He wouldn't be on equal footing with anyone, let alone be able to talk with them.

"Don't think you can die so easily."

Miroku-bosatsu's voice echoed in his head.

Sora thought about his brother's world when he lived among others. When he was in their presence, his perspective would have been like this—looking up from below. That was his present reality.

"Woof, woof."

"Let's go."

Once he'd had a good look at Fuuka's world, Sora planted his feet firmly on the ground and stood up. He took a step forward, ready to face whatever lay ahead in the future.

On Friday afternoon, Sora visited the Kouichi Koudera Tax Accountant Office in his dark-navy suit. With Natsuki leading the way, they made their way to Odajima Construction on foot. It wasn't very far to Nerima-Takanodai—just one station over.

"You know that old man at the liquor store? Watch out for him; he'll grab any chance to hand out blank invoices like little pieces of candy. If you want to fill one out, make sure you don't put down any big, clean numbers or numbers that are just low enough not to require a stamp. The tax office has their eye on that shop, you see." She pointed out the owner, who looked like the type to do exactly that.

"I wouldn't do that..." Sora sighed.

"You'd be surprised how many shop owners are like that around here in Shizukuishi."

Apparently, dealing with those owners gave Natsuki a headache. She walked with purpose in her greige pantsuit; her glossy, flat, black shoes struck a brisk, staccato rhythm on the road.

They covered a distance that would have normally taken twenty minutes in fifteen and came to a tall building a little ways away from the train station.

"Is it because you're based in a neighboring town?" Sora couldn't help but ask as he looked at the sign proclaiming ODAJIMA CONSTRUCTION on the rooftop above the twelfth floor. It was unusual for a company of this size not to have an office in the center of the city, but he could tell they had close ties with general contractors.

"What do you mean?"

"Well, I apologize for being blunt, but even if it's only a subsidiary, the main company seems too large to hire a tax accountant from a small town as its consultant."

Sora was treading carefully, keeping his distance from Natsuki. It wasn't as though her tone had any edge to it, but she was someone who would force you into giving her a contractual thumbprint.

"You're sharp. I'm impressed, Mr. Oushuu. I knew I'd picked the right fraud examiner," she declared with a nod, though Sora doubted she'd had any other choice. Carefree as she was, there was no knowing what she'd do next. He couldn't trust her at all.

"Mr. Odajima's a drinking buddy of mine. To be more precise, we met at the bar just over there. Near the station."

"So he was chatting you up..." Sora's voice was laced with fatigue now. Natsuki's pace was truly exhausting.

"No, no! He ordered this expensive sake for me, his treat."

"That's just flirting..."

"He's like that with everybody! That's the way he is! As soon as he takes a liking to someone, even just a little, he'll treat you to *anything*. Sometimes he doesn't even pick up the receipts. The waiter asked if he wanted one, and he just went, 'Oh, I'll skip it today,' so I was like, 'Hold up, man.' And that's how he asked me to work for him."

Sora had never heard of someone flirt-scouting a tax accountant like that, but coming from Natsuki, it sounded believable.

"So as you can imagine, he's our biggest client. Well, I say that, but we're only in charge of the subsidiary company up in the northeast. As for Mr. Odajima, he's an old man who doesn't even glance at his account books."

Sora followed Natsuki into the entrance hall of the company building. Before he walked in, he caught sight of the cornerstone and saw that the structure had been completed fifty years ago. The interior showed the years, but he could feel the modern air-conditioning. They must have done large-scale renovation at some point in the past.

"What are you doing? Follow me," called Natsuki, gesturing to him. She'd picked up an ID for each of them while Sora was staring at the high ceiling.

"Anything interesting up there?" Natsuki asked as they waited in the elevator hall.

"This building was completed fifty years ago, but—"

"How did you know that?!"

"It's engraved on the cornerstone. But the AC system seems new, and the ceiling is well maintained. That's a sign the company is comfortably in the black."

"Way to go!" Natsuki suddenly slapped his back in full force.

"...!"

"I like it! You don't miss a trick! I live by intuition, Mr. Oushuu, so I wish I could hire you."

"Living by intuition seems completely unreliable for a tax accountant, but hiring..."

I wouldn't say no to that, Sora thought, but he didn't say it out loud.

The elevator was as spacious as the building, a large and speedy box.

Sora heaved a big sigh. He had a feeling that kind of broad-stroke intuition was important to succeed as a business owner. The way he worked involved focusing on minute details, and that was leading him into a financial bog.

"As a construction company, the condition of their office building is the first step to gaining trust."

"Don't you think it's a waste of space, though? They've got several departments in the headquarters, too, but the ones in charge of the large-scale public construction projects are all successors in regional branch offices. If all Mr. Odajima has to do is hold meetings and foster ties with clients, I feel like it's enough for him just to have a small office in the city center."

As they talked about the company, they reached the twelfth floor.

"But he says this is where he started, so he likes this place. I get how he feels, but still."

The twelfth floor in Nerima afforded a view over a variety of things. Clusters of office buildings spread out before them, skyscrapers rising in the distance. On a sunny day, you might even see Mount Fuji, but the distant parts of Tokyo were faded today.

"I'm starting to see why you get along with Chairman Odajima, considering how you feel about high-rises," observed Sora, looking out at the scene. The greenery was sparse here—neither an urban cityscape nor a traditional old-town neighborhood.

"We've been awaiting your arrival, Ms. Koudera."

A woman neatly dressed in a suit greeted them with a smile, standing in front of the elevator on the top floor, where the chairman's room was located.

"Hello, Ms. Miyaizumi. How are you?"

"I'm always in tip-top shape. You've brought company today, I see."

The woman, who looked close to Natsuki in age, turned to Sora and bowed graciously.

"Nice to meet you. My name is Oushuu."

He returned her bow and was about to take out his business card when

Natsuki gave him a sharp jab with her elbow. Ah, right. If he revealed his true profession now, they would be on the alert.

"This way, please."

Miyaizumi led them to the chairman's door and opened it gracefully without a sound as Sora bowed.

"Hello! How are you, Mr. Odajima?" said Natsuki brightly.

"My name is Oushuu. Nice to meet you."

When Sora looked up, he saw a heavyset man in a suit around his seventies, sitting at an old-fashioned wooden desk that brought back memories of a previous era. He was mid-laugh, holding a fountain pen in his hand. And on the guest couch, there sat another visitor. The visitor and Sora had just seen each other that morning.

"Tamuramaro! What are you doing here…?!"

"Hey, Sora."

There he was, lounging on the couch in a black suit. Tamuramaro had been surprisingly faithful to the contract with the credit company, which stipulated that he should go to work every day.

"You know him?" asked Natsuki. "Mr. Tamuramaro? Or, um, Mr. Maro Tamura?"

Evidently, she wasn't aware that Tamuramaro was Sora's lodger, and Sora stood speechless, pinching the bridge of his nose.

"Hi there, Natsuki. This is Mr. Tamura, our prospective consulting lawyer. His name really is Tamuramaro, if you read it all together Japanese-style, isn't it, Mr. Tamura? It's quite a name." Odajima gave a deep, booming laugh. Sora already wanted to go home and escape this chaos in the chairman's office.

"My parents admired Sakanoue no Tamuramaro."

"That so. Are they from Tokyo, your parents?"

"They're from Nara."

"Indeed. I've heard people from the northeast despise the sei-i taishogun," Odajima joked; perhaps he was old enough to know and have an interest in Japanese history.

But Sora, who knew firsthand why northeastern people would despise the famous commander in chief, said nothing.

"I'm not surprised. It's only natural they should hate him." Instead of laughing it off, Tamuramaro answered with a melancholy smile.

"And who's this? Quite a handsome young man. You look like a Kabuki actor," Odajima said kindly. "Come—do sit down."

"He's my assistant. Still getting his business cards ready. And I can make him perform the Heron Girl dance if you want." Natsuki laughed. The dance of the Heron Girl was her favorite scene in Kabuki theater.

"I'm sorry; it's true I don't have a business card at the moment, but I won't do any dances. I'm pleased to make your acquaintance."

For the first time in a long while, Sora felt like he was getting buried in a forest or carried down a river. Natsuki had struck him as the type to get overwhelmed, too, but he still sat obediently next to her and across from Tamuramaro.

Sora glared at Tamuramaro, silently demanding an explanation, but Tamuramaro went on laughing and pretended not to notice.

"Here you are," said Miyaizumi, slipping back into the room and offering cups of tea to the newcomers with efficient ease.

"Thanks."

"Thank you very much."

Things like this gave a hint of the long history the company had.

"So you found an assistant," Odajima remarked. "You've been dealing with our accounts all by yourself all this time, Natsuki, but it's a wonder you could pull it off without a helping hand."

Odajima was rather tall and broad-shouldered for his age, and Sora could guess that he'd started out as a hands-on worker in the construction industry. The fountain pen, which he absentmindedly toyed with as he spoke, looked vintage.

"I do have helping hands, though. I wouldn't manage otherwise. I share the work with the office."

"Well, it's been a great help to us, since I found you just as our previous accountant was retiring. But the laws are changing all the time." With a slight creak of his chair, Odajima swung around to survey the view from the top floor. "Maybe it's high time we closed up shop. Oh, not you, Natsuki. My company. Well, me, to be specific." He turned back to the room with a cheerful laugh.

"What are you talking about?! You're still young!"

Even if the company was performing well, Sora thought Odajima was old enough to retire. He sighed a little, getting a sense of what kept a man of his generation in this position: encouragement and support from people like Natsuki. It wasn't uncommon for business managers like him, from the days of the postwar economic boom, to stay in office well beyond retirement age, which often led to illegal practices in their account books. Some people of that era genuinely weren't aware of more recent changes in the law.

"Oh, I don't know, Natsuki. Let's see, your glowing assistant hasn't come here to dance the Heron Girl. And I bet he's not a tax accountant. A prosecuting attorney?"

He'd hit the nail on the head. Natsuki didn't say anything, but her face said, "What gave it away?"

"Why in the world would I bring a prosecutor here?" she said aloud.

"...Ms. Natsuki," Sora whispered. "Chairman Odajima seems too much of a veteran not to see through me, so I have to confess. I actually used to be a prosecutor."

"Mr. Oushuu! You should've told me that in the beginning!" Natsuki screeched.

"Er, should I do the Heron Girl dance or something...?" Sora suggested the only way out he could think of before her loud outburst made the situation irreparable.

Although he was determined to choose a new path, Sora couldn't help but think it was an unfortunate turn of events that his first business partner in this fresh chapter should be Natsuki. He didn't even have a clue who the Heron Girl was. Natsuki was on a completely different wavelength.

Maybe I'm not good with women, he wondered. It was rare for him to spend time with them. That might explain why this was so exhausting.

"I wouldn't say no to that," Odajima said with a laugh. "Anyhow, Mr. Tamura made an appointment with me the day before yesterday. Normally, I wouldn't be interested in seeing any self-promoting consulting lawyers, but he asked me if I had anything troubling me."

"Oh! Hang on! This handsome-but-totally-not-my-type Mr. Tamura... Gosh! He came to our office two days ago! I thought he was just passing by on his sales route, flirting with Miku!" Natsuki leaned forward and stared at Tamuramaro as her memory rushed back.

"Nice to see you again. I had a nice chat with Ms. Kawaguchi, your excellent tax assistant."

Tamuramaro bowed in response to her accusatory look, and Sora was finally starting to get the picture. Tamuramaro had likely sniffed out the news that Sora had some work with the Kouichi Koudera Tax Accountant Office and reached out to Odajima in anticipation. He really was keeping a close eye on Sora.

"Just in case, I assure you that Ms. Kawaguchi didn't leak anything. I tricked her by claiming to be with Oushuu and wheedled her into telling me about the client," Tamuramaro explained to both Natsuki and Odajima, so as not to tarnish Miku's reputation.

"I'll have you know, Mr. Tamura, it doesn't matter how good-looking you are, Miku's definitely not into guys like you. She doesn't fall for the manly type."

"Ms. Natsuki...I don't think that line of attack works on him," Sora intervened.

"Actually, I'm surprisingly hurt. I'm very proud of my manly looks, you know." Tamuramaro sighed, then drank his tea. It was impossible to tell whether he was joking or dead serious on that one.

"So, you see," Odajima went on, "this dashing lawyer with a majestic name came to our company. And your Heron Girl is apparently a law practitioner, too. My reading is that they know each other very well."

He seemed to have guessed how things stood between them from their initial reactions, but instead of being angry, he looked amused.

"My identity is changing by the minute," Sora remarked. "I'll hand him my business card, Ms. Natsuki."

"As you like."

Now that her plan to sneak Sora in as an assistant had been immediately foiled, Natsuki threw caution to the wind.

Sora took out his business card and stood up. "Please excuse my lack of courtesy. My name is Sora Oushuu." He walked over to Odajima and held out the card.

"Thank you very much. Oushuu Law Firm—a certified fraud examiner, I see. It's the first time I've heard of such a profession, but I have a vague idea what it's about. *Fraud* is quite a weighty word."

Odajima gestured to the sofa, inviting Sora to sit down again in a well-practiced manner. For the first time, he left his fountain pen untouched on the table.

"So here I have our consulting lawyer, who thinks I'm in some trouble. Ah, well, I guess that settles it, Mr. Tamura. I do seem to be in trouble, so I'll hire you. And here we have our tax accountant, who brought along a former prosecutor and a current law practitioner."

Odajima surveyed the three guests gathered there with a helpless smile.

"I suppose it won't be long now," he said simply, still amused.

"Don't give up, Mr. Odajima!" Natsuki cheered him on recklessly. She sounded slightly desperate, but Odajima himself didn't seem to care whether he stayed or went.

"But, Natsuki, you brought young Sora here because you thought he was necessary, didn't you?"

Though Sora was startled by Odajima's almost fatherly use of his first name, he stayed silent to observe how things unfolded. He still had a long way to go in terms of learning about human nature, and Odajima's character was a mystery.

"I'll be totally honest and tell you what I'm concerned about." Natsuki braced herself, straightening her back to disclose everything. Perhaps she'd known from the beginning that little tricks weren't going to work on Odajima.

"Go right ahead," said Odajima, toying with his fountain pen again without writing anything down.

"For the last two years, the income and expenditure of your subsidiary company has been unstable. There are too many instances of unspecified expenditures in the books."

"We're an upper-bracket tax payer. We might make it onto around the end of the list." Odajima smiled wryly, guessing what Natsuki wanted to point out. "We've come a long way. You said we should sell off this land to a home improvement store, but we started out here as a small construction company, just a subcontractor. We didn't even know about the economic miracle while it was happening—we just grabbed all the deals we could and climbed up from the bottom rung. We used to do so much more bid rigging back in those days."

"You have an outstanding company, Mr. Odajima," Natsuki assured him quietly. "The work you take on is important, and you do it thoroughly, with care and attention."

"Now we do." He sighed, smiling. "I wouldn't have minded retiring, but then that disaster happened. Our longtime subcontractor was half-destroyed. Couldn't operate, at least. So I bought them and turned them into our subsidiary, and then there was all that post-disaster special demand. No better time to build than after a crash, as they say."

The last phrase seemed to sit awkwardly in his mouth. To Sora, it sounded like Odajima hadn't quite accepted those words, or he could have also been poking fun at himself—Sora couldn't tell which.

"Have you been to the regions that were hit by the disaster?" asked Odajima, to no one in particular.

Both Natsuki and Tamuramaro replied in the affirmative.

"...I'm sorry. I've only seen it in video footage." Sora had lived in many towns, but he'd never thought about living in the northeast.

Twelve hundred years ago, he had promised himself to return to his homeland once he found a way to turn Fuuka back into a human. But his people quickly assimilated into the culture of the Imperial Court, and there was no longer a home to go back to. Those who were awaiting his return all passed into the Pure Land before he knew it.

"Videos capture the worst and the best. The real lives of the people sit somewhere in the middle, you could say. Not that I go there often myself—only once in a while." Odajima waved his hand, reassuring Sora that it was fine not to have seen it firsthand. "The point is, it takes some years to clear it up, first of all. You have to level the ground, reinforce it, and so on. The plans for the actual building can keep changing, too."

"Why is that?" asked Sora. He'd learned a bit of the present reality of his long-lost motherland.

"And sometimes people who should've returned never do," Odajima went on.

Sora was caught off guard by how much the comment affected him. He felt as if Odajima was talking about him.

"It can't be helped. You know, it's like our plans changing from one day to the next. That's just how it is, living life. It's nothing terrible," he explained to Sora, slowly spinning his fountain pen.

"...Very true," murmured Tamuramaro, lost in his own memories.

Natsuki had brought Sora here because Odajima was supposedly doing something wrong. But, for some reason, the chairman reminded Sora of a tribal leader. A leader, for Sora, was someone who was right. Someone just and reliable.

"When you're working on big buildings, that's just something that comes with the job. Sometimes, by the time you finish the project, there's no one there to use it. I didn't mind things like that, back in the old days. Once something's done, you go on to the next and the next."

Sora could easily imagine the vigor and energy of his youth—his speech still had a bounce to it.

"And laws change, too. Around when we'd been working in the northeast for ten years, there was a moment when I could see how everyone had been running on empty. When you're working too hard, there comes a time when you just...break. Some of us passed away."

For Sora, who had come on a long journey, it was very difficult to picture how people's emotions could fluctuate so much in a mere ten years from the crash—first tense, then relaxed, then fatigued.

"Right when I wanted to say, 'This is it. This is where we start,' I couldn't bring myself to say anything to them anymore."

Perhaps Odajima was a leader who supported a multitude of people, more than Sora could imagine. Meanwhile, Tamuramaro was watching Odajima and seemed to understand how he felt as a leader—feelings that Sora couldn't fathom.

"Just when the cogs were starting to turn, they told us that we need highly specialized technicians. There were fewer and fewer jobs I could pass on to our subsidiary company."

A leader was just, and a just person didn't make mistakes. Sora's leader had been betrayed and killed by the man in front of him. It was extremely difficult to make all instances of what was "just" fully consistent. As he listened to Odajima, Sora wondered vaguely whether justice itself was inconsistent by nature.

"But...," Sora began. He understood where Odajima was going. He'd read about it in the papers. If he wanted to eradicate the concerns that led to harmful rumors of nuclear waste contamination, it was dangerous not to have expert technicians. "Isn't that what *restoration* is?"

As soon as he said it, he hated himself for his choice of words. There was no word of sympathy he could find in his excessively coherent view of justice.

"...!"

Before he could kick himself for the remark, Natsuki stomped on Sora's foot.

"You're quite right," Odajima answered. "If we put a name to it, that's what it is. In reports and newspapers, they call it *restoration*. But what's needed is immediate work."

Sora thought Odajima was trying to mislead them by leaving out the agent in that sentence, though he couldn't fathom why—it should be Odajima Construction that needed the work.

"I haven't grown my company this big by playing clean. We can stay afloat for a while using some tricks."

Odajima was clearly refusing their investigation, demanding they leave the company alone. A heavy silence fell over the room, and Sora glanced at Natsuki beside him. She was the one who'd brought him to Odajima, but her expression showed that she wasn't ready to step in any further at present. Sora decided to follow her lead, since she was his employer for the time being. He was making choices he would never have been able to make before, but now he was fumbling in the dark and finding his way to them, one by one.

"Why did you choose your profession, Sora?" Odajima asked, putting down his fountain pen and looking at Sora's business card. "You don't see many certified fraud examiners."

Though Odajima may have meant to change the subject to something safe, it actually touched on the heart of all this.

"Um..." Sora was at a loss for an answer. The only answer he could think of would be relinquishing something that he had finally been able to grasp just now. But he couldn't help it—the core of his nature stirred into life again when he was asked. He had chosen and longed to follow another path, and yet...

Sora opened his mouth, hoping that maybe, somehow, saying the answer out loud might still change something. "When I was a prosecutor, this area was what I considered to be the most pointless crimes, so I thought I wouldn't have to hesitate to pass judgment."

"What area?"

"Embezzlement, corruption, misappropriation, illicit donations, bid rigging. Profitless and useless crimes."

One form of hope was to seek a kind of justice that didn't break down on itself; everything he'd said was the honest truth. He found himself wishing that, if Odajima was involved in any of the activities he'd just named, he would stop immediately. Even though they'd only been talking for a short time, Sora could understand why Natsuki was so fond of Odajima. It was an emotion he'd never experienced before. He recalled perfectly that he had never felt a trace of sympathy for anyone who might deserve punishment for a crime.

"Profitless and useless, eh?" Odajima was still smiling.

This time, Natsuki didn't stomp on Sora's foot, but she was leaning back on the sofa, her eyes closed.

Tamuramaro's expression remained unchanged.

Sora couldn't let go of the idea of an invulnerable justice so readily, and he was once again hoping it would right the wrong.

"Your eyes look red, Sora," Odajima observed.

"What?" Sora sucked in his breath in surprise. The one who had red eyes was Fuuka, when he killed without hesitation.

"It's like there's a fire burning in you. You must be keeping a righteous anger inside you."

Sora could immediately grasp what Odajima meant.

"That's not a bad thing, though," Odajima went on. "Anger is a power that can control others. If your anger is righteous—well, that's tremendous."

"Control others?" It sounded far from positive to Sora.

"Isn't anger the driving force behind change? To change things or people you think should be different. Whether it's in the form of a revolution or political activism," Odajima said gently. "A righteous power… is a double-edged sword."

There was no hint of criticism in Odajima's voice, but the words pierced through Sora like a blade.

"…That's why I work in law."

I'll never trust myself to decide what is just and what isn't. That was the conclusion Sora had come to at the end of *ritsuryo*.

"And you're smart, to boot. Why is it that you respect justice, Sora?"

The man sitting across from Sora answered Odajima's question for him.

"Because he believes justice will make many people happy."

Sora looked at Tamuramaro, and he sensed a parental warmth in the other man's eyes.

"You saw it happen?"

Odajima's brief question dug the sword deeper into Sora's heart. He stopped breathing. For a long time, he had held on to justice. He'd believed with absolute certainty that justice would bring happiness to a multitude, just as Tamuramaro had said. But what Sora had seen when his heart had first burned for justice was a mountain of innumerable corpses. And forty years ago, when Sora had sympathized with the revolutionaries, the kind old lady next door had nearly died.

"Chairman," Tamuramaro suddenly said in a loud voice, and Sora remembered to breathe again. "A certified fraud examiner is expensive to hire. You better have him on your side. Sora is very competent."

Whatever Tamuramaro had in mind, Sora couldn't figure it out. Perhaps it was a strategic move by a martial god who excelled in battle. At the moment, it was hard for Sora to imagine the god of war suggesting any false move to the leader he served.

"And how can we do that? Bribes won't work for him, I reckon. Who's going to pay for those high fees, then? Not Natsuki, surely?"

There was no one else who could possibly be the employer, and Odajima was watching Natsuki with wide eyes.

"I don't want you going to prison, Mr. Odajima." Her voice was serious for a moment, but she brightened up again. "You're our biggest client, after all!"

"I won't let you suffer. If anything happens, I'll have you work with a different company. Oh? Have you already hired the Heron Girl?"

Odajima's tone suggested he had some idea for what came next.

"I haven't been hired yet."

Sora wanted to leave as soon as possible. His blood was running colder and colder, and he was haunted by the scene of Awata-guchi as if it had happened only moments ago.

"He signed a contract. The Heron Girl lives with a big dog, so he needs money." Natsuki mentioned his household finances, which was common knowledge among the Shizukuishi townspeople by now.

"That so?"

"Yes."

Odajima's voice was gentle. Even when he'd asked Sora, "You saw it happen?" he was gentle.

"Everything about him is expensive, so I'm short on money." Sora had no choice but to confirm what Natsuki said. It wasn't a lie, after all, and he no longer had any handle on words.

"Ha-ha, that's nice to have a big dog." Odajima was already done with discussing the main subject.

"He's a family member, not a dog."

If that fire in Fuuka's eyes that Sora had seen all those years ago was merely his own anger and obsession with justice, what did Fuuka's heart desire now? What did the heart of his precious little brother want? Had that heart been born in the first place?

"Family, eh. You know, I'm a fan of dogs. Why don't you come out here for a walk and bring him along with you sometime? I'd like to meet your family."

It was a realistic distance for a walk, and Odajima really meant it. When Sora glanced at Tamuramaro, he signaled, "Better not," with a small wave of his hand. He probably wasn't sure yet which way the wind would blow.

Although he spoke to them with a magnanimous air, any fraudulent practice by the chairman of this large construction company would likely be of an incomparable scale. Even as he joked that he'd be done for soon, he was still resisting liquidation.

"I can't give you an answer at present."

Sora didn't need a reminder from Tamuramaro to imagine that if something like the burglary were to happen again in the midst of such a case, there would be a real danger of Fuuka slashing someone's throat open.

Perhaps Fuuka, with a newborn heart beating inside him, was

beginning to walk yet another path from Sora. But why did he still not think twice about killing someone? Was the fire still burning inside him? Would it never be extinguished? Sora couldn't bring himself to think that the fire belonged to Fuuka, who had no will of his own. How was it possible that the flame survived even now, after he had witnessed its devastating, irreparable consequences? In his mind's eye, he saw the red fire that could ravage people's lives when fanned by a wind.

"You don't need power *to kill. You need intention. To will and to believe."*

Was he still hanging on to that belief?

What do I believe in? he wondered.

After Natsuki and Sora returned to her office on foot, he sat at the computer, examining Odajima Construction's papers for the last three years. Eventually, he threw up his hands in dismay.

"I'd need to look at all the remaining receipts and invoices, all the actual papers that are still left. Otherwise..."

"You can't trace anything from these documents?"

On the first floor of the office, Miku and Hiraga were going on about their work as usual, and in the conference-slash-reception room on the second floor, Natsuki was standing next to Sora, peering at the screen in front of him.

"As you're very well aware, if the accounts are this chaotic, there's definitely something there. They've been doing something secretive for the last two years."

"Of course. I knew that already, but I'm asking you to do something about it. It's a request from your employer."

"That contract is invalid. Besides, what do you mean by 'do something'?"

Natsuki had taken the leap and suggested liquidation to Odajima in good faith, but he had refused. Even if Natsuki's contract with Sora could be seen as valid, the only option left for her was to bring the charge against Odajima to the Public Prosecutors' Office.

"I told you that already. Hunt down the evidence of the malpractice and make him stop."

For the first time since they'd met, Natsuki was talking like a petulant child, complaining about not getting her way. He couldn't tell what she was after, or whether she was simply grumpy, so he shifted the subject.

"There was one thing I found surprising. That was the first time a tax accountant's office of this size had such a thorough understanding of what my work involves from the very beginning."

At this point, she was already breaching her nondisclosure obligation as a consulting tax accountant. She had probably forced his thumbprint out of him so that she could use it to defend herself: If he was an employee, she couldn't have kept the confidential information from him.

"Well, of course—I researched what kind of professional would do the job I wanted them to do."

"...I would never murder anyone, just so you know."

"I didn't mean it like that! I told you—I like Mr. Odajima! He's a sweet, generous old man who treats me to pricey sake! Come on—do something! Please help me out here!!"

She was saying it over and over again. Even though Odajima had declined her proposal, she still wanted to save him.

"His profit has actually been going down in recent years. You know what they say—ill-gotten, ill-spent. If we can use that point to persuade him, he'll understand, too. I'm sure he'll see that it's better than getting taken in by the district prosecutors."

"I understand what you're saying. Except..."

Even if Natsuki wanted Sora to save Odajima, Sora was reluctant to acquiesce, considering the records of the last three years.

"You're a competent tax accountant, Ms. Natsuki," he said. "I looked at the accounts from three years ago, when you said things were still normal, but from a quick glance, his methods of lawful tax avoidance seem to have been right on the border. You really have been protecting him."

"He saw what I was capable of, and that's how we came to have a long working relationship."

The accounts showed that she had been putting the ethics of her profession on the line to stretch the legal limits of tax evasion as much as possible.

"And now you're asking a stranger for help," said Sora. "You must know you're asking for the impossible."

"...What's going to happen to him if things go on like this?"

"Since the unspecified numbers make a substantial sum, the National Tax Administration Agency will find him suspicious. I'm surprised he hasn't been investigated already. He's also involved in public construction projects in the disaster-struck regions, so he's also harming the public interest."

Sora regretted the last words as soon as they slipped out of his mouth. It was hard for him to change his own personality or habits.

"Harming the public interest, huh." She sighed, mulling over the phrase as she gazed into the distance outside the second-floor window. "Hmmm... Rare, I think," she murmured out of the blue.

"What do you mean?"

"Oh, sorry, it's nothing." She waved her hands, clearly surprised by her own comment.

"Do you mean it's a rare case?"

"I wish. If it was, I doubt they'd even notice. I've run into things like this all the time, more or less, both now and when I was a corporate tax accountant. It's fine if they were just being sloppy or careless, but sometimes they try to pull you into their malpractice. It's usually someone from that generation—the people who've outlived the economic miracle."

So these cases were far from rare, she explained. "But you can't lump them all together and blame them the same way. They're the ones who didn't look back and built the foundation of the society we have now, where a girl like me can get a decent education. Look at my father—he worked himself to death when he was still young. Still, it's tough to deal with. I want to line everything up in black and white with clean numbers."

Natsuki had been forced to accept all of it, both the good and bad—and that had been a source of stress for her over many years.

"That must have been hard," Sora murmured without thinking. He wouldn't have been able to bear such work.

"But they still have so much power, that generation. A lot of the time, I can't go against them. So when someone gets on my nerves, I burn them at the stake."

"What?!"

"In my head, in my head. Then I feel better. I pick different levels depending on how corrupt or dishonest they are. When I'm really pissed off, I slowly roast them over two weeks till they're well-done. If they're not too bad, I kill them before I burn them. When they're exasperating, but I want them to stay alive, I just cook them rare."

"The fact that you've constructed these levels like actual criminal punishments makes me shudder."

This inadvertent peek into Natsuki's mind really did send a chill down his spine.

"It's just to get it out of my system, you know. They're usually old men, so I call it the Grandpa Grill Bill. Cute name, right? Like a barbecue joint. If one of them has a devoted daughter who would rush out and plead with me not to burn her father, I'll lock him up so that he doesn't wreak havoc on society, and he doesn't have to burn."

Even though it was all a game in her private thoughts, it seemed as elaborate as if she was drafting an actual law. Sora's words about Odajima "harming the public interest" seemed to give rise to a familiar, sharp pang in her heart as well.

By his own colossal effort, Sora had come to a realization through the course of this case. Now that he was working with a woman one-on-one, he had suspected he wasn't very comfortable with women, but he'd been mistaken—Natsuki was quite a warrior. He wanted to apologize to women as well as to Natsuki for making assumptions.

"Your work must be really demanding. I don't know what to say."

She took things in stride with a smile on her face and a joke up her sleeve, but now that Sora knew the legal code she was writing in her head—he could tell how rough the waves were that she had to fight through in her work.

"As for Mr. Odajima," she began in a wavering voice, "I'll take responsibility for locking him up. Just...please, Sora, do something."

Hearing her voice break with emotion for the first time—as she called him by his first name, just as Odajima had done—Sora thought he could finally understand why Natsuki was so distressed by Odajima's refusal.

Even though ten years had passed since her father's death, the office still held her father's name.

"Ms. Natsuki's always going on about it."

Sora remembered how gentle Hiraga had sounded, lending an ear to Natsuki's woes, and that Hiraga had been her father's business partner. She was probably seeing a shadow of the father she'd lost in Odajima.

"You're a rather fierce and devoted daughter."

"Whoever hands down a judgment on Mr. Odajima, I'll forgive them."

Sora looked up at her as she sat leaning on the edge of the computer desk. He peered at her profile, trying to fathom how she felt as she tried to protect a man she cared for as a father figure from his own misdeeds.

It wasn't as if Sora himself had no parents. Someone must have brought him into this world. For 1,200 years, he'd tried not to dwell on them as much as possible, but now that he lived with Tamuramaro and Fuuka was developing his own self, fragments of memory were rising to the surface in his mind, day by day, whether or not he wanted to think about them.

When he met Odajima, Sora could guess that he was probably doing something wrong, but he'd also reminded Sora of Aterui.

He thought of Fuuka, who might not have existed before, and himself, an orphan who was raised by Aterui's clan. Who was Aterui, really? Who was the leader who had resolutely stood with the people, the justice for the people, the kind of justice to which Sora himself was probably still blind?

"Even if I were a devoted son, I'd cook him all the way to well-done."

He felt as if he'd already figured out the answer to that question long ago, and he was taken aback by the chill in his own voice.

"But not while he was alive," he concluded. He would show that much mercy, at least, but he would still burn him, even if the man in question was his own real father.

"...I wish he'd never gotten involved in the post-disaster work," she murmured tearfully. "He's old enough to retire and enjoy himself. But he started on the work because of the subsidy from the government under a special measures law."

"A special measures law... Was that for removing the debris and raising the banks? That part is finished, isn't it?"

"He was at it to the very end. *Restoration* is still there as a term, but like he said himself, there's nothing left now that Odajima Construction can do." Her hoarse voice didn't sound like her anymore. "Why does he do it?"

If he were still his old self, Sora would have begun to persuade her to alert the Public Prosecutors' Office.

He'd only had one answer for everything, always. No matter what twists and turns there were in a situation, no matter what conversations occurred, he always arrived at the same answer. It was the only goal in his journey. And so he'd never hesitated to cast aside any less direct routes as a waste of time, a source of unhappiness.

"I wonder why there's not much profit."

He turned his attention back to the accounts on the computer screen and noticed one significant point that he would have missed had he been bent on that single answer.

"Well, as I said. Ill-gotten, ill-spent."

"I've heard of other cases where companies participated under the special measures law and were later prosecuted for malpractice. They found a new route toward profit, and they pooled money from bribery, formed corrupt relationships to receive certain commissions, and more. In all these cases, the profit was what attracted them to remain in a region where work opportunities were destroyed and to engage in illegal operations."

"...What are you saying?"

Sora couldn't answer just by looking at the orderly numbers in the records.

"Money gained from bribery wouldn't appear in the books, of course, but it doesn't connect to loss of profit. In fact, they would normally line up the numbers with their records from the previous year to make it look more natural. If there was some corruption, profits should be rising."

The records that had attracted Natsuki's attention showed many orders for constructions, purchases of building materials, and costs for staff, but the source of the funds that paid for these were ambiguous. The numbers looked chaotic because they were trying too hard to balance the books, but in the end, profit was plummeting.

"I've never heard of fraudulent activity that doesn't result in profit. I'll take these records home and reinvestigate."

"Really?!"

"Ms. Natsuki," Sora began.

He'd always stuck to a single answer in the past, but now that he was open to other possibilities, he was finding that answer might not necessarily be the only one.

"At the moment, I can't predict where this will lead," he said. "If you're willing to accept that, we can draw up a proper contract this time."

It was also the first time he had no idea what the end result would be. He actually felt frightened to think back on the man he used to be, who had so adamantly pursued a single answer and nothing else.

"Thank you."

For someone who seemed to be brimming with energy most of the time, Natsuki sounded strangely lonely in her earnestness. Sora hadn't meant to come into contact with such deep emotions from someone else. Perhaps he'd done it before, but only now was he capable of feeling it.

"I need the work, too. And this case would actually require more than a million yen in fees."

"What?!"

In reality, this case involved a large-scale malpractice at a major company linked to general contractors, even if the specific company under scrutiny was only a subsidiary. The fee that Natsuki was presenting to him now would be nowhere near enough, even for an initial investigation.

"But this is a learning experience for me, so I'll give you a discount."

"What do you have to learn? You can do so much already… I'll pay you in full, though."

She looked determined to pay him the amount he'd suggested, but he didn't think it was realistic to charge so much.

"I'm learning a lot already."

At first, he was simply being tossed around by this incomprehensible woman, but now he could feel a profound emotion in another person. He'd learned that there were multiple answers that didn't fit neatly into an idea of punctilious, perfectly consistent justice.

The moment he touched on the boundary between himself and others, he could see the distinction more clearly. Without touching it, he would never have realized there was a difference at all.

Perhaps it was his confusion about being "different" from Fuuka—how he and Fuuka were no longer two in one—that had shown him this distinction.

Maybe, just maybe, he was beginning to walk a new path on his own two feet.

Shakujii Park stretched east to west over a wide area, enveloping masses of green and water.

"This park has so much nice shade even when it's sunny."

It was a bright, cloudless weekend in the latter half of September, and Sora was walking with Fuuka in dog form from the west side of Shakujii

Park closest to Shizukuishi, making their way across the crowded, midday park.

"Woof!" Fuuka wagged his tail, excited to be outdoors.

"Though I'm dead tired after two full days of desk work… Slow down, Fuuka. I'm a little wobbly."

He had been looking over from scratch all the suspicious details in the papers he'd taken home from Natsuki's office, and before doing any investigations in person, he'd researched everything he could online, examining relevant projects and public constructions. Even governmental institutions made the information public in data form, which almost made him suspect they were trying to avoid probing searches on purpose. By the time he had gone through every single one of them, the long autumn night had passed into dawn.

"Woof…"

Sora could see that Fuuka was itching to run around the park, delighted by the lush trees all around them and the refreshingly misty lake.

"I wish I had a big piece of land…"

If only he could let Fuuka off his leash—but he knew the sight of such a large dog running around untethered would cause a terrific hullabaloo in no time.

"Woof?" Fuuka looked up at his brother with a quizzical look.

"No, that's not the way to go, is it, Fuuka?" Sora laughed, stroking Fuuka's head. They didn't need land. Once Fuuka was a human being on his own, he could run free wherever he liked.

"It's hard to find your way on a new path. Okay, let's walk… Phew, all-nighters at the computer can really get to you."

Though he had slept a little toward the morning, his whole body felt stiff. He managed to loosen up as they walked, and when they were finally trotting past Sanpouji Lake, they saw a familiar face slouching on a bench and looking as drained as Sora.

"Hey. Sunlight makes your eyes hurt, doesn't it?"

Tamuramaro, wearing cotton pants and a pair of setta sandals, had seen them first and raised his right hand in greeting.

"You're the picture of a dad on a lazy Sunday. I guess even a sturdy man like you is no match for modern inventions."

He knew Tamuramaro had been locked up in his room on the second floor, wandering the rabbit holes of the internet just like him. He shuddered at the hazards of the digital world.

"I miss the days when I was working on my feet," Tamuramaro muttered, though he was always easygoing and rarely complained. "But at least it's sunny out. That's some comfort for a day like this."

Sora was puzzled for a moment. Tamuramaro was unusually tired, and what's more, he was dispirited. But of course, he could never forget what day it was. It was the day Aterui had been executed.

"You saw it happen?"

Odajima's gentle question echoed in Sora's ears. The question brought home to him the fact that his determined belief in his own justice had left him blind to so many things around him.

Sora sensed that Tamuramaro was seeing Aterui's execution in his mind's eye—the death of a man he had begged to be saved.

"...So the sky wasn't clear—"

—that day. Sora left the rest of the sentence unsaid and looked up at the shining rays of light filtering through the leaves. Both the zelkovas and the maples were still a deep green.

"Why don't you walk a little, too?" said Sora.

He couldn't bring himself to ask Tamuramaro about the memories that might be on his mind just then. Sora had seethed with hatred fiercely enough without having witnessed the execution. It worried him, even now, to think what would have happened if he had.

"Yeah. Let me join you, too, Fuuka." At Sora's suggestion, Tamuramaro got up from the bench, rubbing his neck.

"Coo." Fuuka whined.

"I wasn't inviting you to come with us. We're already living under the same roof, pursuing the same case from opposite directions."

"Are they opposite?" Tamuramaro laughed, as though he could see through everything.

"You really are keeping an eye on me. Don't you get tired of it?"

It couldn't have been by pure chance that they'd confronted each other in the same projects; Sora wasn't fooling himself. But when Tamuramaro had told him that he'd actually been watching him, he was honestly surprised.

"I consider it the life's work of the sei-i taishogun. Though I guess it's no joke to throw around my title too casually in this park."

There were several shrines near Shakujii Park, as well as some small ones scattered through the park itself.

"After twelve hundred years, I don't even know what's a joke and what's not anymore," murmured Sora. He wondered whether these words came out of the ambiguity he'd recently learned to embrace.

They passed by elderly people playing a game of shogi on a portable board and others painting the scene in watercolors. They made their way toward Hyoutan Lake, where children were eagerly searching for crayfish with their parents.

"Oh, how lovely. Taking a walk, you three?"

As soon as he heard her voice, Sora knew who it belonged to. "Ms. Tatsuko, thank you very much for the delicious hot pot the other day," he said with a bow. She was sitting on a bench by herself.

"Yes, I couldn't *believe* how amazing it was. Even the zosui rice porridge at the end was so good, I savored every bite! I'm so glad I moved to Shizukuishi!!" Tamuramaro was finally back to his usual buoyant self as he also thanked her.

"Woof, woof!"

"I'm happy to hear that. Did Fuuka have some of it, too? Better not eat anything with bones or strong flavors," she said as she stroked Fuuka's cheek.

"Are you by yourself today?" Tamuramaro asked casually, since it was a Sunday.

"Some days I want to wait alone." Tatsuko was gazing toward Hyoutan Lake, as if she was waiting for someone to come.

Tamuramaro flinched, regretting his words, and fell silent.

"I see you've heard the story, too, Mr. Tamura?" she asked without any surprise.

"It wasn't me…!" Sora blurted out. "Oh."

For a long time, Tatsuko had been open about her wish to divorce Rokurou. Everyone in Shizukuishi knew why, but no one brought it up in front of the couple.

"…I'm sorry."

"Why apologize?"

About forty years ago, when the residential district of Shizukuishi had largely become what it was now, a three-year-old son suddenly appeared at the Kashiwagis'. They were in their late thirties at the time. The adorable boy looked just like Rokurou, so everyone could surmise how matters stood, but from what Sora heard, there were very few who gossiped behind their back.

The Kashiwagis hadn't been able to conceive a child for a long time, so it was understandable that Tatsuko loved that boy even more than a biological son. She doted on him, raising him with the sternness of a truly loving mother, and everyone agreed that she went above and beyond what any woman would do for a child born of her husband's adultery.

"Mr. Lawyer, you should be the one to do the divorce settlement between Ms. Tatsuko and Mr. Rokurou."

Keita, who was younger than their son, probably remembered him from when he was little.

"I hope you're going to take care of Ms. Tatsuko's divorce."

For Natsuki, the son might have been in the same year at school, or a friend in the neighborhood who was a couple of years older than her.

"I know. He's never coming back, but still, I can't help waiting."

At seventeen, the son had discovered that he was born from his father's affair. He'd been sympathetic to Tatsuko and furious with Rokurou, and he'd stormed out of the house. He had been gone for twenty years now, as everyone knew.

They did everything they could to find him when he disappeared. In this day and age, when someone couldn't be found after all the avenues had been exhausted, they could only assume the worst. By the seventh year, when the missing son could be legally presumed dead, everyone found it painful to see Tatsuko still awaiting his return.

Sora had picked up from various sources that Tatsuko had begun talking about divorce after seven years of waiting, unable to forgive Rokurou.

"Let's say, for example…," Sora began cautiously.

Everyone in Shizukuishi took care not to touch the subject in front of the Kashiwagis, and they probably told the story to any newcomers who became close to the couple so that no one would open old wounds by accident. Many of them saw Tatsuko sitting here, staring absent-mindedly, still awaiting her son's return. Very few of them seemed to believe he was still alive.

"What if he…can't return for some reason?" Sora went on, touching on the forbidden subject.

"I doubt it. It's been twenty years, you know."

"But suppose…when he came back…he'd be happy to find you waiting for him together."

It was completely out of character for Sora to say such a thing to Tatsuko. She'd always waited by herself; she wanted to get a divorce. But he meant what he said. If the son returned, even after twenty years, and saw his mother waiting for him, surely he would be happy. Sora wanted Tatsuko and Rokurou to live on in Shizukuishi, just as they'd always done, and that was only one reason. This was his honest wish.

"What a dream," Tatsuko said with a lonely smile. "I still have dreams like that, where that boy comes home. But he's never older. Still seventeen."

She sighed. Even after twenty years, her love for her child hadn't changed at all.

"I'll wait here forever. As long as I live. I'll just wait."

Tatsuko was gazing at Hyoutan Lake. There was no sign of her son on the water.

Sora imagined how heartbreaking this must be for her, and he wanted to pull her away from all the children playing with their parents in the water. Their laughter rang out in the air as they looked for crayfish, wild with excitement. Many of them were boys.

"Once you become a parent…you never lose your love for your child." Tatsuko gazed out without blinking, listening to the voice of each child.

"…I said more than I meant to. I'm really…"

Sora couldn't find the words to apologize enough for going too far, and he stood frozen in place. Instead, Fuuka plopped his chin on Tatsuko's lap.

"Oh, you want some skritches, dear Fuuka?"

"Coo, coo." Fuuka cooed sweetly, and Tatsuko stroked him with her aged hand.

"Coo," he murmured softly, leaning against Tatsuko and swishing his tail.

Tatsuko's hand remembered where she needed to caress to comfort a child, as vividly as if it were yesterday. Tatsuko was a mother who had been given a child, then lost him.

"…I'll pay you a visit soon to return your cooler bag," said Sora, desperately looking for a way to change the subject.

"Let me stuff it with something again and bring it to you."

Fuuka pressed his head against Tatsuko's belly, asking for more.

"Thank you for always looking out for Sora and Fuuka." Tamuramaro bowed, as though it was the most natural thing in the world.

Tatsuko smiled quizzically, but she didn't press why. Perhaps she was weighed down by her dream about her son, destined to remain seventeen forever.

"Coo." Fuuka whined as the three of them walked back to Sanpouji Lake. His voice carried Tatsuko's sadness.

"I really shouldn't have said that," muttered Sora, staring at his toes.

"I'm sure many different people have tried to console her all kinds of ways. But words are meaningless in the loss of a child. Don't worry about it," Tamuramaro said, patting Sora's back.

"What would you do, Tamuramaro? If they asked you to settle their divorce."

Since the Kashiwagis had welcomed him into Shizukuishi and cared for him fondly, Sora had harbored an affection for them before he learned about their history.

"If Ms. Tatsuko really tried to get a divorce, in legal terms, it could happen immediately. She'd have the advantage."

Although they were half-joking, the Kashiwagis had often asked Sora to mediate their divorce. For him, it wasn't an exaggeration to say the matter weighed on him as if they were his own parents.

"I would follow my own heart rather than the law," said Tamuramaro in a low voice. From what he had observed recently, Sora expected as much.

"But it was your side that created *ritsuryo* and spread it across the country in the first place," Sora pointed out. He couldn't easily buy into Tamuramaro's reasoning after 1,200 years.

"Those codes of law were made by people. That feels truer than ever to me today."

Tamuramaro's voice clouded over just a little as he mentioned "today."

"Where did my obedience to *ritsuryo* get me? I had to watch as my friend, who surrendered because he believed in me, was executed. And then they put his head on display," he muttered, his eyes fixed on the small shrine in the distance, though he didn't know who it was for. A shadow fell over his face. "That's why I decided to follow my own heart."

Sora couldn't say anything as he stared at Tamuramaro's profile for a while.

"Coo," Fuuka murmured at Sora's feet. Sora knelt down, rubbed his cheek against Fuuka's, and ruffled behind his ear.

"Tamuramaro," said Sora. He was encouraged by the presence of Tatsuko, who embraced her own loss yet still stood strong and continued to wait. He decided to put into words something he'd suspected for a while, perplexing as the idea was. "You've been bringing us up, haven't you?"

Tamuramaro turned to him in surprise.

"You brought us up like we were your children, didn't you? I realized for the first time that I don't have any recollection of growing up with my own parents, and it's because you raised us."

He thought of Tatsuko again, who was probably still sitting on the same bench. His experience was the opposite of hers, but similar, in a sense—he wouldn't have discovered his own lack if he wasn't given what had been missing.

"You taught me patiently what it meant to have a parent, so when I moved to this town, and Ms. Tatsuko and Mr. Rokurou were so generous with me, I could understand what it was. I could embrace it. I'm glad I've been able to connect with people and get to know them… I'm grateful."

It was brief, but for the first time, Sora thanked Tamuramaro for bringing them up. And Tamuramaro didn't tease him with jokes about sudden hail like he would have normally.

"Once I started learning new things, I found there were more and more things I couldn't understand. It shook everything I believed in, and I got so scared I ran away from your house."

"You're starting to see the world, I think."

If what Tamuramaro had said was true, Sora was starting to see Fuuka, too.

"The more I knew, the more I knew that I didn't understand anything. That was a frightening thing for me, and I've been running away from that fear for a long time."

But now he was trying to seek out a new path, along with Fuuka.

"I'm still running away," he went on.

Perhaps he was clinging to Fuuka so much because he didn't want to change. If he was going to follow a new path, he wanted to do it with Fuuka.

"Then I'll keep you company," Tamuramaro answered.

"Why?"

Tamuramaro had said he was keeping an eye on him, but that wasn't quite true. Even Sora had to admit, after many years of denial, that he was watching over them to protect them.

"A friend's last words."

Sora could guess what he meant.

"Back then, I didn't know it was about you. I didn't know you'd be so young," Tamuramaro went on. He'd seemed to have in mind the day they'd first met 1,200 years ago. Sora wondered what words this friend had left behind.

"Well, you're not so little anymore, are you, Sora? You've grown into a man."

Tamuramaro stopped by the edge of the lake, colored by delicate shades of green, and looked straight at Sora. Eventually, he met Fuuka's eyes, too.

"I remember his eyes that day. They were blue as a deep lake," said Tamuramaro, kneeling down before Fuuka and peering into his eyes, putting a hand to his cheek. "And I gave my promise."

Fuuka stood still, and for a second, Sora felt as if he wasn't the Fuuka he knew anymore. Anxiety gripped his heart.

"Ow!"

But the moment passed, and Fuuka chomped on Tamuramaro's arm, half in jest, half serious.

"Stop, Fuuka! I told you—no munchy-munchy!!" Sora grabbed him and pulled him away, glancing around to check if they'd been seen.

"Woof!" Fuuka barked grumpily and snuggled up against Sora's legs.

"Don't expect Fuuka to warm up to you just because his eyes have turned blue," Sora said with Fuuka's leash in his hand, laughing more lightheartedly than ever before.

He'd finally managed to offer the thanks that had been stuck in his throat for a long time. There were still important things that he hadn't been able to say out loud. He had to go one step at a time, but he felt like he might never bring himself to say the most crucial thing of all.

"It's a big deal, though, those eyes changing color. His jaws are too powerful!" Tamuramaro cried out as he rubbed his own arm.

Where was that friend Tamuramaro had just mentioned?

For some reason, Sora had a fleeting feeling that the spirit of the man he had always deeply loved wasn't in the Pure Land, either.

With a few well-placed forehead nuzzles, Fuuka convinced Sora to buy a few Kyoto vegetables from Keita on their way home for another round of chicken hot pot.

"Your hot pot was close to Ms. Tatsuko's, Fuuka. I'm impressed," Sora said after he'd cleared away the bowls and did the washing up in his unpracticed way, just as he'd promised. At the clean table, Tamuramaro was now teaching kanji to Fuuka.

Though both Sora and Tamuramaro were busy with the Odajima case, Tamuramaro never missed his daily after-dinner reading and writing lessons for Fuuka.

"I didn't simmer it for three days, though," Fuuka answered. "I boiled chicken with bones and kombu kelp stock for around three hours, then put in some salt and the other ingredients. And I only checked on it a few times, 'cause I wanted to practice kanji."

Ever since his lessons began, Fuuka had been an eager student, reading easy books on his own, too. He'd told Sora that he enjoyed being able to read hiragana.

"Really? Your hot pot was something special," said Tamuramaro. "The chicken broth was so rich, but the meat melted in my mouth, too."

"It was truly delicious," Sora added, wiping the clean bowls in the kitchen. One almost slipped from his hands, but he managed to catch it just in time.

"Wonder if Ms. Tatsuko was in the kitchen for three whole days," Fuuka said, suddenly pausing his writing. "I kinda felt like her. It made me want to keep simmering for three days, too."

"What kind of feeling was that?" Sora asked, coming back to the living room with three glasses of barley tea on a tray.

"It's a secret." Fuuka laughed in a somewhat melancholy voice as Sora placed the tray on the table. He still talked like a little boy, but his blue eyes had a look far beyond his apparent years.

"Aren't you cold in that outfit?" asked Sora. Fuuka had been constantly wearing his favorite blue outfit that Tamuramaro had given him, washing it often. Seeing him in it made Sora worried for no apparent reason.

"It's so cozy. I love it." Fuuka tilted his head to one side, puzzled at himself.

"But the temperature's really going to drop soon," Tamuramaro chipped in. On this particular day, it seemed as though he couldn't bear to see blue-eyed Fuuka in that blue outfit.

"Say, Fuuka, you've mastered putting curses on me. What kanji do you want to learn next?" Tamuramaro asked, nudging him to start writing again.

Fuuka mulled over the question for a while, as if tracing back a long-lost memory, then he looked up.

"Sheath."

"Sheath?" Tamuramaro asked back, unsure what he meant. Sora, who was listening next to them, also wondered what this was about.

"It's the first word I ever heard," Fuuka said, though he didn't say from whom.

"You mean the sheath of a sword?" Tamuramaro asked again to make sure.

A strong gust of wind blew across the deep autumn night outside, where a crescent moon shone like ice over the garden. There was a sudden chill in the air.

"I dunno." Fuuka shook his head evasively, though he looked like he knew more than he let on. "I heard it means I'll protect my older brother."

"...Who said that?" Sora asked, fearing the answer he might hear. It was the first time Fuuka had said anything like this.

"Am I doing a good job of protecting you, Sora?"

Fuuka didn't answer Sora's question. Sora couldn't tell whether he simply didn't know, or he had no intention of telling him.

"You do protect me," said Sora, stroking his brother's hair. At the same time, he felt there might be only one answer to his own question. "But don't kill anyone to protect me anymore, Fuuka. Can you do that?"

Sora hoped these words would reach Fuuka for the first time. Fuuka seemed to be talking about their fate at the very beginning of their long journey.

"That's impossible. Sorry," Fuuka said simply.

"Why?" Sora leaned forward, trying to find a way to dispel the fate they'd been burdened with. It might be possible if Fuuka remembered how it had begun.

"When I kill someone, I don't have any time to think," Fuuka confessed helplessly, first to Sora, then to Tamuramaro. "There's nothing in my head. My body just moves. I'm not even thinking about killing or not killing."

He never intended to kill. He couldn't change an intention that was never there in the first place.

"Then who's doing the thinking?"

Just as the question escaped Sora, Tamuramaro interrupted by saying Fuuka's name. Gripping the pencil with his large hand and pressing the hard lead against the notebook, he wrote a single kanji character in one smooth, swift motion.

"That's *sheath*."

He wrote the character big on the paper, laying down each stroke and dot very clearly.

"Looks hard..."

"It's made up of the characters for *leather* and *to imitate*. Probably because the sheath is where you keep a sword, and there was a time when they used leather to protect the blade."

"'To imitate'—what does that mean here?"

"To become similar, to resemble. To become the same."

"Sheath." Fuuka picked up his pencil and wrote the character slowly, intoning the word as if to drink in its meaning. He wrote *leather* for protection on the left, and *imitate* for becoming similar on the right, then carefully came to a stop.

"Sheath." Fuuka smiled blissfully.

Sora studied his brother's profile. He was certainly so much more than a sheath. He promised himself that he would protect his beloved brother's path, wherever it led, no matter what.

It was long past midnight, and the crescent moon was a thin sliver of silver in the sky. Sora, who had been staring at the computer screen in his office facing the street, sensed the presence of a man standing on the threshold that led to the main part of the house.

"Our bodies have such a troublesome design, don't you think? We get hungry; we get sleepy. We feel pain; we get tired. Wrestling with a laptop for long hours kills our eyes and shoulders. But we can't die. What a punishment," Sora told Tamuramaro, who was standing behind him.

"I have to agree with that. And I'm the great sei-i taishogun. People all over sing praises of my valor, and I feel like I'm dying when I look at a screen for too long."

After his lesson with Fuuka, Tamuramaro had gone upstairs again to examine all the information. He looked utterly exhausted as he came to Sora's side with a tablet in one hand.

"But we never die."

He pulled over a navy office chair next to Sora, who was sitting at his wide desk, and sat down. The office was about 290 square feet, fitted with dark-grained wooden floorboards. Instead of a set of couches for receiving guests, there was an office desk with four nicely designed office chairs.

"Gotta say, your office is minimalist at best," Tamuramaro remarked, carefully regarding the space for the first time and shaking his head.

The shutters were down over the entrance, and the wooden indigo blinds above the window that looked out over the little garden path was the most the office could claim as interior decor. The opposite wall was lined with bookshelves containing books and documents.

"I never imagined I'd have so few visitors. I even set up separate male and female toilets." Sora sighed, regretting the unnecessary money he'd spent on the bathroom during the renovation. He'd stowed away the partition long ago, and he didn't even remember where it was anymore.

"Ms. Koudera can use the women's toilet. Tell me, young Sora, what's in that document case of yours? It looks like it's about to explode."

"Maybe it's inappropriate for you to be my lodger after all, Mr. Tamura." Sora was actually relieved that Tamuramaro turned to talk about work without bringing up Fuuka.

"You know how competent I am. We're researching the same thing. Don't you think it'll be faster for both of us if we shared information?"

"Faster to do what?"

This time, Odajima's consulting tax accountant had officially hired Sora as a certified fraud examiner. It was his job to audit the internal records of the subsidiary company as a third party.

"That's what I haven't figured out yet," Tamuramaro replied.

Teaming up with Chairman Odajima's consulting attorney was out of the question as far as Sora was concerned.

"But it's one way to find the best path—a point of compromise where we save as many people as possible from misfortune."

Until now, Sora would never have chosen such a path.

"Right when I wanted to say, 'This is it. This is where we start,' I couldn't bring myself to say anything to them anymore."

Earlier that day, by the lake in the park, Sora had confessed to Tamuramaro that he was still running away. And Tamuramaro had smiled back at him, saying he'd keep him company.

He'd heard Natsuki's voice, too, as she spoke of Odajima as though he were her father.

Even if he was lost, he didn't want to run away anymore—not if he could make good things happen.

Sora turned his screen toward Tamuramaro to show him the website he was looking at. Without throwing any questions at Sora, who had just managed to take a step toward a different path, Tamuramaro simply smiled and peered at the screen.

"I haven't heard about this," Tamuramaro said, once he carefully read through the page. He'd slipped back into his role as Odajima's consulting lawyer and was pointing at an elegant, wooden structure presented as a prospective roadside station, a rest area along a major road designated by the government.

"Maybe he's keeping it a secret? A new prospective roadside station called North Station, opening this autumn. I found this when I was looking through new construction projects in the area where Odajima Construction's subsidiary company is operating. The label that says To be built by Odajima Construction is embedded in the image, so it won't show up in a search."

Roadside stations were designated by an application system in which the Bureau of Public Roads in the Ministry of Land, Infrastructure, Transport, and Tourism registered the sites that fulfilled the eligibility requirements.

"It meets all the requirements of a roadside station perfectly," Sora went on. "A resting space that can be used for free, twenty-four seven. An expansive parking area. Hygienic toilets, and this one has the newest models installed. A well-equipped place for people with babies. The shop will stock local specialty products and souvenirs, and several restaurants that used to be in the area before the disaster will open nearby."

"All that's left is getting registered," Tamuramaro observed. He was staring at the building on the screen with his palm pressed against his mouth. The structure had a wooden look that blended in well with its natural surroundings: the kind of building that would become a familiar, well-loved place in the local area while also attracting visitors from afar.

"For a start, I checked all the extant documents from the last five years, but there aren't nearly enough purchase requisitions for the corresponding construction fees, and no deposit to cover the fees for the building works, either."

"But even if it's not a public construction project, they must be going through the local government."

"There's no way they wouldn't be. They have to for the registration application process, and besides, the construction work is right next to local roads and waterways that belong in the non-statutory public properties. They must have applied for permission from the city's construction department. Even if we were to disregard all the paperwork, it would be impossible to pull off a building project of this scale without the consent of the city or its citizens."

They racked their brains together to figure out the narrative behind this case.

"So there was a plan for the roadside station to begin with, but it went out the window, and Odajima Construction built it anyway because that's what the chairman wanted. Is that what this means?" Tamuramaro suggested.

"Likely. Since he was familiar with the procedure, he arranged the application, and neither the local government nor the citizens suspect anything behind the new roadside station candidate. Though the chairman probably has support from people there, including some in the local government."

"What a force of nature, that old man!"

"Don't underestimate the elderly. When I found this, I shuddered." Sora's mouth twitched in a slight smile, as if he was making an uncharacteristic attempt at a joke. "I'm glad you came down."

"Don't leap too far all at once. You'll trip." Tamuramaro shrugged, joking that hail would be the least of their worries then.

"But I just don't understand where the funds came from," said Sora. "The most virtuous scenario would be Chairman Odajima being a super volunteer and putting in money from his savings stashed away at home."

"Those savings would mean he was hiding his income, wouldn't it? He can't get off the hook for that. But this construction project would cost at least in the hundred millions, if not a billion. Personal savings wouldn't cover it. I suspect the funds came from here."

Tamuramaro opened his tablet and showed Sora an article he'd saved.

"'No Bids for Investor Relations: Exclusive Win for Odajima Construction'?" Sora read the headline out loud. "But it says this comprehensive resort project has both pros and cons, and with the resistance from the locals, it's at a standstill. Even though Odajima Construction was assigned the project, they wouldn't have received the funds yet, right?"

"IR is desperate to get this built. But it keeps getting pushed back further and further, and there's no telling when it'll come through, so general contractors withdrew from the project. The IR side wants to establish a fait accompli, so they've already paid the initial funds to Odajima Construction. Seven hundred million."

"With seven hundred million, the roadside station would be possible—and all they have to do is get it officially registered, and the owners can pay back their debt in the future."

The figure of seven hundred million that Tamuramaro had pointed out was in the public records as the outcome of the bid. Most data on public construction tenders was made public online, so anyone could view it if they wanted to. On the flip side, no one would look into it if they didn't have a reason to, so it was perfectly possible that anything suspicious in the records would remain overlooked until the data retention period was over, and it passed into obscurity. That is, it could go unnoticed if someone deliberately put a stop to any close inspection by the nation's Board of Audit or the Public Prosecutors' Office.

"On top of all that, there's a member of the Diet named Yamagata who's rumored to have helped bring about the exclusive appointment for Odajima Construction in the resort bid. And when you trace back their relationship, Yamagata and the chairman have always been close." With a shrug, Tamuramaro tapped through all the documents he'd gathered.

An expansive shopping mall that Odajima Construction had worked on ten years ago was located in Yamaguchi Prefecture, where Yamagata was from. There were articles from twenty, thirty years ago with rumors of monetary contributions and corruption over public construction projects.

"When smoke rises, they put it out. Looks like that's been their method with these rumors," Tamuramaro observed.

The two of them were silent for a while. It wasn't so difficult to construct a clear narrative with the information they'd collected, but it took time for them to process the implications.

"Ummm. So the chairman pretended to take on the project from IR that no one else wanted, then appropriated the funds to draw up plausible application papers and went right ahead with building North Station?" said Sora.

"Looks like it. And it's opening to the public soon. Actually, it's really soon, the week after next."

They'd both witnessed most kinds of malpractices in their 1,200 years, but it was the first time they'd encountered such a large-scale and reckless operation.

"I have no idea what to do," Sora said, utterly stunned.

Tamuramaro chuckled.

"What's so funny?"

"Not so long ago, you would've come up with just one answer for a case like this."

"...Now that you say it, that's true. We just tracked down a large-scale case of fraud, and I don't know what to do? Ha-ha."

Sora burst out laughing, too. He couldn't believe he'd said that. They dissolved into laughter for a while but suddenly fell silent.

"It's completely beyond me, but do you think you can find a point of compromise in this case?" Sora asked.

"I don't think Chairman Odajima can come out of this unscathed, but he also likely doesn't want any dirt on the roadside station that's about to open. So let's look for a way there."

Tamuramaro invited Sora to think of a solution together. Sora had never tried to look for a compromise, so nothing came to him. But he fully understood that if they were to censure this malpractice publicly, there would be a risk of extinguishing a light of hope that had finally flared up in the aftermath of the earthquake and tsunami.

The protector and the protected, the right and the wrong.

In his mind, Sora repeated to himself the same words that had been wavering inside him.

"You saw it happen?"

Odajima's quiet, gentle voice haunted his ears as if he'd only heard it a moment ago. It was the kind of voice that suggested the depth and breadth of the speaker's experience.

Every time Sora heard an echo of that voice, it struck him. He hadn't been seeing anything. No. Even if he could see, he had shut it out of his heart, never admitting to himself that he saw it.

He remembered standing at Awata-guchi 1,200 years ago, where he'd resolved never to forgive and witnessed the loss of all those lives.

He remembered the elderly woman who fell amid the roaring voices of idealists calling out for reform.

In truth, Sora had been watching all along. It was there in his world, too. But he had excluded from his view everything that didn't match up with the justice he believed in. That was who he was.

"Before…Fuuka said he wasn't thinking about anything when he killed."

Sora had always sought justice, even when it meant blowing out the light of hope.

"When Fuuka killed people, the one who was doing the thinking was always me."

There was no equal, no alternative to that justice, and Sora had clung to it in his belief. That justice itself would bring people happiness. It took him all the strength he could muster to admit that was the person he had been.

"It took me twelve hundred years." Sora couldn't breathe, but still, he faced Tamuramaro directly. "I am sorry for what happened to your soldiers."

He bowed his head, but the lives that were lost that day, razed to the ground in a moment, would never come back.

"You said you'd trained some of those soldiers yourself. Knowing you, I suppose you regarded some among them as your own children, too."

Sora could never forget the look on Tamuramaro's face from 1,200 years ago, when he pushed his way through the soldiers. He chose to remember it, even if he hadn't understood what it meant.

"Back then, I believed they needed to die. It was me, my thoughts. I am sorry, I really am."

But he had never thought a day would come when he could bring himself to apologize.

"Finally…I can say it and truly mean it."

There was no response from Tamuramaro, and Sora kept his head bowed.

A few moments passed in the chilly light of the moon.

"Whatever you might think—to me, you were just a child then. You couldn't have understood," Tamuramaro began in a reassuring tone. "They were my soldiers. I let them die, and I let you kill them out of my own carelessness."

He touched Sora's head lightly, like a caress, and lifted his face.

"I ordered them to erase from the records that Aterui's eyes were blue," said Tamuramaro, recalling his friend and the recent anniversary of his death.

"Right. It wasn't written in *Shoku Nihongi*, and I'd wanted to ask you why sometime." Sora had been thinking that Tamuramaro probably knew Aterui better than he himself did, since they had confronted each other over a long period of time, in different ways. They'd even spent his last hours together.

"I implored them to leave it out. Back then, I thought if people knew his eyes were blue, they wouldn't realize what a brave and honest leader he'd been."

But Sora was too scared to hear about Aterui from someone who had known him so well.

"Times change," Tamuramaro went on. "Nowadays, he'd be an even more celebrated hero if they knew his eyes were blue. He was truly…a precious friend."

Tamuramaro sighed, fixing his eyes on the air in front of him, seeing something out of his memory. "I couldn't keep my promise to Aterui. I was watching him until the very last moment. His eyelids never closed. His eyes remained that clear, deep blue. They made the people of Yamato shrink in fear."

Even though he hadn't seen it himself, Sora had always loathed that day of execution more than he could say.

"But even now, I have no regrets. None," said Tamuramaro.

Only the day before, Sora had thought to himself that there was no knowing what he would have done had he witnessed it himself. But now he merely listened quietly to Tamuramaro's words.

"My friend spoke of the same thing that Miroku-bosatsu did. That a power that was too strong was born in the north. One that would become a leader who could destroy a whole nation by himself. Aterui asked me to protect his heart, and I promised I would. But…" Tamuramaro's gentle eyes gazed at Sora with a worried look. "I had no idea how young he was. It was only after that incident at Awata-guchi that I realized who Aterui was talking about."

"I want to turn Fuuka into a human," said Sora.

Aterui had recognized the mark of fate, the burden in this figure. Now Sora understood who it was.

"Sora."

"Not turning him *back* into a human being. Just into one. When I said I wouldn't mind if he killed me…it was because I knew that would be the end of both of us."

Sheath. Fuuka had said that was the first word he'd ever heard.

A sheath was made to catch the blade.

And the sword was Sora himself.

"But I think I would mind now," Sora said. "Fuuka is my little brother. If I'm allowed to, I want to live with Fuuka, with people."

Sora had journeyed for a long time, protected and nurtured by Tamuramaro, who'd made a promise with Aterui, who had in turn seen the burden of the fate on Sora. He had come to know the people of this town, and now he felt hope rising inside him.

I want to live side by side with people.

"If that's your wish now, I would've thought your burden had been lifted."

Tamuramaro's words sounded reasonable to Sora, too.

"I wonder if Fuuka would ever kill without hesitation again...," Sora murmured. After all, Fuuka had admitted it was impossible for him to stop. "Even though I don't believe in it anymore."

"...Believe in what?" Tamuramaro asked.

At his question, Sora lifted his eyes and looked straight ahead.

"That all the wrongs of the world reside outside myself," he answered. In that moment, he was sure his eyes weren't red. "That there's only one true justice."

At long last, with the care and help of many people along the way, Sora had come to realize what beliefs had been at the core of his heart. And that heart was capable of killing innumerable people all on his own. He'd come to this discovery in the small hours of the night after the anniversary of the death of a man who was, in all likelihood, his own father.

"Mr. Odajima. Just wow. You're really something. A legend. You nincompoop."

On a Saturday afternoon, a week before the grand opening of North Station, Sora, Tamuramaro, and Natsuki were gathered in the chairman's room at the Odajima Construction headquarters.

"Now, you don't hear 'nincompoop' very often in real life. Not even me, and I've been alive for over seventy years." Unfazed, Odajima sat at his desk, toying with his fountain pen as usual.

"The things you do are so big, the thrill is killing me!" cried Natsuki.

She'd heard Sora's explanation back in her office, and before they left to see Odajima, she'd downed a shot of bourbon as a pick-me-up.

"Slow down, Ms. Koudera," Tamuramaro chimed in. "It was a really nice place, North Station. I saw the preopening. Old eateries that had no choice but to close up shop or leave town are back, along with cafés run by some younger folks, and they're already attracting people from the surrounding neighborhoods."

Tamuramaro had been itching to get up and move around, so he'd rented a car and gone to see North Station in person, as well as interview people from the construction department of the city hall.

"Wish I could've gone with you… I saw the website. I'd love to try that seafood set with some sake."

Even before the official opening, the website was already thriving with vibrant, mouthwatering pictures of set meals and ramen and gelato made from locally sourced fruits. Natsuki had to resign herself to merely enjoying the food vicariously through the screen, and she was mad about that, too.

"I think your registration application will be approved. It's attracted attention already, so if my estimate of the number of customers is accurate, there will probably be enough profit to pay back the debt very soon."

Sora had done a provisional calculation of the flow of money based on the rough estimate of the construction fee and the initial funds from IR.

"That's great news. I want to have some sake with that seafood set myself. I can't wait to go," Odajima said, swirling his fountain pen with a mellow expression, as if he'd already had a taste.

But Natsuki cut in fiercely, interceding as a devoted daughter would. "If you think you're going there anytime soon, then you've got it all wrong!"

Miyaizumi brought them tea as they sat on the guest couches, same as last time. She didn't seem much different from before—just a bit more worried.

"If you don't mind, could you tell us the whole story in your own words?" Sora asked Odajima in a mild tone.

For a long time, Odajima gazed at the motley view of the city outside his twelfth-floor window.

"Do you know what they mean when they say shit rolls downhill?" he asked kindly, turning back to the three of them.

"Yes."

"I do."

Both Natsuki and Tamuramaro sighed and nodded.

"I've heard of the phrase, but I don't exactly understand in this context," said Sora.

"Well, we're a subcontractor of major general contractors, too, and we started out as a much smaller company. We know what it's like to take the brunt. But we were fairly quick to grow our company, and once we got big, we were in the position to let *our* shit roll down—our subcontractors, the subcontractors under them, and the manufacturers of the building materials that we order from."

Odajima added that doing so hadn't always been a burden to him. "To lower the price of the bidding, I'd ask our subcontractor to lower their personnel expenses or another company to lower the cost of the materials. If we couldn't land the project even then, it was those small companies who'd have to find a way to survive the lack of work. Small companies can quickly collapse, so they have to lay off employees to survive."

Looking back at all the things he had done and seen, Odajima continued telling the story as his own responsibility. "But you know, I just got sick of it somehow. I wanted no more of it. That's why I made one of our subcontractors a subsidiary company for the time being and started work in the disaster-struck areas. We had the government's budget, after all. We could use as much as we liked, and we could guarantee work to the people while pushing forward the restoration. There was nothing but hope—at least, that's how I felt."

"I..." Natsuki choked up. She had wished Odajima had never gotten involved in post-disaster projects.

"There were real plans to build the roadside station. Once that was built, it would generate work for maintaining the place and other facilities nearby, so my plan was to cut ties with the subsidiary company at that point and let them go. Ah, by the way, I've made the arrangements to cut them off already. Sorry I didn't talk to you first, Natsuki."

"Don't worry about me."

"No, no, we can't have that. I don't want anything rolling downhill. Everyone's doing their best to survive, so we should try not to let anyone get hurt. You're going to keep up this business your father left behind, aren't you? I'll ask you to be a consultant for another branch, so don't you worry," Odajima assured her with a smile.

"I know things are off to a good start even in the preopen stage, and the future is bright," he went on. "I can't be happier about that. It wasn't me who thought of the whole thing—a roadside station that wouldn't rely on exaggerated reviews but stay true to the neighborhood and showcase local products. We invited a specialized consultant to come in, and our top priority was making use of what was available in the local community." Of course, Odajima was well-informed on the project, and he looked very pleased with how it was turning out.

"What happened to the initial plans for the construction? Why did it disappear?" asked Sora.

Retrospectively, the project seemed to be destined for success, but Sora realized again that it had only become what it was through the hard work of the professionals and the locals, and Odajima had held the key to it.

"Unfortunately, it came up as a topic of discussion in a parliamentary meeting, and they argued that no one would come to a roadside station in such an out-of-the-way spot. There were huge issues about nuclear waste and decontamination getting the spotlight then, so I suppose they wanted to divert everyone's attention to a different agenda. Who knows what was going on in their heads," Odajima concluded. He looked unusually disgusted by the Diet. Perhaps he had been disappointed or stabbed in the back many times in the past. "Of course no one would come unless you built an attractive facility there. I suppose they don't stop to imagine how many people would lose their jobs from that one big project fizzling out. As for roadside stations, people will come a long way to visit a really nice one. But, well, I can't go barging into parliamentary assemblies myself."

He put down his fountain pen and scratched his head. "So I decided to go ahead and build one anyway." He laughed without holding anything back.

"Wow. What a guy. Seriously, a legend. I'm blown away..." Natsuki groaned with her head in her hands. This time, she did not call him a nincompoop.

"You never know what old people will do, eh? All that's left for us is dying, so we've got nothing to lose."

Sora had to agree with Odajima and smiled wryly—if everything but death had been checked off your life's to-do list, most things wouldn't scare you anymore.

"How did you get permission from the local government? You must have...supporters among them." It was impossible to assume otherwise, and Sora continued with the inevitable questions.

"I pushed it through their department. It's all my doing. I did it by myself." Odajima showed no intention of confessing any details there.

"Are you planning to take all the blame?" Tamuramaro interjected. "I've met the department manager in person. He was fully prepared to do however many years in prison he'd get, with no regrets."

The Diet and the local government might have looked the same to ordinary citizens, but in reality, one made the political decisions while the other conducted those affairs on the ground. The manager of the construction department was a civil servant on the latter side. His job involved passing documents in a clerical process, but he held no executive power himself. If he had transgressed his administrative position and moved some documents forward without permission, that would be another serious crime.

"I'm afraid I don't know what you're talking about," Odajima replied. "I'm sure there are all sorts of people among the Diet members and civil servants, but the ones who work hard give everything they've got to every job they have. They deserve retirement allowance, especially the civil servants." He was adamant in respecting the path he hadn't chosen for himself. "I used to think civil servants were the dullest of the dull back in the day, but listen to me now." He chuckled.

All three around him understood that the "back in the day" he had in mind was more than thirty years ago, when he had been fervently climbing the ladder in the construction industry.

"Times have changed. And so has the world. Well then, I've cut off the subsidiary company. The roadside station is about to open. The locals can take care of the rest. I have no regrets. Am I headed for prison?" Odajima asked the three of them. "That could be fun, too."

"There's one thing I'd like to ask." Sora spoke up. His task for the day was to make sure they didn't miss any points to clarify, so they could fully defend themselves during the next steps. "The source of your funds was the initial payment from IR for the resort construction, wasn't it? That means a private enterprise is backing the construction of a roadside station that's come to a deadlock. Hasn't the Diet investigated this?"

"There's all sorts in the Diet—some honest ones, and those who're only interested in their rights and how they can profit from those rights. We've got a bad crop these days, and there's more of the latter. They only brought up the construction as a way of diverting attention from other issues in the first place, so they couldn't care less. They wouldn't even notice." Odajima shrugged.

"All right." Now that the rough outline was clear, Tamuramaro had determined their strategy for moving forward. "Let's make it a story of heroism," he declared, grinning like a devious salesman.

"How?"

"I know a journalist who writes influential articles. We already have the evidence to corroborate most of the account you just gave us. Let's have the Diet take the fall, not the roadside station. I'll have the journalist write about misappropriating the funds from IR, but the people's opinion of IR is largely negative right now. So people will take it as a hero's story."

Tamuramaro explained the general structure of the article, since he had already prepared the materials that would serve as a springboard for it.

"I think that's the best way forward, too. There won't be any lies in that," Natsuki agreed with a deep sigh.

"Ms. Koudera, if we could have a comment from you as consulting tax accountant A, who'd been concerned about Chairman Odajima, that would be helpful."

"Of course. That's not a lie, so I'm happy to talk." She nodded earnestly. "Even today, I was so worried I downed a shot of bourbon earlier."

"You know, when Mr. Yamagata asked me to take on that investor relations project, I had no intention of embezzling the funds to build the roadside station. I just figured, if no one else was going to do IR, I'd do it. Though to tell you the truth, I thought they'd be better off getting some foreign capital, since Japan doesn't have much money right now," Odajima explained. He seemed anxious that everything was getting arranged so neatly. "IR's funds are the country's money, too, even though national sentiment doesn't want them."

"The nation is merely a box," Tamuramaro said. "In a hundred years, everything in it will be replaced. We simply deal with what's right in front of us—but who can say whether that's going to make the box stronger or weaker?"

As always, he left much unsaid and didn't assert any opinion of his own. Tamuramaro had learned the important lesson of not knowing long ago, Sora recognized.

"Never done time before. This'll be a first," said Odajima.

"You'll have to stay in detention for a while, but as for the term, I'll do my very best to secure a suspended sentence for you. All that remains is to decide who should be obligated to repay the debt." Tamuramaro lost no time working out the next steps, suggesting that the subsidiary company could be the one to repay, since they were likely to yield a steadily growing profit.

As Sora gazed at Odajima, who would probably step down from the front line now, he couldn't help but see him as a good leader of his people. "Wouldn't you have been a good politician?" he asked suddenly.

"What's gotten into you, young Sora? I did my own work, that's all." Odajima laughed. "You might look at me now and think I'm an old man who's done a good deed. But I only did what I did because of the special measures law after the disaster, and I saw the places where everyone's lives had been destroyed. That aftermath... Just one look at it would change anyone's life."

Odajima's life had changed, and he didn't consider it anything of his own doing.

"I've been doing this work for more than half a century now," he went on. "I've let others take my shit, and some hanged themselves down the line. It doesn't feel quite right to have things tied up in a neat bow, here at the end. I figured I wouldn't be allowed in the Pure Land anyway, so I've done many deeds I'm not proud of in my time."

"'Even a virtuous person can attain rebirth in the Pure Land...,'" Tamuramaro told the obstinate Odajima, "'...how much more easily a wicked person.' Words from Shinran, a Buddhist monk from the thirteenth century. Most people are basically wicked. Virtue and evil live side by side in us. Is there anyone in the world who has only one or the other?"

"You talk like an old man for one so young, Mr. Tamura."

"Buddha will take care of the rest. There's only so much humans can..." Tamuramaro trailed off without finishing his sentence. "Well, you've done enough. I'll call the journalist now," he said instead, asking for Odajima's confirmation to put his plan into action.

"Hmm." Odajima twirled his fountain pen and looked around at the three of them. "I do think I'd better go to prison. If you ask me."

"That's up to Mr. Tamura's abilities, so I'm sure you could do some time if he plays his cards right," said Sora, just to comfort Odajima, though he expected that any penalty would be mitigated by extenuating circumstances. It was a half lie. Sora found it extremely difficult to lie, and that hadn't changed, but he did his best.

"Virtue and evil live side by side in us. Is there anyone in the world who has only one or the other?"

"You could've told me that earlier…," Sora muttered at Tamuramaro with a sigh.

"Hmm?"

Tamuramaro grinned as if he knew perfectly well what was on Sora's mind, and Sora decided that he was as irritating as ever.

"Hmm…," said Odajima.

"Is there anything else you're worried about?" asked Natsuki. Her tone was gentler than any of them had ever heard from her.

"Hey!"

"It makes me uneasy when you're so sweet to me, Natsuki."

Natsuki laughed at Odajima's quip, but Tamuramaro and Sora did not.

In late September, two days before the article about Odajima Construction and the post-disaster region was to be published, on the Saturday when North Station officially opened its doors, Fuuka's dinner was authentic-style ramen, by his own request.

"Ramen's always so yummy. I love it so much," Fuuka said, savoring the aftertaste as he took out his notebook for his writing lesson with Tamuramaro. Sora was full of guilt as he listened, washing their bowls and porcelain spoons in the kitchen.

"Oh yeah. That soup flavored with your soy sauce and that char siu pork—man, they were out of this world!" Tamuramaro, also guilt-ridden, sounded like he was trying too hard to please.

From time to time, Sora and Tamura sneaked into Ichirou and Tarou to enjoy some ramen—not the homemade "authentic-style" ramen, but the real deal. In fact, for lunch that very day, they had found themselves slipping into Ichirou to have some soy sauce ramen after meeting at Natsuki's office to do the final check on Odajima's article.

"You sound weird, Tamuramaro." Fuuka sniffed at him even though he was in his human form, sensing the smell of something tasty.

"Nah, I'm okay. By the way, aren't you getting cold in that outfit? Want me to look for a winter version?" Tamuramaro attempted a smooth segue into another subject. As he spoke, he glanced down at an app on the tablet in his hand, which he'd been constantly keeping an eye on these days.

"Is it cold? If you say so, maybe I am?" Sora tilted his head and looked down at his blue clothes. "Time to make hot pot again. Now that I've learned how to make chicken stock, it's fun to make the soup. Ms. Tatsuko said she uses scallions and ginger, but I don't put them in 'cause I feel like the meat my brother buys for us these days doesn't smell."

"Now that you say it, I think so, too." Tamuramaro nodded. He'd been cooking for himself sometimes, so he knew what Fuuka was talking about.

"You're right," Sora joined in. "When we started living by ourselves forty years ago, we didn't have any money, so we got whatever we could get our hands on—the kind of food you couldn't eat if you didn't prepare it properly. I don't really see things like that in the stores these days."

Now all the products in the shopping street and supermarkets looked clean and decent with meticulous expiration dates. Perhaps that was thanks to the development of the distribution system and technology.

"After we left your place, you know, we didn't have any money, but we couldn't help getting hungry," Sora added to Tamuramaro, who was listening quietly to their conversation.

"When you think about it, our current state really is a curse."

"Tell me about it. In the beginning, I managed to find some work each day, and I'd cook for both of us, although I was pretty clumsy. After a while, Fuuka started cooking for us while I was out, and he'd be waiting for me with dinner. He said he had plenty of time on his hands."

"Wow, Fuuka."

"I messed up a lot at first, though, burning things and making it too salty and stuff," Fuuka said.

With hands that had only just started to grow, he had chopped vegetables into pieces that were too chunky, and his flavoring was trial and error. Even so, he kept trying for forty years, teaching himself to manage everything in the kitchen.

"It made me so happy when Sora liked my food."

Fuuka looked back at that time forty years ago when the two of them had begun their new life on their own. Of all his 1,200 years of memories, that one felt the most distant.

"I wouldn't have minded if those days went on forever."

These days, there was something lonely and sad about Fuuka's expression. Sora wondered when it had begun and what had triggered it, but nothing came to him. He couldn't be sure what was on Fuuka's mind. But he liked Fuuka even more now, more than he had when they were an inseparable pair. He wanted to stay with him more than ever before. He wanted to know what Fuuka was thinking. *It's because we're starting to live our separate lives*, Sora told himself with conviction.

"We never used to talk about the past when we were by ourselves, Fuuka." Sora suddenly realized that his brother had been talking about many more things lately.

"Fuuka's reading a lot of books during the day now," Tamuramaro remarked, thinking about how important that really was. "Maybe he's learning how to articulate his feelings because of all the words and stories that he's taking in."

"What does that mean, 'ar-tic-u-late'?"

"Ah, sorry, Fuuka, hang on a second." Tamuramaro looked at his tablet and stood up. "I better get the car."

Sora sensed what was happening and rushed toward the door with him.

"Woof?" Fuuka transformed into a white dog, even though there was no one else in the house.

"Sora!"

They heard Natsuki shout from behind the front door. She had apparently pushed through the small gate by force.

Sora and Tamuramaro exchanged a glance. Tamuramaro was already at the door, with Sora close behind. As soon as they opened the door, still shoving on their shoes, they saw Natsuki standing there in a sweatsuit.

"Mr. Odajima's gone missing! He's not picking up at all!!" she cried. "Oh! Mr. Tamura! What are you doing here?!"

Her eyebrows rose as she took in Tamuramaro in his jacket, standing in the doorway next to Fuuka the dog. Neither Sora nor Tamuramaro had told her about his lodging situation, since it was obviously inconvenient for the case.

"Just stopping by for dinner after we looked at the article together. Anyway, what was that about Chairman Odajima?" Tamuramaro said quickly, looking at the tablet in his hand.

"You could've called me…" Sora checked the history on his phone, which he'd had close to him the whole time. "I guess you panicked, Ms. Natsuki."

"We live so close anyway, and I'm really worried. I know it's not like him to run away!"

"As his consulting lawyer, I had the same understanding. So, of course, I hid a GPS tracker device on him."

That was what he'd been checking on his tablet: Odajima's current location.

"I hired someone to keep a close eye on him, too. I'm sorry, Ms. Natsuki. I thought it would worry you even more, so I didn't tell you. I hardly expected the Diet member who'd been so friendly with the chairman all these years to accept our heroic tale without a fuss."

Sora checked the location of the lookout sent by Tamuramaro, but the dot on the map was still in front of Odajima's house, likely detained.

"You're both shockingly efficient and calm somehow…"

Their stolid manner steadied her nerves, and she seemed to be breathing a bit easier now.

"Ms. Natsuki, you can scold Mr. Odajima later. He probably knew this was coming," said Tamuramaro.

"Oh." Odajima's doubtful expression as she asked him her last question—*"Is there anything else you're worried about?"*—flashed through her head.

"Where did you hide the GPS?"

"In the body of the fountain pen. He often puts it in his breast pocket, and I thought he'd have it on him at all times. I slipped it in when I asked him if I could see the pen."

Tamuramaro determined the pen's location, and it was one of the places that he'd already listed as possible destinations. "As clichéd as a movie," he remarked, half incredulously.

"Is it by the bay?" Sora peered at the tablet.

"You mean Tokyo Bay? That's where the IR resort would've been built… Are they trying to sink him along with IR?!"

"We'll rescue him before that. He's still close," Tamuramaro assured her.

"But they've already passed through Tokyo Circular Route 8, heading toward Route 7," said Sora. "Maybe they're trying to avoid the security cameras on toll roads."

"In that case, we'll take the Metropolitan Expressway. We've got a rental car ready, so don't worry, Ms. Natsuki. You can wait here."

They'd only had the car on standby just in case, but now their hand was forced. Sora picked up the car keys by the entrance.

"I can't just wait here! I'll have a heart attack."

"Woof!" Fuuka, now caught up on the situation, put his paw on Sora's shoulder and demanded to be brought along.

"No, Fuuka. You look after the house while we're gone."

Fuuka fully understood that Sora was going somewhere dangerous, and he wasn't about to let him go alone.

"Ms. Natsuki. Please, could you wait here with Fuuka?" Sora wanted to reassure Fuuka by reminding him that he couldn't die, but he stopped himself in Natsuki's presence.

"Woof, woof!" Fuuka refused to stay behind, and he snatched away the car key.

"Am I doing a good job of protecting you, Sora?"

Perhaps Fuuka had been cursed to protect his brother. If it *was* a curse, Sora wanted to free him of it. Sora caught his breath and looked to Tamuramaro for his opinion.

"I guess it's all right," Tamuramaro murmured. Instead of his usual open way of talking, his words were tense with anxiety.

Tamuramaro probably understood better than anyone: Sora had now discovered the sheer danger his belief in a single, irrefutable justice had posed. Throughout history, too, the belief in one absolute justice had sometimes led to the deaths of multitudes.

"That's impossible."

Fuuka's actions must have followed Sora's emotions in the beginning, but now he had said he couldn't stop himself of his own will.

"Fuuka. You remember what I asked you not to do, don't you? If you do, I'll let you come with us."

Sora knew it wasn't something to bet on, but even so, he wanted to believe in a future in which he and Fuuka could walk on a new path together.

"Wait, you're taking Fuuka with you?" asked Natsuki. "Some thugs from a gang that Representative Yamagata sent over are about to drown Mr. Odajima where IR's resort was meant to be built, right? What if something happens to your doggo?"

"You have a thorough understanding of the situation and well-developed skills for articulating it, Ms. Koudera..." It was no time to be impressed by such things, but Tamuramaro couldn't help it.

As for Sora, he was staring at Fuuka. Natsuki's question had come as a shock. He'd always been too busy worrying about whether Fuuka would kill someone that he'd barely had any time to consider whether Fuuka himself would get hurt.

"Fuuka," he called to him and wrapped him in a tight embrace. "I'm sorry."

"Coo." Fuuka whined.

"If you're gonna sit around hugging your dog, you better take me with you, too! I know I'll get in the way, but I could keep hold of his leash at the very least!!" Natsuki stomped her feet impatiently.

"Well said," Tamuramaro agreed. He didn't tell Sora that everything would be all right, but even so, he gave him a pat on his back.

Both Sora and Tamuramaro had a driver's license, but they decided that Sora would drive while Tamuramaro kept his eye on the GPS tracker in the passenger seat.

"How does it look? He hasn't been buried yet, has he? Not drowned in the bay?" Natsuki and Fuuka sat nervously in the back of the hybrid rental car.

"The police and an ambulance are on their way. The watch stationed at Mr. Odajima's house was beaten and tied up, but he's alive. There was no time for them to kill Mr. Odajima on the spot, and we'll be with him in five minutes," Tamuramaro explained patiently to her as they entered the bay area, lit by rows of artificial lights by the sea.

"Coo..."

Fuuka whined softly, staring up at the lights streaking past as if he was seeing something otherworldly. It was the first time Fuuka had seen such a cityscape at night, Sora realized. Living side by side all these centuries, he'd been so obsessed with the idea of turning Fuuka back into a human being that he hadn't gotten around to showing Fuuka how much there was in the world. His chest tightened at the thought.

"I never realized how unreal the view is here at night," Tamuramaro said, though it sounded out of place in such a tense moment. It was probably a coincidence that their thoughts aligned.

They crossed over the bridge, where artificial lights glowed in evenly spaced intervals, and Sora thought he caught a glimpse of a train running over the sea. The tall, narrow skyscrapers stretched out along the bay, the lights from their windows reflecting on the water here and there. It was hard to believe that this place, here and now, was connected to the past they had been born in. For a moment, Sora felt as though he'd been drifting in a long dream.

"Surreal, isn't it? The Yurikamome train runs over the sea, and there are people living over there. It's like a fantasy," Natsuki murmured, though the place would have already existed around the time she was born.

"Do you think so, too, Ms. Natsuki?" Sora asked in surprise.

"It's a pretty view, but I grew up in Shizukuishi, you know. It feels like a different world to me. I bet Mr. Odajima feels the same way, too! He was born in Nerima, after all. They better not drown Mr. Odajima all the way out here!!"

"We won't let them!"

Prompted by Natsuki, Sora pressed down on the gas pedal, and the car sped into the Aomi Container Terminal. Aomi was a candidate for the IR resort location, but the container terminal was a wharf where shipping containers did their loading and unloading. No one would go there just for fun.

"Sora, turn off the headlights and slow down. We don't want them to hear our engine," Tamuramaro said as he reached over to switch off the interior lights completely. Sora followed his orders, letting the car move forward in gear. Only then did he realize that Tamuramaro had told him to rent a hybrid car because of the quieter engine. As usual, he was slightly annoyed at Tamuramaro's competence.

He could make out a tiny light at the tip of the terminal. There were shadowy figures, at least two men.

"Stop here. Leave the engine running," Tamuramaro said quietly, carefully pushing open the door on his side.

"Ms. Natsuki, please wait in the car with Fuuka," Sora whispered as he followed suit. He knew it was too late, but he was regretting bringing them here. After all, these people were trying to get rid of a man. It was dangerous.

"It'll be all right," Tamuramaro said quietly into the dark, as if he could sense Sora's anxiety. "But there's bound to be more of them waiting in cars. If it's just one car, we can expect two or three people at most, but don't let your guard down."

Now that he could see the enemy in front of him, Tamuramaro could probably make a rough estimate of the situation. Neither of them could shut the doors completely because of the loud sound, and this worried Sora. They edged toward the shadows along the containers.

"You know, they're going to find my body pretty soon if you drown me in a place like this."

Sora let out a sigh of relief at Odajima's leisurely voice.

"What do we care? Let them find a drowned corpse."

Apparently, there were arrangements in place for the politician to use Odajima's death as a warning to suppress the article due to be published in two days and make the press lay the full blame on Odajima's embezzlement of IR's funds.

"See, we've drawn up a will for you. Sign here."

"All right, all right. Let's see—'I pocketed the money from the IR project and spent it all,' eh? I must've had a grand old time using up seven hundred million all by myself."

"Shut your trap and sign!"

The whole job must have been a familiar drill for the man, but even he seemed ruffled by Odajima's blithe manner as he pulled out a fountain pen from his breast pocket.

"I'll get him in one hit," whispered Tamuramaro. "Keep Mr. Odajima safe. Don't forget, they definitely have backup waiting nearby."

"Got it."

No sooner had he spoken than he darted out. He kicked the man on the side of his head with his hard, leather shoes to get him off-balance, and it was perfectly aimed to give him a concussion.

"...!"

The bulky man toppled to the ground, and Sora pulled Odajima's arm while he was dutifully signing the will.

"Whoo. This is like a movie."

"Do you realize what danger you're in?!"

"Well, it's nothing I didn't expect. I did call Mr. Yamagata up and ask—we've already done some creative accounting, collusive bidding, bid rigging, arranging public construction works, you name it, so how about we do some time in prison together? But he didn't like that."

"If he'd said, 'sure,' he would've been a true friend...!"

Two men who had been hiding in a station wagon on the other side of the containers sprinted over, but Tamuramaro kicked one down in no time.

The enormous second man lunged at the escaping pair. Sora dug his elbow into the pit of his stomach, but he didn't budge. Instead, he swung a billy club at Odajima, and Sora flung himself between them. The weapon hit him square in the shoulder, knocking him down onto the concrete.

"Sora! Dodge!!" Tamuramaro shouted, twisting around to look at Sora as he wrestled with his opponent.

The man who'd struck Sora raised his weapon again to land the final blow on his head. Sora writhed on the ground, knowing he wouldn't die but steeling himself for the hit—and then he felt a gust of wind.

Fuuka had leaped out of the half-open car and effortlessly thrown the man onto the ground.

"A w-wolf?!" he yelped under Fuuka.

"Fuuka!"

Sora's shout didn't reach the snarling wolf. Tamuramaro struck down his assailant, but he wouldn't get to Fuuka in time to stop him.

"Fuuka...!"

Right before his teeth sank into the man's throat, Fuuka froze.

Time seemed to stop in Sora's eyes.

He felt like everything had stopped altogether. Never before had Fuuka held back from killing someone from Sora's voice alone—not once. But the police sirens were rapidly drawing closer, indicating the passage of time.

Fuuka had managed to stop by his own will.

"Stop right there." Tamuramaro pushed down the man who was about to flee from Fuuka's feet. "That guy's got ropes for tying up the chairman. Sora, you tie their hands behind their backs."

Sora wanted to rush over to Fuuka, but at Tamuramaro's orders, he bolted over to the man on the ground with a concussion, grabbed the rope, and tied him up.

"Give me some rope, too." Natsuki held out her hand. Sora hadn't even noticed that she had rushed out after Fuuka.

"Ms. Natsuki…we asked you to stay in the car."

"I'll deal with the police. I'm Mr. Odajima's consultant, after all. I won't let them take Fuuka away. It's true he was attacking the culprit, but we never know what they'll think."

Natsuki had seen everything: how Fuuka rescued Sora and nearly bit into the man's throat.

"Thank you…for saving Mr. Odajima," Natsuki added.

"I really owe you one," Odajima chimed in. "Thanks, everyone. And this adorable doggy you have here."

"I'm not letting you off the hook, Mr. Odajima!" Natsuki cried at the easygoing chairman.

"Thanks, Natsuki." Odajima knew full well that Natsuki loved him as if he were her real father. "Sora," he called calmly, gazing at the red flashing lights approaching them.

"…Yes?"

"Those crimes you said were profitless and useless—they'll be snuffed out soon enough. They really are useless now. The judicial system is moving in that direction. Our old ways won't work anymore."

As they listened, Sora and the others realized that Odajima had been planning to end not only his work as a chairman but also his life.

"When I started on the ground, I was mad with envy to see the higher-ups sitting in the president's room holding fountain pens. I wanted to beat them and get what they had." Odajima looked wistfully at his own fountain pen as though it was some relic from the past. "But you know what? By the time I'd climbed up high enough to hold a fountain pen myself, everything became electronic. And now, there's not much use for these except times like these. I suppose I don't need it anymore."

He swung back his arm to throw the fountain pen into the sea, but Natsuki grasped his hand in a tight grip.

"Let's drink together at the roadside station, Mr. Odajima, and have that seafood set. Treat me to some good sake!" Natsuki declared. Her voice was full of its usual exuberance, most likely for Odajima's benefit.

"Right." In a moment, light came back into Odajima's eyes, which had turned dull and dazed as if his own life had been taken away along with his fountain pen. "I haven't seen that place yet. There's still something I want to do before I die, after all."

"Exactly!" she replied. "Sora, you can go ahead. I'll tell them I drove the car and came here by myself." Natsuki hurried him, looking at the police cars about to arrive.

"Will you be okay by yourself?"

"The police are here now. I'll be fine."

Sora and Tamuramaro looked at each other, then made sure the three men they'd tied up couldn't get away. They decided to leave with Fuuka, who was watching quietly.

"I thought you looked like a kid when I first met you, but you've grown up somehow, Sora," Natsuki said, holding Odajima protectively as Sora started to walk away.

Sora glanced back at her for a moment, then broke into a run with Fuuka and Tamuramaro to get away from their parked car. They stopped to watch the police arrive from a distance, arrest the three culprits, and bring Odajima and Natsuki into their protection.

"They're about to start their on-the-spot inspection. Let's head to the other side for now." Tamuramaro pointed in the direction of Sea Forest Park, which normally wouldn't have been the kind of place for anyone to walk in.

Sora was silent, searching for the right words to say to the wolf padding along in between them.

Fuuka hadn't killed anyone. He had bared his powerful fangs but stopped himself. He had learned not to kill.

"Brother."

Sora stopped in his tracks at Fuuka's human voice. He turned to see his brother standing between them as a man in white robes.

"Fuuka…you're a human outside? Are you completely human now?!"

Although it was deserted around them, it would have been impossible for Fuuka to retain his human form somewhere they could encounter people.

"This is great… Fuuka, you're finally a human…!" Sora choked back tears of joy and flung his arms around Fuuka.

But Fuuka said quietly, "Sora. It's time…"

"Huh…?"

"I have to say good-bye to you here." Fuuka smiled and looked around quizzically. "Wonder where we are?" He gazed at the Sea Forest Waterway nearby, then at the hotels and ships glittering like stars. "It's so different from where I was born."

"Yes, Fuuka. Now that you're finally a human…let's go back to where we were born. Let's go up north together. Right?"

To Sora, Fuuka looked like a man contemplating the view around him for the very last time before his death. He grabbed Fuuka's hand desperately.

Tamuramaro looked on, remembering the last farewell between him and his friend in the distant past, though Fuuka didn't know it.

"I'm not going to the north. I need to part ways with you here, Sora. I hope I'll be able to break myself."

"Why? What do you mean, break yourself?!" Sora gripped Fuuka's arm tightly, determined never to let go.

"You see, I'm your sheath…," Fuuka began, voicing the word *sheath* carefully, lovingly. "But you're not a sword anymore. You don't need one."

"Of course I need you! You're my precious little brother!! You're right;

maybe I'm not a sword anymore. So that means you don't have to kill anyone ever again, Fuuka. You did it—you stopped yourself back there."

"It's only because I learned how to write *sheath* from Tamuramaro the other day. It popped up in my head, and I went blank. Just a fluke," Fuuka explained. He hadn't stopped because he'd intended to, but only because he was carefully tracing the strokes of the character in his mind.

"Can I butt in?" Tamuramaro asked hesitantly. "Doesn't that mean you could stop because you learned something? If you keep learning about people, you'll have more and more things to think about, and then you'll definitely be able to stop yourself before killing someone. Every time."

He usually left things unsaid and rarely asserted anything, but this time, he was firm.

"I dunno. Who can say for sure? If I killed someone again by accident, Sora would say he'll break himself with me."

"Fuuka..."

"I wouldn't mind if you ripped me apart, Fuuka."

That's what Sora had told him when the thugs broke into their house during the previous case.

"If you ever want to kill someone, kill me."

Now Sora realized just how much his words had been tormenting Fuuka.

"I bring you pain when I'm with you. It's okay, Big Brother. After all, I started out as—"

Sora squeezed Fuuka in his arms before he could say the rest. Fuuka didn't hug back as he always would. Tamuramaro only looked on and didn't intervene again.

"I have taken your name for safekeeping."

"Fuuka?"

Wind swept past them as Sora looked up at the sound of Fuuka's voice, weaving together words that weren't like Fuuka at all.

"I have taken the part of you that wields power to burn everything you touch like fire in the wind. I am a sheath for the sword that you are."

Sora listened in stunned silence.

"Those are the words I learned. The first words I ever knew. But I couldn't say them out loud till now," Fuuka confessed, scrunching his face in a grin. "Up to a certain point—I don't know when—that was all I was. But since you cherished me so much and tried so hard to turn me back into a human and loved me..."

"So a soul was kindled in the sheath?" It was Tamuramaro who asked.

"I don't really know myself. I used to be just a sheath for my brother in the past. I was made to stop Sora, to keep his power bottled up. But now I just want to be with him like an ordinary brother."

"You *are* my little brother. I don't care if you're a dog or a wolf or a human. You'll always be my brother."

"But you're better off without me. I mean, I was made to seal in your fate, the burden of the fire you were born with."

Fuuka was suddenly speaking resolutely, like a grown man.

"I'll take all your hatred and sorrow with me," he gently reassured Sora with a smile.

"Aren't you saying that out of love? The love you have because you're my brother? Just forget everything you heard in the beginning!"

"I think Lord Aterui created me. But he probably made a mistake and failed to seal in your fire completely."

Perhaps Fuuka was always meant to disappear when his duty was done and there was no sword to sheathe any longer. When Sora looked back, he remembered what a gentle, sweet little brother Fuuka had been; whenever Sora clashed with anyone because of his insistence on what was just and right, Fuuka would do everything he could to calm him down. He had been the place where the sword could rest without hurting others.

"Maybe Aterui did make a mistake," Tamuramaro said, "but it's also possible that Sora's fire that time far surpassed anything Aterui ever imagined. The sheath only covered the sword; it couldn't keep it contained."

Sora understood Tamuramaro's theory that the seal had broken at Awata-guchi.

"But that fire was mine!"

"Could be… But I feel like I already had some will of my own that day. When I was born, I wasn't even fully formed in a human shape," Fuuka said, speaking of things that Sora had no recollection of. "You always took care of me and loved me so much as a brother, Sora. Sometimes you'd even quarrel with people just to protect me, you know. So I think what I did that day also came from my own desire to protect you—my big brother. Even though I was never even human."

Fuuka laughed sadly.

"But the fire was always mine," Sora protested. "I think I've found a way not to be so fixated on one sense of justice. My fire that was sealed in you is probably…gone, too. So you're just my little brother now!"

"Yeah. I wish I could've always been your little brother."

Sora's words didn't reach Fuuka, who was already seeking the next step in his journey.

"Hey now…"

A familiar, airy voice they hadn't heard in a long time echoed through the Aomi Terminal.

"You're back, you sloppy Miroku-bosatsu!" Sora shouted toward the voice as if they were the root of all evil.

"Don't give me such a weird nickname. It's been a little while. Was it you who called me?" Miroku-bosatsu looked straight at Fuuka.

"Yes," Fuuka answered in a clear voice.

"Don't go, Fuuka… Don't take him away from me, Miroku-bosatsu!"

As always, Miroku-bosatsu was clad in their vestments, floating in the air in a sitting pose, joining their fingertips in a circle.

"Does that boy truly have a life of his own, or is he merely a vessel to seal in your fate? It's easy to check, you know."

"What?" Sora, still clinging to Fuuka, was puzzled at the abrupt suggestion.

"In fact, I've known the answer to that from the very beginning. I sent you off on your journey regardless. There's not much in the world I can't handle, but there are things I find interesting to observe."

Sora could only feel frustration at Miroku-bosatsu. He was about to lose his precious little brother, his companion throughout their long journey, and Miroku-bosatsu's opinion of the matter was that it was "interesting."

"I mean, suppose I fixed every failure and made everything whole—what next? The world would come to an end, wouldn't it?"

As irritating as they were, Sora couldn't find the words to defy Miroku-bosatsu at the moment. He bit his lip.

"Your journey didn't turn out as long as I'd imagined. I thought you'd take eternity."

"Yeah. Sorry," said Fuuka. "I knew it'd make things easier for my brother if I said the words I remembered, but I couldn't."

Clinging to Fuuka, Sora could sense his brother's unwavering resolve through his fingertips. But he couldn't feel the heartbeat he'd often listened for anymore. He couldn't find his pulse. Warmth was dissipating from Fuuka's body. Perhaps this signified that the burden Fuuka had carried as his sheath was being relieved.

"Sora, you don't have to think about me anymore. I'm happy as long as you're happy."

"Well then, shall we?" Miroku-bosatsu called to Fuuka.

"Yes, please," Fuuka answered.

If Fuuka had been created against the laws of life, the burden placed upon him should have been Sora's from the beginning. For a long, long time, Fuuka had walked on their journey carrying a heavy, painful load for Sora. As he said, he was going to take away all the hatred and sorrow with him—which meant he had been carrying the weight that should have been Sora's to bear for 1,200 years.

When they'd left the house that night, Sora had brought him here because he wanted to liberate Fuuka from his curse. He had to free his precious little brother.

"...Sora?"

He knew that letting him go was the right thing to do, but he wrapped his arms around Fuuka from behind in spite of himself.

"My little brother, Fuuka. That's your name."

An unfamiliar sensation slid down his cheek and dripped onto his toes.

"You want to stay with me, don't you, Fuuka?"

He felt something wet trail down his skin for the first time in his life.

"You like your big brother, right, Fuuka? I love you, Fuuka. I can't—"

When he realized he was crying, he got a lump in his throat, and his legs turned weak as his embrace tightened.

"You don't want to go anywhere, do you, Fuuka? You're my little brother."

"...Sora."

Fuuka lingered, turning around to touch Sora's tears.

"It's the first time you've ever cried." His voice grew teary, too. "It's because you're sad, right? I'll take away everything with me, all the sadness and tears."

"What kind of person doesn't have any sadness or tears?" Tamuramaro interrupted, breaking his silence.

"Tamuramaro. Look after Sora—"

"Ramen!" Tamuramaro yelled out a single word that was completely out of place.

"Ramen?" Fuuka asked with a bewildered look as Sora still held him in a tight embrace, unable to speak.

"You haven't had ramen before, Fuuka."

"Yes, I have. I made that authentic-style ramen with fresh noodles. We just had it today."

"That was an authentic-*style* ramen. But not the real deal."

"Huh?" Fuuka let out a little gasp in pure surprise. He'd made ramen often because he liked it so much.

"You've never had it at a ramen shop, have you? Let me tell you, the stuff at a ramen shop is, in fact, at least twenty times more amazing than your homemade authentic-style."

"You're exaggerating..."

"No, I'm not. Especially in Ichirou and Tarou in the Shizukuishi shopping street. They take a huge stockpot and make broth from the bones of ten chickens at once, stewing it for half a day. They're extra careful scooping out the scum, and the soup turns golden, with big, clear rings of fat from the chicken."

Just listening to Tamuramaro made Fuuka's mouth water. Even Sora's stomach nearly growled, though it was no time to be thinking about food.

"In the pot next to it, they stew the char siu. A huge block of juicy, fatty pork meat, tied up tight all around with a string. They told me the other day that they stew it in sake, soy sauce, and raw sugar. That meat's so melty you can easily tear it apart with chopsticks. They lay the slices on top of translucent, curly noodles freshly made by hand."

"It sounds so…out-of-this-world yummy…"

"Well? You'll regret never tasting it if you leave now! Your brother and I have been going there to eat in secret!!" Tamuramaro proclaimed as Fuuka's stomach finally growled.

"What?! How could you, Sora?!" Fuuka cried at Sora clinging to him.

"I know, I'm awful… But letting you have ramen someday was my… my…dream." Sora managed to squeeze out the words and buried his face in Fuuka's chest.

"You know, all you people bring up ramen at times like this. It must be quite a delight." Miroku-bosatsu sighed dreamily, wishing they could have a taste, too.

"I wanna eat that ramen. I wanna have it with you, Sora."

Sora's tears were soaking through Fuuka's shirt, and as the heat in those tears finally reached him, he wrapped his arms around Sora in a tight embrace.

Now Sora could hear his heartbeat again. He pressed his ear close against where Fuuka's heart would be to make sure the pulse was really his.

"'Cause I love you, Sora. It makes me happy when I eat yummy food with you."

Blood rushed back through Fuuka's veins, and warmth returned to his body.

"You're Sora's little brother, Fuuka, right?" Sora asked one more time, gazing straight into eyes as blue and deep as a lake. Those eyes gazed back at him, too.

"I don't know. It's not for me to say."

Even so, Sora knew for certain now that Fuuka wished for his own happiness as well as Sora's.

"Stay with me, Fuuka. If you weren't my little brother anymore, I'd be—"

Perhaps it was time for Fuuka to set down the heavy burden he'd been carrying for a long time.

"I'd be devasted, lonely, and heartbroken."

Sora knew he was making it hard for Fuuka, but he followed his heart. He allowed himself to express what he felt, which was unending love for his brother.

"Sora. I can stay with you?"

"How many times do I have to say it?"

But Sora was ready to say it as many times as it took—that even if Fuuka hadn't been a human being in the beginning, he was undoubtedly his dearest brother now, and Sora would never let him disappear.

"Miroku-bosatsu. Ever since ancient times, they've said that spirit dwells in all things. Even if Fuuka was a sheath created for Sora, Sora has loved him as a brother for twelve hundred years. Surely life has been breathed into him by now?" Tamuramaro asked in an unusually tense voice.

"Yes, that's not impossible, I'd say. A spirit dwells in all things in the universe."

"Then doesn't that mean Fuuka has turned into a human being?"

Even Tamuramaro was holding his breath. Sora realized his intent: He was imploring Miroku-bosatsu, who had the power to touch everything in the universe, to endow Fuuka with a human life.

"...Please. Please turn Fuuka into a human," Sora begged Miroku-bosatsu.

"I wanna eat ramen," Fuuka blurted out.

"When a heart is bent on an excessive belief in justice, it mostly creates more troubles," said Miroku-bosatsu.

Sora could understand what that meant now. In history, and in the present world, rulers and leaders who killed multitudes likely never thought they were doing something wrong. If anything, it was because they believed they were right that they could enact such atrocities.

"However, there are rare cases in which it does come to some good. This boy did some wonders for you. You had someone to love, someone small to protect. Your father made a good sheath."

Miroku-bosatsu didn't tell him openly that his father was Aterui.

"But he couldn't seal you completely. Things like this never can be, you know. There's still something left."

Sora wanted to think that he'd set down his burden. But perhaps the fact that Fuuka moved by impulse meant it would never be completely gone—the fire burned too fiercely.

"Never mind. You can't snuff out a fire that ferocious. You did well, toiling for twelve hundred years, but it's not something you can extinguish completely. If I take this boy with me, the one who has accepted this fire inside him, you'll be able to return to the path of a human being again."

"The path...of a human?"

Sora had journeyed for so long that, for a moment, he lost sight of what that path was in the first place.

"Isn't that what you're starting to wish for now? To grow old like everyone else, to live together with the people around you—and someday die. That path," Miroku-bosatsu explained, making the shape of their fingers even rounder.

"What happens if I ask you not to take away my little brother?"

"Well, that's not up to me anymore. Can you rejoin human time? Can this boy become a human? That's got nothing to do with me, so you better deal with it yourselves."

"Please don't take Fuuka away."

Now that Sora had learned of another path, he had no doubt about which one to take.

"Sora…" Fuuka stared at Sora in surprise.

"So you'll choose a more difficult path?" asked Miroku-bosatsu.

"Yes."

The difficulty of the path was nothing to Sora. Fuuka was his own little brother.

"It's funny…" Miroku-bosatsu smiled, pensive and amused. "I sent you off on your journey because your fateful burden could've turned either way. You know how you could see me that day? It's because there was a little bit of uncertainty in you. Besides, you tried to kill yourself when you saw the mound of corpses."

Sora also remembered vividly how he had tried to take his life and Fuuka's at Awata-guchi. Perhaps Fuuka still carried that thought as a painful memory even more than Sora did.

"You had the capacity to become a dictator or a king who ruled over the world with a good government. But you chose the life of a normal person. Is it that good, this life?"

"Yes." A thin smile finally crept onto Sora's lips.

"I'm glad to hear it."

"Huh…? Miroku-bosatsu!"

By the time Sora called out their name, Miroku-bosatsu had vanished into thin air.

Fuuka, who should have been standing next to him, had also disappeared from view. Sora's heart stopped, and his legs quivered.

"Coo."

He heard a soft coo. On the wharf, now completely back to reality, there stood a white dog, wagging his tail and looking as though being a dog was the best he could do.

"Fuuka." As his strength left him, Sora dropped to his knees and flung himself around Fuuka's neck. "Fuuka."

When he thought Fuuka was gone, his heart had actually stopped. Dog or human, it didn't matter anymore—Sora was content just to have Fuuka with him.

"Coo," Fuuka murmured softly, snuggling his cheek against Sora's.

"Hey, did Miroku-bosatsu forget about me?" Tamuramaro realized with a little gasp. Surely *he* was the one who should've been taken along to the Pure Land after laboring hard for 1,200 years.

Without uttering a word, Sora stretched out his hand and gripped the hem of Tamuramaro's pants. Tamuramaro could sense the young man's desperation and let out a helpless sigh.

"...Well, that's true. Maybe you're still a bit shaky."

"I've only just learned how much I don't understand, you know," Sora muttered through his teeth, although it vexed him to admit it.

"And there's so much ramen out there that I haven't eaten yet." Tamuramaro laughed as an excuse.

"I guess we have to walk home."

They had been left behind in the middle of the night at the Aomi Container Terminal, and they couldn't take any public transport because Fuuka was a dog and they didn't have a carrier case. Tamuramaro couldn't think of any other way.

"Let's go, Fuuka." Sora let go of Fuuka and looked into his blue eyes. "You too, Tamuramaro," he said, rising to his feet.

The three of them started walking toward the lights.

Sora took his first step with a firm stride. He would walk a completely different path from now on. There were no signposts. Until now, he had believed that if he kept working hard, someday he would live in human time, and Fuuka would become a human being.

"You better deal with it yourselves."

Sora looked at Fuuka, then at Tamuramaro.

The streetlights that had appeared artificial on their way here gave off a warm glow in his eyes now.

To Sora, the unknown path stretching out in front of them was not a source of anxiety but renewed hope.

"I felt like we were gonna die. Even though we can't," said Tamuramaro, walking through Shakujii Park in the middle of the day in October.

"Yeah, I thought so, too."

"...Woof." Fuuka also agreed.

After they had left the container terminal, the three of them had walked for six hours to reach Shizukuishi. It was dawn when they got home, and right after they finally passed out, the police came to interview Sora, of course, as the renter of the car. And Tamuramaro was back in his role as Odajima's consulting attorney.

Sora somehow managed to convince the investigators that he had dealt with the men by himself. The men kept muttering about a "white wolf," so the police decided to settle for the testimony of the thirty-one-year-old who had rented the car rather than the ravings of the criminals.

"Mr. Odajima's enjoying his time in detention," Tamuramaro told Sora. "People over seventy-five are wild. According to him, anything he hasn't done before is fun."

The article in the weekly magazine was safely published, but Odajima, who had nearly been murdered by the gang sent by Diet member Yamagata, was still under suspicion of embezzlement, so his consulting lawyer had a pile of work to get through.

"Mr. Odajima... He's over seventy-five?" For the umpteenth time, Sora shuddered at what elderly people were capable of.

"Apparently, that was his birthday. So he felt content to die then and there, but now he says, 'There's so many things I have left to do!' He's sprier than us right now."

"He did promise to have the seafood set and sake with Ms. Natsuki at the roadside station."

North Station appeared in the news daily as a brand-new attraction, set to become a familiar feature in the region affected by the disaster.

The tale of its construction excited much public attention and was drawing large crowds to it every day. Sora and Tamuramaro were heartened to hear the local people on TV interviews say that all this bustle was only temporary, so they could keep calm and focus on their long-term goals.

"Everyone's in an uproar about the Diet now. If they don't register it officially as a roadside station, they'll be vilified even more, so I'm sure the application will go smoothly," Tamuramaro remarked. Even though they couldn't round everything off to satisfying perfection, what mattered was taking one step at a time.

"People plus work equals hope," said Sora with a sigh of relief.

"Woof, woof!"

As they reached their usual path by Sanpouji Lake, Fuuka was the first to notice Tatsuko and Rokurou sitting on their usual bench.

"Hello there. Getting along well, I see. How nice." Rokurou smiled to see Sora and Fuuka walking with their lodger.

"We just ran into each other, that's all...," Sora mumbled wearily, but in truth, they always went on afternoon walks together these days.

The reason was nothing other than ramen, plain and simple. Whenever Sora and Tamuramaro got ready go out by themselves, Fuuka would cry out angrily, "Are you gonna eat ramen without me?!" and tag along. As a result, neither Sora nor Tamuramaro had had any ramen since the day they'd walked home from Aomi.

"I've run out of steam...," Tamuramaro grumbled, staring off into the distant sky while dreaming of ramen.

"Natsuki was singing your praises, by the way," Tatsuko said. "She told us you're both so accomplished in your work."

"We couldn't be happier that there's someone in the neighborhood who understands your complicated job, Mr. Lawyer," Rokurou joined in.

"Thank you so much for the introduction." Sora bowed, remembering that it was the Kashiwagis who had brought Natsuki to him.

"If you're that reliable, we'd really love to have you settle our divorce," remarked Rokurou.

"That's right. Brisk and efficient, that's what we need," Tatsuko added, reciting the same line as usual.

They appeared to be their normal, cheerful selves, but to Sora, it also seemed that the many iterations of those same words was wearing out their hearts.

"Tamuramaro." Sora handed Fuuka's leash to Tamuramaro for the first time, since somebody had to be holding it at all times. Then he sat down on the bench beside Tatsuko.

"Divorce isn't difficult," said Sora, looking into their eyes. "Perhaps there's no need to split your property, either. If we follow the necessary legal steps, your home might become Ms. Tatsuko's."

Sora expected that such an outcome was possible and that Rokurou would be content with it. If Tatsuko herself wished to live alone, they likely wouldn't have to go through the hassle of dividing up their property and assets.

"Will we have to go to court?" The couple seemed terribly surprised and alarmed that Sora was finally listening to their request.

"There's a process called mediation before it's brought to trial. From what I've seen, I don't think you have any objections, Mr. Rokurou?"

"...Indeed. You've hit the nail on the head, Mr. Lawyer."

"Honey..."

It was the first time Sora heard Tatsuko address Rokurou like her husband.

"Ms. Tatsuko has the right to that much. Though I'm not an attorney lawyer, I can act as your representative in a mediation." Sora spoke deliberately, expressing his sincerity to both of them. "If you ask me officially to settle your divorce, I'll see it through to the end."

Sora waited until they took in his words. Tamuramaro, standing nearby, and Fuuka, sitting on the ground, waited with him.

"But if I say how I feel...," Sora went on, once he saw that they'd digested his explanation. "My wish is for you to live together always—teaching calligraphy to the kids in Shizukuishi."

Just as he said, that was only his wish. But both Tatsuko and Rokurou were staring at him.

"That's unfair, Mr. Lawyer." Tatsuko sighed, as though at a loss.

"How can we say no to that?" Rokurou sighed, too.

"That's the first time anyone's said I was unfair," Sora replied, breaking into a childish grin.

"I'll bring you some inari sushi later, wrapped in fried tofu skin," Tatsuko said.

"That's very kind of you. Thank you so much. I'm looking forward to it already." Sora bowed to them, then got up from the bench.

"You seem like you've grown much older somehow, all of a sudden," Rokurou observed.

"I think so, too. You're all grown-up," Tatsuko added.

Sora laughed in delight at their words.

"I'd be glad to share the sushi with him," Tamuramaro said brightly, handing back Fuuka's leash to Sora.

They slowly passed by Sanpouji Lake, and they came to Hyoutan Lake, where they could hear the shouting of children at play.

"It's parental love," murmured Tamuramaro, as if to himself. He seemed to be thinking of Tatsuko and Rokurou.

"I suppose so." Though there was a slight hitch in his movement, Sora nodded in ready assent.

"Coo?" Fuuka let out a soft hum, looking up at Sora quizzically. Sora gazed back at him.

"All I wanted was a human death—both for myself and for Fuuka," Sora began. At first, he'd thought Miroku-bosatsu had sent him on a journey he'd never wished for. "But now I want to live out my life properly, growing old and sharing my time with the people of this town. That's my wish."

He had been sent out on a near-eternal journey—not set out, but sent out. He had company, but there were no signposts. Still, he didn't feel any discontent at the prospect now.

"Yeah." Tamuramaro didn't say whether he believed that was possible for them. Instead, he gazed toward the lake, wind sweeping across its surface.

"Hey, Tamuramaro."

"Hmm?"

"It's late to be saying this, but…you knew who my father was, didn't you?"

"Huh?! It's not me!" Tamuramaro yelped, slipping out of character.

"That's obvious. I didn't mean you. I meant…your friend." Sora was thinking of the man who had been Tamuramaro's friend and the great clan leader whom Sora had always loved and admired.

"My father saw that his son was a freak, so he left me—wasn't that child neglect?" Sora asked in all seriousness. The more he thought about it, the more he was convinced that there was no question about it, and the conclusion formed deep furrows in his brow. "Wasn't he awful to me?"

"You've been alive for twelve hundred years, and *now* you wanna be an angsty, cranky teenager?!"

"How modernized you've become, Sei-i Taishogun. But really, I've never gone through that teenage rebellion thing. I had so many other things to worry about, as a neglected child. If I get like that now, it's inevitable." Sora sulked.

Tamuramaro looked at him and smiled helplessly. "Who knows? Maybe he was watching over you the whole time from somewhere close by."

He suddenly stopped in his tracks and peered into Fuuka's blue eyes.

"You're just making that up."

"Japan isn't the only place that believes spirit dwells in all things, that divinity dwells in all things. You can find that belief all over the world. But just like Miroku-bosatsu said, I think there's only one soul for one person."

Tamuramaro hoped that the soul of the person who had created the sheath would dwell again in Fuuka and grow into another life in time—but of course, Sora had no idea what was on his mind.

"Don't make me despair."

"No, I mean— Ow!" Tamuramaro had bent down to stroke Fuuka's cheek, but Fuuka bit his hand in an aggressive jest.

"Fuuka! I told you, no munchy-munchy!!" Sora rushed to pull them apart and flashed a forced smile at the passersby around them. "He sure loves to play," he mumbled feebly.

"Well, the truth is, I don't know, either. That's the only thing I'm sure about." Tamuramaro laughed.

"There's so much I don't understand," Sora grumbled. But he was standing firmly on his feet. He would die in time, but until then, he would live.

He had learned that everyone, including himself, had emotions that mattered. To love his little brother, to be raised as a human being, to live in this town, to grow old like anyone else—that was his wish now. And if it was possible, he wanted to do all of that with Fuuka in human shape.

He could never forget the multitude of lives he'd struck down in order to survive. Was he asking for more than he deserved to cherish such a dream?

"Woof, woof."

Fuuka peered at Sora's face. Somehow, Fuuka looked manlier than before, even as a dog.

Miroku-bosatsu had told him that if they took Fuuka away with them—Fuuka, who still carried the undying flame of his fate—Sora would be able to return to human time. But Sora had refused. He hadn't stopped to ask Fuuka's will in that moment. He could've liberated Fuuka from his duty and the fire forced upon him. Would Fuuka have been happier if he'd gone on to the other world?

No matter how much he mulled over it, Sora couldn't find an answer.

"You're better off without me."

Fuuka didn't know, either. But Sora could see just how deeply troubled Fuuka was. Would it have been the right choice to let go?

Sora caught himself looking for the "right" answer again. It wasn't so easy to cure the nature his father had been worried about.

And he now knew it would never be cured completely. He would never forget that fact.

"Oh."

He heard his bones creak inside him again.

"What's up?"

"Coo?" Fuuka let out a questioning murmur.

"It's nothing." Sora smiled back at them.

Perhaps it was the sound of his life moving forward, the clock starting to tick as it did invariably for everyone. Perhaps it wasn't. There was no single truth for anything or anyone.

Even so, his bones rasped with every step he took.

This path he walked on, a path in which nothing was for certain, was one that Sora himself had chosen to take, rather than something assigned to him. He took a step forward, drawing in a deep breath, listening to the slight, resonant creak of his bones as the breeze drifted over the water and caressed his face.

At long last, Sora had arrived at this discovery—there is no one answer for anything.